ANNABEL LANGONI

ANNABEL LANGONI

Coming to Terms with the Past

Eliza Wyatt

Copyright © 2022 by Eliza Wyatt

ISBN | 978152727470-9

All rights reserved.

Table of Contents

Part I

Chapter One 1
Chapter Two 9
Chapter Three 23
Chapter Four 33
Chapter Five 43

Part II

Chapter Six 55
Chapter Seven 75
Chapter Eight 105
Chapter Nine 121
Chapter Ten 129

Part III

Chapter Eleven 143
Chapter Twelve 147
Chapter Thirteen 155
Chapter Fourteen 167
Chapter Fifteen 179
Chapter Sixteen 191

Chapter Seventeen 203
Chapter Eighteen... 227
Chapter Nineteen 247
Chapter Twenty 261

Part IV

Chapter Twenty-One 275
About The Author 287
Interview 289

Also By Eliza Wyatt

Plays

Chronic Competition
Mirror Images
Blue Sky Thinking
Flowers of Red
Angela Hitler The Housekeeper
Aunt and Adolf
Techno Frantic Love
Gods and Goddesses
Poet's Corner

http://www.elizawyattplays.com
http://www.annabellangoni.com

Film Scripts

Crazy But Stable
A Minor Threat
Cooking the Earth

I never thought, when I casually looked up family connections on Ancestry.com, that time travel to the past would become the subject of my first novel. Like my heroine, I was ignorant of many facts about my parents and am now in awe of what they must have endured during the war and I'd like to dedicate this book to them.

I would like to thank the following for their advice and encouragement while I was at work on this novel: Issy Costa, for her wonderful insights, editorial advice and constant encouragement, and to everyone who read the novel in earlier drafts, Lawrence Ball, Rosemary Bailey, Sheena Faro, Yogi, Marco Zarattini, Paul Chi, Brian Kaufman, Tabatha Stirling, Rob Nisbet, Pat Quinn, Charlotte Chatton, Michael Wynne, Joe Benn, Yassy Fahr, Decima Francis, Carol Parikh, Verity Craig, Linda Jones, Louise Fox, Rose Kingsland, Sally Hindell, Ahmad Fakhr, Peiter Smart, Laura Grierson, Anthony St. Martin, Lenny Pedersen, Michael Hoy, Judith Burns, with special thanks to Stirling Publishing Ltd., Stone Cold Press, and Herstory.Press for making this book a reality.

Part I

CHAPTER ONE

Pain comes in shock waves. I am buried under concrete. I can't move but I am not dead, or my heart wouldn't be pounding like this. Panic stricken voices yell through my numbness; I do not understand what they are saying. Their voices come in waves. Water, waves! I try to think calmly of a lake while sirens are ringing in my ears. Machines bleep, and there's a pain inside my head becoming slowly unbearable until a blinding flash surrounds me with white light.

1984

I wasn't always American. I used to be English, but I married an American and we set up house in suburban Houston. Living with my husband, Ed, and our college age son, David, I was happy and sometimes bored, or bored because I was happy. I often forgot I was English, until someone commented on my accent. That was usually at the Sunny Hills Country Club, where I had a good job as Director of Hospitality, or Director of Hostility as Mara would say. She was the resident pastry chef and kept me healthy by forbidding me her sugary concoctions.

'Annabel, you have to watch your weight,' she warned me.

'You are too short.'

Mara had a comfortable figure. Her weight made her look and act older than she was. Two marriages made her seem wiser. I told her everything. Growing up, I had the odd experience of having two mothers, who were now thousands of miles away, so I didn't object when Mara mothered me. She gave me murder mysteries every birthday and Christmas, but I didn't dream about murder until Donna moved in. I had the perfect marriage until she moved in.

Donna was the only divorcee in the neighbourhood and a traditional blonde. I took exception to Donna's blondness because it reminded me of Vivien. Vivien, my biological mother, became an ash blonde at a time when it was a daring thing to do. 'Blonds have more fun.' She once told me, boasting that her blond hair rated her movie star attention. 'Blonds catch men's eyes!' Well, she should know! Her hair used to be as dark as mine. Her father was Italian, one of the few clues she gave me about her family background. As Mara pointed out, I was small and remained dark haired. Ever since Donna caught Ed's eye, I began obsessing about whether I should dye my hair blond.

At least I was happy and felt appreciated at the Sunny Hills Country Club. When I was asked to make a proposal for refurbishing the club lounge my proposal was accepted, and I made a good job of it. The club lounge was no longer recognisable. Gone were the dusty deer heads, the bone sharp skeletons over the massive stone hearth. The walls were now a cherry tartan, the sofas a soft share of blue grey. The décor was welcomed as a change for the better, and as a reward they threw a party for me. The club thrived on birthdays and celebrations. At the entrance was a banner, Congratulations Mrs. Annabel Langoni Fuego. I was flattered they included my maiden name as a nod to my feminism. Mara must have been consulted. I had worked hard for this and grateful to be celebrated at my workplace, even when people found it hard to kiss me on the cheek without spilling champagne on me.

The event began with a series of toast, which the management proposed in an old-fashioned manner. On the podium they pinned a metal American flag on my jacket, clapping enthusiastically. I looked round the ballroom trying to think of what to say next and decided the less said the better. I thanked my husband, Ed, for his support. He looked down at his shoes. Next to the wrinkled millionaires, Eduardo Fuego's dark hair shone and his skin glowed. Keep away, Donna! She was giving him adoring looks. When I stepped down from the podium, all I could see was Donna.

A group of ladies took me aside.

'We'd like you to join us on the first Tuesday of every month. We take it you're a citizen and that's all you need to qualify for our chapter. Women only! We're affiliated with the League of Women Voters. You do vote?'

Could I qualify? Did I vote? I suddenly realised that they were subtly trying to discover whether I had become an American citizen. No, I did not hold an American passport, still the old green card. But I couldn't tell them that because it would disqualify me from joining their League. Although married to an American, I had kept my British passport, which was still in my maiden name because I hadn't registered my marriage in England.

The majority of Sunny Hill's members were Republicans in the Reagan era, but Ed and I did not criticize them and tried to blend in. Ed had no strong political views, and I kept my radical political past to myself. I was careful to tell no one, not even Ed, that I was once a fledging member of the communist party in London. I dropped out of politics when I arrived in Texas, except for being part of the national protest against the war in Vietnam. When the war was over I watched, at first with concern but finally with indifference, as communism became an undesirable political alternative. We were in a new era, and I was a different person. 'I'll be happy to join your group,' I said gaily, glad to be asked because I felt joining their group was expected of me now that I was their interior decorator. 'Sign me up'.

Donna was waiting to say something. 'So glad to see you honoured like this!'

I gave her a false smile. She could never be my friend and I wanted her to understand this. I loved my husband. I'd met Eduardo Fuego during his school year in London, when I was working as a secretary with little hope of advancement. When he asked me to come with him to Texas at the end of the school year, I was only too willing to leave my bedsit. I thought of my trip to Houston as the start of a great adventure and was surprised when I gradually fell in love with Ed, the shrug of his shoulders, his 'don't sweat the small stuff' and his 'do it if you want' attitude. Cool dude, I thought, not realizing that if you lived in such heat you had to play it cool.

I had trouble with the constant heat and also with freezing air-conditioning. 'Never happy', Ed commented, but I didn't take him seriously. It was Donna's air-conditioning that Ed offered to fix. The temperature last August reached a hundred and two degrees and stayed that high for weeks, the kind of heat guaranteed to take down anyone's pants. Although I told Ed I understood all this, I found I was quite unable to forgive and forget. For me his unfaithfulness was as devastating as David's injury had been. Both were a test of our marriage. In his last year of high school, David made a big play in the annual Thanksgiving Game and fractured his hip. I seemed to suffer his injury more than David did. Ed kept telling me not to blame myself. This was far from being the case. I blamed everyone and everything. Ed had taken the trouble to teach me American football, but after David's accident I insisted soccer was a much safer game. I had told them this repeatedly before the accident, but I was not taken seriously. I was English and they were Texan. I was often out gunned by the two men in my life.

****

After the Sunny Hills celebration, I did not understand why I couldn't enjoy a good night's sleep. My insides were raw and bleeding, probably worse for the aspirin I had downed. In the bright sunshine of the next morning, I dosed up on coffee and went skating. One of my delights in Houston was being able to go from intense heat to the cool of the shopping mall, which featured a large ice rink. I often went in my lunch hour, timidly trying small jumps alongside some fierce would-be Olympic competitors. The speed and refreshing cold soothed me, and so did meeting up with Mara. She was a good friend and I knew she was worried about my marriage. I gave her a wild wave and attempted a jump. Showing off, I said to myself, as I came crashing down on the ice. Mara hurried up but I waved her away. I didn't want her pitying me.

She knew I was angry at Ed, but I was also angry at Mara. In one month she was moving to El Paso with her new husband. They were starting up a bakery and she was going to be his pastry chef. We had commiserated at length about how much I'd miss her at Sunny Hills, but that didn't alter the fact that I felt betrayed. We were now at the stage of joking about her 'unfaithfulness' but feeling her sympathy across the table made me feel like crying. 'Okay, I sound like a broken record but let me tell you that Ed shocked me at the Club last night. He wanted her, I know he did, so it's not over. And I feel like murdering her.'

Mara took this calmly. 'I'd suggest some Valium.'

'I don't think that would do it.'

'Not for her, for you! Give yourself a break, don't go back to work, take a week or a month off and go back to England. That would give Ed the jolt he needs.'

'And let her move in?'

'Test the waters. I don't think Ed wants a divorce, and it would give you some perspective. Go back home, everyone needs to go back home sometimes.'

'I have no home in England. My mother's a basket case, and my foster parents left the country. They're living in Australia with their son.'

'What about your father?'

'Non-existent, and always has been. My mother never told me anything, so I imagined he was a one-night stand.'

'Don't you have any grandparents or cousins?'

'Vivien's whole way of life makes her the soul of discretion, desperately secretive. What I don't know about my mother's family would fill a book. She told us she had no relatives because she was raised in an orphanage.'

'No parents? Even orphans have parents somewhere.'

'Not her!' I said grandly. 'She gave us the impression she rose up from the sea like Venus on an oyster shell.'

We laughed about this, but I realised Mara was right. I was homesick. Houston was not where I wanted to be.

'Where do you want to be?'

'I don't know.'

'That's a reason for therapy. You need a therapist.' According to Mara, a workshop entitled The Transformational Weekend had saved her life when she was suffering through the abuses of her first husband. My problems were different. I still loved Ed. 'That's okay,' Mara assured me. 'You'll be working on what you want.'

'I hate the idea of therapy,' I insisted. 'They always blame your mother.'

Mara and I, being feminists, tried to avoid blaming women for what went wrong in our lives.

'They don't always blame your mother, but you do have a special case because you have had two mothers. That must make life difficult.'

'Not at all! I have two mothers to blame. But what's the good of talking about it? Won't stop Donna putting the moves on my husband. Look, I had a happy childhood. People don't understand that being raised by devoted foster parents does not make you an abused child.'

'Okay, but it wasn't normal.'

'It had advantages. If you have two mothers, you can compare them. I have a big comparison book here in my head. And now I'm comparing the Ed of today with the Ed of yesterday.'

'Stop that!' she said sharply. 'It won't end well. You can't throw away twenty good years like that. No one wants to talk about their feelings. especially you, but you've got to do something positive. Go to the transformative weekend I told you about. That therapy saved my life.'

It was because Mara's recommendation came from the heart that I reluctantly agreed to do some work on myself.

CHAPTER TWO

My trip started off badly, with my Cherokee Jeep spluttering and chugging as if it had better things in mind. I turned up the volume and sang along with Bonnie Tyler's Faster Than the Speed of Light, which made me feel like a teenager instead of a woman with marital problems. When the song was over, I heard the engine thump thump. Mara was wrong about me not being in touch with my feelings. I was outraged by this betrayal of my beloved blue Jeep. Cars were supposed to work. Worry confused my sense of direction, and I soon got lost on the wide deserted roads. I could tell by the setting sun that I was going in the wrong direction, but this deep into the Texas hinterland there are no cars and no signs. This was as far as I could get from the English countryside of my childhood. I turned into a roadhouse gas station for help.

No one appeared. A battered notice for Cold Beer on the wire-grill door gave me courage to go inside. The shelves were covered with dusty cans or sardines and baked beans; there were rattlesnake skins and rusted spurs for sale, making me feel like a tourist. A shuffle alerted me to the appearance of a scruffy mom and pop, their white hair fluffing out from lookalike faces which made them look like friendly gremlins. Pop said he'd fix the car and Mom offered a cup of Joe. I'd been in Texas long enough to know this meant coffee. The campfire is Fred, the rain Pete and they call the wind Mariah. I compared this mom and pop to my foster parents, Sidney and Brenda, who also earned their living from their homestead, in their case a market garden, in their own backyard.

This Mom was no talker because she was too busy smoking, and she had a nasty cough. Pop wiped his hands on a greasy rag every now and then and every time he did that, he took a swig from his hip flask and shooed away the chickens.

'Chinese Silkies,' Pop informed me. 'Blue meat, that's what.'

'He won't eat no blue meat,' Mom chipped in.

While I waited for my car, I took a walk out the back. Compared to the fertile earth of my Sussex childhood, I could see no vegetable growing could be done here. The landscape was dotted with gnarled oaks and short bushy cedar trees. Deer lived here because there were hoof prints in the fragile sandy soil. A lime green gecko ran across my path, and I wondered if the Texan outback was like the Australian. I tried to imagine my foster parents, Brenda and Sidney, living in the Australian outback. I was in shock when they sold up and left, but this was not unusual in England, the English were always running off to warmer drier countries and maybe this was what I was searching for in Texas; this dryness that warms your bones and lulls you into a dull acceptance.

Was that what I always needed, a place where I could relax and open my arms wide?

The gas station pay phone was actually working, so I called my therapy group to say I was running late. When I got past the answering machine to talk to someone, I made my apologies to a thin voiced woman called Fiona. She told me she was the workshop leader and that I should start the exercises by writing about my two mothers.

'I not only have two mothers, I have three now, a mother-in-law!'

Fiona's forced laugh was not reassuring.

'The woman with three mothers, that's a challenge! You'll have a lot to say. Try and go back to your very first memory. You'll be surprised by how much you remember.'

I doubted whether childhood memories would solve my problems and heal my marriage, but I was willing to try anything. Waiting in the sun for my Jeep to be fixed, I disappeared the Texan landscape and went back to Warmdene Village. I saw myself: picking strawberries in my foster parents' strawberry patch, the ground usually wet and muddy and the strawberries delicious. Child labour? No, I ate more strawberries than I picked. Then suddenly, in stark contrast, there were day trips to Vivien's London. I would be hurried to the zoo and whisked from plush hotel foyers to famous restaurants where I would order a soft boiled egg; a strange kind of spoiling. I did not like the days in London with my 'real' mother, but they hardly merited the word traumatic. A vivid memory was trying to open the door of a London taxi. Vivien grabbed me and gave me a vicious shake. That may have been the beginning of my dislike and distrust. Why did I open that door? Because I didn't want to be in a London taxi with her! I wanted to be back in Warmdene running through the grass into the arms of Brenda, my foster mother. Vivien knew this. She guessed I wanted to escape her, that I've always wanted to escape her. That was probably the reason I was living in Texas.

Yes, that was the sort of information therapists wanted, but as I went through those childhood memories, I knew I would hate confessing in front of strangers how little I knew about my biological mother and the fact that I didn't have any blood relatives. I never dared challenge Vivien's desire to keep her secrets. She would put a finger to her lips whenever I asked an awkward question. Nor did I want to reveal that my biological mother never had a respectable job. She was a fixture in exclusive London night clubs, partying the night away in the hope of finding a man to pay her rent. My foster mother, Brenda, once warned me that Vivien was immoral because she took money for sex. 'That's why you must never go and live with her.' I agreed. I had no wish to be a part of my mother's chaotic life; punctuated by miscarriages, according to disapproving Brenda. My family history was more complicated than Mara's, and surely all this was too much to relate to a weekend therapy group? Especially since it happened so far away in London.

I was afraid that group therapy would not be as comforting as my feminist consciousness-raising group of sympathetic women. If there were men at this workshop, and why wouldn't there be, I'd have trouble talking about Ed's fling with Donna. I would also have to confess that Ed had sworn 'Nothing like that will happen again' and that I still couldn't forgive him.

My obsession with his unfaithfulness did not make much sense out here in the wilderness. I felt peaceful in the empty stillness, punctuated only by the company of nonthreatening Mom and Pop.

'Should hold you!' Pop concluded, reaching into his hip pocket for his flask.

Partly in thanks, I wanted to buy something from their store. I took another look at the dusty glass cabinets. When Lou saw I was attracted to a pile of arrow heads thrown in a heap, she took one out of a pile and gave it to me. I wanted to pay for it, but she said, 'They don't belong to nobody. We found 'em whereabouts.'

I accepted her gift. The sharpened stone, with its three points, lay in my palm like a living memory.

When I climbed back into the Jeep I was overcome with a desire to go home, but I gritted my teeth and turned into the setting sun. I got lost several times and grew impatient. Surely this therapy group was not going to save my marriage. I needed to talk to Ed. I needed to forgive him. I made a decision to go back to Houston and made a U-turn, but a few minutes later I saw cars speeding towards me. I wondered why Texans were so crazy, driving straight at me, hooting and hollering. I slammed on the brakes and when I looked around, I saw that I'd mistaken the massive four-lane highway for a dual carriageway, and that my Jeep was facing the oncoming cars. I turned the car round and cursed myself all the way back to Houston. 'You're losing it, you nearly drove yourself off the map.'

I didn't feel safe until I pulled into our carport, but when I went to the fridge for a comforting Coke it became clear I was not home safely. There was tell-tale evidence of a homecooked meal in a saucepan that wasn't mine; orange cookware, the label half peeled away. The sound of Ed's car driving up reminded me how angry I was. When I came out of the shower, I saw that Ed was washing out the orange crock, explaining that he had been helpless to prevent this ruthless invasion of Donna with a dish of mousse.

'Mousse? Chocolate mousse, as well as this stew?'

Ed laughed at my mistake. 'Moose! The animal! Her brother shot it in Wyoming. She made mountains of stew and brought some over.'

The scale of this country never failed to surprise me.

'I couldn't help the fact she came by. I didn't invite her in.'

'Where's David?'

'Still camping with Tracy.'

We suspected camping with Tracy was a sexual tryst. David had met his girlfriend at church, and they were both religious. We hoped camping was David's opportunity to romance his girlfriend, Tracy. Neither of us totally approved of an overly religious girlfriend.

'I'm sure he only converted because he liked her.' Ed was safe with the subject of David. 'Typical sophomore behaviour.' Never having been to college, I was unfamiliar with these rites of passage. We worried the night away in our separate beds, watching re-runs on television. At five o'clock we heard the roar of David's motorbike. We both leapt out of bed to greet him.

David said, 'Stop the fret!' He began to unpack panniers full of camping gear, and lumber them into the house. I was already mixing pancakes.

'Did they mind you camping on the beach?'

'Galveston is much colder than Houston.'

David never answered a question directly, and turned his back to us when he said, 'There was a phone call from England, with some bad news. I didn't want to leave a note, or have it spoil anything.'

By anything, he meant his tryst with Tracy in the tent. We faced him down.

'Your mother's committed suicide,' he informed us. 'The police called... I took the call, and no one was here and no one showed up before I left. I didn't want to leave a note.'

I knew immediately he meant Vivien had committed suicide, not my foster mother. I sat down heavily on the kitchen chair, not able to take the weight of my emotions. Ed hovered over me, distractedly rubbing my shoulders.

'Oh my God. I better make you a cup of tea.'

Ed had been in England long enough to know the routine English response. David was pulling bits of paper out of his pocket.

'I wrote the number down. But I didn't think I could just leave you a note. I didn't know what else to do. I knew it would ruin the weekend.'

Ed put a hand on my shoulder. 'We better call the English police.'

David was eating his pancakes too calmly. I turned on him. 'You didn't want the news to ruin your weekend! You only ever think of yourself. Someone may have been able to save her life!'

'Not if she was already dead from sleeping pills.'

Sleeping pills had such a familiar ring. Somewhere in the back of my mind was the memory that she had taken sleeping pills before. 'Did they say why she took sleeping pills?'

'Of course not. Why would they know?'

Ed leaned over me. 'You mustn't blame yourself.'

'I have no intention of blaming myself. My mother never bothered to look after me, so it's too much to expect me to look after her.' I didn't want Ed's sympathy. I heard myself saying, 'I'll have to go to England.'

They both stared at me, as if they suddenly realised I wasn't born in Texas.

'Sorry!' I had to smile as I said that. Very English, saying sorry when you are telling someone something that they don't want to hear.

Ed stroked my head. 'Look, she was your mother even if she didn't take care of you. Of course you have to be there for her funeral.'

I never got any sympathy from having a bad relationship with my biological mother. Everyone who met Vivien liked her. She was charming. When Ed met her he was impressed by her fluent French and Italian, her couture clothes, and was lured, as were most men, by the sad expression in her enormous dark eyes. David, when I took him to England, was also happy in her company. He was a sociable kid, who knew how to behave with a grandmother. They got on well, until Vivien came to visit. The only time my mother came to Texas was something of a disaster. It was Christmas and she drank steadily through the festivities. David found her passed out on the bathroom floor. We suggested she return to London because we were trying to protect David, a thirteen-year-old who had already been caught smoking pot. That was the start of Vivien's downward slide. On one occasion the London police called me in the middle of the night. She had been 'disturbing the peace'. That referred to her having too much to drink at the local pub and creating a racket that disturbed the neighbours. Then she began calling me in the middle of the night, forgetting the time difference. She complained about not being able to afford aspirin for her headache.

We sent her what we could afford, hoping she'd buy aspirin and not Smirnoff. We discussed inviting her to live with us, but that seemed an insurmountable problem, complicated by trying to protect David. Our problem was always deciding how much to tell David about his grandmother. At first it was easy, she was just a grandmother in England who wanted his photographs and spoiled him with presents. As David grew older, Ed decided to keep her means of earning a living a secret from him. David was a kid raised on gross television stereotypes; escorts to him were Las Vegas strippers, call girls who knocked on bedroom doors with fetish clothes. He would not understand that his grandmother moved in high circles during the post-war pleasure boom. She claimed her men-friends simply offered her gifts and that she never accepted less than a diamond bracelet. I thought that was a dishonest boast. When I heard her talking on the phone I learned that after a friend's introduction, a man could have a good time with her if he 'passed muster' during an expensive dinner and night on the town. I was too young to work out how she got to this exalted, if morally dubious, level of the good life. Her career took place in a very different era, a time when there was no sex before marriage and maybe very little after it.

Ed was now trying to get me to drink some wine. He was also doing me a favour by explaining to David that I had to return to England. David was resisting the idea.

'What are you going to do?'

'Go to her funeral. Clear out her things. Maybe I'll find some clues about her life, and who knows... maybe even something about my real father.'

David gave me a horrified look.

'You mean you're going to go through her things?'

'Yes, that's my right.'

David had more questions. 'Where is the funeral going to be? Suicide's a sin so I wonder if they're going to allow her to be buried in sacred ground?'

Ed also had a question. 'Do you have any idea why she did it?'

'No! But I'm going to find out. Maybe it was a murder.' If Vivien swallowed sleeping pills, it did not sound like murder; but I was an avid reader of Agatha Christies.

Ed knew the idea of being a detective appealed to me.

'Maybe it was the result of a tragic love affair. You told me she hit the bottle after her love affair with that Frenchman, so perhaps another one broke her heart.'

'With Jean Paul? That was years ago.' 'Jean Paul?' David had a lot to learn.

'Jean Paul was the only man she really loved, and the reason she changed her name to Vivienne, spelling it the French way.'

'I wish you weren't going to London,' David complained. 'Buildings are always being blown up. Didn't they just blow up that hotel where that woman prime minister was staying?'

I was impressed he knew about Margaret Thatcher's miraculous escape from the Grand Hotel, even if he did not remember her name.

'I'll be fine,' I assured them both. 'Anyway, aren't you two going to be hunting in Hill Country? I'll only be gone for a week.' During the hunting season, Ed and his brothers took off in search of wild deer in the surrounding hills. If they were lucky, they managed to stock their freezers with wild deer to last the family the rest of the year. They sometimes trekked almost as far as Mexico, and often brought home a boar, or wild turkey. David joined them as soon as he was old enough. I went with them last year, and had no desire to repeat the experience. The rifles are heavy, the deer smart, and the ground hard to sleep on at night.

'I don't have anything warm enough for England.'

Ed unlocked the gun closet and took out a wool sweater with antlers on the chest. It was not flattering but I needed the warmth of that in London, in December.

The Sunny Hills Country Club gave me a week off for the funeral. Everyone commiserated. Donna swung by in her tennis outfit to say how sorry she was.

'I'm sorry too,' I countered, 'but it could be fun. As fun as a funeral can be.'

Ed was helpful with the preparations for my departure. When he saw I was pleased to be going back to England, he suggested we have sex before I left. He was kissing me on the back of my neck when I saw Donna bounce by our house. She was walking her three small dogs. I pointed that going by our house was too much.

'Don't concern yourself about Donna. We'll be far from temptation, hunting in Hill Country.'

I took exception to the word temptation, as if it was an inevitable fact of life.

'Look at the way she hangs around, deliberately walking her dogs past our house. But I'm not going to protest any more. I'm getting out of your way.'

'What do you mean?'

'Let me know when you've worked it out.'

'There's nothing to work out.'

'There is! Something or someone has to change, and it may be me. I may not come back.'

Ignoring the look on Ed's face, I had an announcement to make. 'I've got to make a cheesecake.'

At the second meeting of the League of Women Voters, I had been asked to bake a cheesecake. Donna graciously attended this meeting, and I was happy to see her breasts subdued by a jumpsuit, even though it was a nauseating pink. She sat next to me and said, 'I've just met your wonderful son David. I didn't know he helped out in the Pro Shop.' She certainly knew how to upset me. I gave her a sideways tilt of my head and foolishly put my hand up to make a cheesecake. When Donna applauded me, I whispered to her. 'Don't forget I'm a murder mystery fan: it may be laced with arsenic.'

Cooking calms me. I decided on two cheesecakes, one raspberry for Ed and David, one strawberry for the League. Surrounded by electric appliances and broken eggs I realised two cheesecakes were one too many, but it was too late to stop. I dropped my wine glass, which shattered into micro-balls. Ed came running in and seized the dustpan and brush. I shouted him out of the kitchen, grabbing the dustpan from him.

Donna smiled cautiously when I knocked at her door. She invited me in for coffee, which I refused. Her house smelled of lemon furniture polish.

'The girls love cheesecake.'

I hoped they would all get fat on it. I was surprised how easy it was to understand Donna, and also how unable I was to forgive Ed. I did not think of myself as an unforgiving person, but I was. Perhaps I had too much to forgive.

CHAPTER THREE

I have no notion of where I am. It's an exhilarating feeling. The nurses come and go, talking about my comatose state. I cannot see them because my eyes are covered. I realise I cannot feel my hands. The nurses are talking about contacting my mother. I wonder which mother they mean, Brenda's in Australia and Vivien's in London. I don't want Vivien to visit me. When she visited, she always complained that I don't know how to dress, forgetting I never had money to buy good clothes. What would she think of me wearing white bandages? In a burst of angry energy I catapult myself to the ceiling of my hospital room and look down at myself lying on the bed, trying to get some idea which hospital I am in. Hopeless. The window looks out onto a brick wall.

Ed and I said a fond farewell at the airport. I hoped he didn't notice the jaunty way I walked through the departure gate because I was looking forward to being alone in England. I was thrilled to see Houston and the Astrodome shrink to toy size and the horizon see-saw up and down. I was only sorry my foster parents were in Australia. It would have been comforting to be greeted by them, to sink into their lumpy armchairs and tell them about David becoming a born-again Christian. I was upset when they sold up and left, but never blamed them for following their son to Australia. They wrote regularly at first, but last year I only had one letter. Brenda wrote that Paul was getting married, and she hinted Sidney had a touch of dementia. She told me she had made very supportive friends. She is a friendly woman.

My hotel room was dusty and a disappointment. The single bed looked back at me accusingly. From the square piece of sky allotted me, I could see cloud cover was complete. The sense of freedom that I'd longed for was going to be a challenge. Leaving your family behind is surely the ultimate feminist fantasy but I still had a responsibility to myself. Not wanting to be a tourist in the 'old country' I badly needed a job. If I succeeded in earning a decent wage, I would stay in England because it seemed I could never forgive Ed. Working and living in London would remind me of when I was a young woman with a future ahead of me. I simply told people I was from Brighton and they assumed that's where my parents lived. Unlike school, no one in London needed any more information. I was accepted. I was forever going to interviews for the perfect job, even if I was in no way the perfect secretary.

My old temporary employment agency was in Oxford Street, above a dress shop, run by my friend Marcie, a friend from my political past. As teenagers Marcie and I had sat at the feet of energetic, bearded communists, and learned about the socialism that was to be found in Marx and Engels. Not able to afford a university education, those free classes were the only ones I attended after high school. The Trotskyists were more appealing to the foreign students and nationals, but I was faithful to the originators, and found it impossible to change sides. The Trotskyists had a global reach, Che and Simon Bolivar. The South Americans especially had a passion for Trotsky that I envied. They held much better parties which went on for days, resounding with romantic and revolutionary songs in Spanish. It was at one of these parties that I met Eduardo Fuego, who felt at home with the language and the music, but not the politics. He was American.

Those days were long gone, and I sat in the employment queue listening to a litany of female complaints from every painted mouth. When I was admitted to the inner office, Marcie kissed me on both cheeks as if she were French. Had that custom come to England? Her cheeks were lightly rouged. 'You've come from the U.S. to work here?' she shrilled, her clipped manner now a razor-sharp edge. 'Haven't you heard about the miners' strike?'

'No.'

'Aren't you American now? Can you work in England?'

'Yes. I still have my British passport in my maiden name.'

Marcie was flipping through a Roladex file system. 'Thatcher's on the throne, and the industries are up for grabs. Things have got much worse since you left. Everyone's looking for work. If you've got a Green Card and a job in America, you don't know how lucky you are.'

'Okay, then how about a job abroad? Greece? South Africa? South America?'

'Job in a million you mean? And a million applicants! Do yourself a favour and go home.'

This was not advice I wanted to hear.

'Sounds like you've been living the American Dream.' Sitting opposite my old friend in her employment bureau, it was clear she had also given up politics to become a businesswoman.

'Times have changed. Not going to be so easy for secretaries today.'

I said goodbye and headed towards Tottenham Court Road, which was under construction like it always was. The glamour and glitter of Oxford Street shop windows challenged Marcie's idea of an economic recession. I remembered the fashion buzz here in London with the mini skirt. To me, London looked the same. Carnaby Street was full of tourists, unlike Houston. And there I was, doing my comparisons again. My London was multiracial and multi-ethnic, a city famous for its diverse neighbourhoods as well as boasting glitzy neighbourhoods, like Mayfair and Knightsbridge where my mother once had a penthouse flat.

My jeans and jacket were not enough protection against the penetrating cold damp of England, and I soon gave up wandering the streets. The cold weather made me dread the funeral. Green Park was white with snow, which crunched under my feet. I greeted the bare trees like friends and crossed Pall Mall to make for St. James's Park, which was where I'd walk with my mother parading our newly bought summer dresses. Graceful on high heels, Vivien could not walk in a park without attracting male attention. I was too young to know this was calculated, but I don't remember being jealous of the attention she received. She had an hour-glass figure, being one of the first to have her boobs lifted at the London Clinic. That was back when she was the mistress of an Admiral, a wrinkled eighty-year-old man, who was madly in love with her and rented her a penthouse in Sloane Street. While in that luxurious abode, she invited my foster family to spend Christmas day with her. They came up on the train, Brenda, Sidney and Paul Long, and the day became a good example of was what is now called a culture clash, the townie entertaining the country mice; the mice disdainful but resigned. Of course, it was Brenda who cooked the turkey roast.

On the path ahead of me, a woman wearing a chic blue coat with a fur collar reminded me of Vivien, she had the same confident walk. Except that when I thought about it, Vivien's confident walk was a lie. This unwelcome insight made my legs feel weak, or was it jet lag that made me feel dizzy? Before I fell, someone took hold of my arm and led me to a park bench. A green glow danced in front of my eyes, and then I saw I had been rescued by an old-fashioned city gent, an attractive older man with grey hair.

'Are you all right now?'

'Sure, I'm fine.'

I cannot easily explain my reaction to his smile or the power of his blue eyes. I used to fantasise about being rescued by a distinguished-looking man, a doctor who could save me from a terrible illness. Unfortunately, I've always had perfect health.

'Visiting from America?' He sounded ordinary.

'I am, but I'm not American. The English always think I'm American, but I was born here.'

He edged closer as if he was hard of hearing, which made me sorry that he was old enough to be my father.

'I'm here for my mother's funeral.'

'Sorry to hear that. That must be distressing.'

He sounded too quaint to be real. I had to enlighten him. 'Not really. She topped herself.'

I expected my casual attitude to shock him out of his English cool, but he continued to gaze at me as though he had something to say. His attentive attitude prompted me to be talkative.

'That's why I'm here in England. That's why I'm lodged in London in some awful hotel room.'

'Sorry about that.'

'Her funeral's tomorrow.'

'If you want a better hotel, go to Adelphi Square. There's a good, reasonably priced hotel there.'

'I could use a better place.'

'And you'll be safe there. There are guards everywhere. The whole place was built for members of Parliament. There are buzzers in the rooms to alert MPs when the division bell is sounded.'

This felt like information from another century and so carefully delivered I suspected something. 'Are you a politician?'

'Because I live in Adelphi Square?'

'Oh, do you?'

I had caught him out, him and his intentions. His blue eyes twinkled, but then I saw that wavy green line again. I covered my eyes and made a disapproving face, which made him limp away. I went back to my hotel and found a taxi. When I told the driver Adelphi Square, he gave me an all-knowing wink.

'Everyone knows Dolly Square! the government scandal, right? you must have heard about the Profumo affair.' He wanted to talk about Christine Keeler and

Mandy Rice Davies, to bring them back to life in his dingy black cab but for me it was old news from Vivien's society girl era.

'Those girls were taken advantage of,' I objected like a maiden aunt. 'Sixteen, seventeen... they didn't know they were being used by Russian spies.'

I didn't tell him that things like that didn't happen if you were discreet like my mother. She knew many celebrities who were called personalities back then. She would point them out to me on her small black and white television, which we called the box. Because she knew people in the music industry, she suggested I become a pop singer, until her friends in the music industry heard me sing. Never on a Sunday hit the charts. According to this song, Sunday was the only day a working girl took a day of rest. Her friend, the music producer, wanted my reaction. Would the younger generation buy it? 'If it's a hit everywhere else, why not England?' Not a very original remark, but I did not crave originality. Looking back, I see now that he could have been in cahoots with my mother. They did not want my opinion for the song, so much as to inform me of my mother's source of income. As if Brenda hadn't already warned me!

Adelphi Square took up two city blocks, complete with shops and restaurants, but I wasn't deceived by its façade of solid respectability. I knew what went on behind closed doors. Before her income dried up Vivien lived in expensive city blocks such as this, Richmond Court, Imperial Mansions. My hotel was part of the Adelphi Square residential complex. The room was decorated in exquisite beige, which prompted me to go downstairs to explore. The manager gave me a sideways glance as if I was making his lobby untidy. I slipped out a side door into the ambitiously signposted English Garden. It was freezing outside. To find some warmth I went down some steps to the basement. There I found a maze of underground passageways, hung with heavily lagged piping. I wondered if they led to the House of Commons. The very sturdiness of Adelphi Square prompted me to question how long it was going to last, when the fortress would crumble. These were the kind of thoughts I used to have, crossing Pall Mall on my way to communist meetings. Why now? As if I was being chased, I ran along the corridors with the eerie feeling of being haunted. It came as no surprise when I saw Vivien running ahead of me. I knew it was her ghost, but I didn't care. I ran after her. She was wearing her Chinese silk dressing gown. I always liked her in that pale pink dressing gown. It meant she was in a morning glow, having her first cigarette. Like any good ghost she turned a corner and disappeared, but not before she'd spun around and given me a sad smile. I didn't understand why her ghost appeared in Adelphi Square. As far as I knew, she'd never lived here. I was left staring at the white walls, feeling dizzy in the airless passageways. I frantically found the stairs, and burst through a heavy metal door to collide with a man in uniform.

'And what might you be doing a-down there?'

'What a place!' was my reply.

He did not repeat his question, but I could tell from his searching look that he was making mental notes. 'You mean the underground corridors? Yes, history has a way of being made in those corridors. And where are you off to now?'

'The place is crawling with guards,' I remarked.

He nodded wisely and said with a heavy Irish accent, 'We have to watch out for insurgents, don't we? Protect the Government's VIPs.' As he walked me back to my room, he wanted to impress me. 'Some MPs still have bachelor pads here, convenient to sleep over before taking the morning train to their home constituencies. If they ever go home! When the division bell is sounded, it's the signal for the Members of the House to go and cast their vote after the debate.'

'After the debate? You mean they don't have to show up for the debate?'

'Don't be too curious,' he warned me, as I firmly shut my room door on him.

CHAPTER FOUR

The nurses are talking about someone who has gotten rid of my clothes. There is a scandal about it because I am not dead, only in a coma. Why do American nurses speak in English accents, or am I no longer in Texas? If I am in England, how did I get here? Then I remember being in some crummy hotel room, giving my passport to be inspected and seeing my name.

The next day was the funeral at Wood Vale cemetery. I was curious about who would be there. Ed had told me to look out for any family members in case my mysterious relatives had heard about her death. I doubted that. Perhaps there would be a few friends. I hoped to see her closest friend Cleo, the one friend of my mother's I liked, but I knew most of her friends had been alienated by her drinking. Would I be expected to say a few words? Did I have the courage to tell the story of an orphan who made good, that she was a Party Girl who reached the peak of her dubious profession? No, that sounded wrong. What did I really know about her life other than a few likes and dislikes, that her favourite film was South Pacific? that she liked dancing, her taste being for Latin rhythm, and not rock and roll. Maybe it was better to describe how she looked because looks were important to her, how she loved custom-made suits and low-necked blouses, how her bleached hair became a tasteful ash blonde when she moved uptown to Knightsbridge.

As I was pondering my speech over breakfast, I was summoned to the lobby where I was very surprised to find Cleo. We hugged, and I hoped she was going to accompany me to the funeral. No, she was on her way back to Rome. Funerals were not her style.

'Ed called me about your mother,' she informed me, but immediately understood I didn't want to talk about him. She was the picture of elder chic, her short black hair carefully groomed, her lips bright red. I was sixteen when Vivien took me to Rome where the two friends were both fixtures on the Via Veneto. As the day drew to a close and the streetlights came on, the two expensively dressed women were to be seen al fresco drinking champagne, waiting for a man smart enough and sure enough of himself to speak to them.

'Do you still live in Rome? Is Rome still the Mecca of the glitterati?'

'Not anymore, the rents are too high in the *citta antica*, which of course is good for business.'

'That's right, you went to work for your boyfriend, Savo.'

She pouted. 'Yes, now I'm a real working girl in real estate. We work fifteen hours a day.'

I asked if she knew why my mother committed suicide.

Cleo raised her pencil thin eyebrows. 'You know she became something of an alcoholic.'

'Of course I knew, but even if alcoholism is a tad suicidal, that doesn't mean...'

'She was never an alkie before Paris. I blame Jean Paul: he kept her in that Paris apartment with nothing to do all day. You can't be a mistress of a married man!' Cleo shook her head, as if professional women should know better.

'Why suddenly end her life?'

'Maybe she didn't want to get old. Maybe she was sick with something.'

'I never thought of that. She didn't leave a suicide note!'

Cleo slowly lit a cigarette. I noticed she no longer used a cigarette holder. Cleo and my mother used to belong to the cigarette holders' club.

'It made Vivien sad,' Cleo said carefully, 'seeing you grow up with Brenda, and not being able to get you back. She did what was best for you. Remember that old song? She had the Lp.'

'Please don't sing it!' Useless to protest, it was Cleo's farewell to her friend. With tears in her eyes, she sang, 'When the bells toll the end of the day, I want you here, I want you near me. The name I hear in the wind is yours, Annabel. The bells toll the hours of the day, but you're far, far away.'

When Cleo saw I was upset, she said: 'She never blamed you.' She checked her watch, and reminded me she was on her way to Rome.

'I sent flowers, so look out for them. By the way, the funeral parlour warned me that the crematorium only allows fifteen minutes for each service. I mustn't delay you.'

She was trying to make up for making me listen to that song. She pouted her lips to give me an air kiss without smudging her make up. I reluctantly waved her goodbye.

I hated going by the Tube, watching people's gaunt faces shakily reflected in the dirty windows. I had never been so free, but I had also never been so depressed. I'd lost a mother and deserted a husband and son. Janis Joplin was right: freedom's just another word for nothing left to lose.

When the train stopped at a dimly lit station, I was surprised to see crowds of people in fancy dress. Anything is possible in London. The train doors opened and I ran to exit, but was it the right station? I hovered on the train step, looking down at the gap. The doors behind me slid together with a hiss. I leapt back and fell into the carriage.

'What station do you want?'

'Wood Vale.'

'Two more to go. I'm getting off there.'

I fell back into my seat. On looking up, it was a man with long hair looking sympathetically down at me. Why am I noticing handsome men? Was it because I needed to attract a man now that Ed had taken another woman? As the train rumbled on, so did unwelcome thoughts. That's the trouble with the Underground. My thoughts go underground. I tried to grieve for Vivien. What did her departure mean to my life? It meant there would never be another bed for me in one of her flats. Vivien moved every few years as her bank account thrived and dived, but there was always a bed for me. Sometimes I had my own bedroom, and sometimes I shared her sumptuous king-size bed. The beds were dream beds, richly adorned with organza or muslin ruffles in pale, fairy colours. I'd only be invited to stay one night. Two nights were one too many, and then she would discreetly suggest I leave. Business, I would say to myself. Now all I had to look forward to was seeing her face in the coffin.

The handsome man was nudging my elbow.

'The next stop is yours, Wood Vale. That's the stop for the crematorium.' He nodded in a superior way, or maybe I only presumed it was superior because of his plummy accent. He fell into step beside me. 'I'm going there, too.'

I was grateful for the company, but who was he?

'I thought I recognised you. You're Vivien Langoni's daughter.'

'Yes, have we met?'

'She showed me your photo. I'm a friend of hers.'

I should have known handsome men would attend, although maybe not a man quite so young.

'My name's Adrian. I met your mother at rehab. Alcohol rehab, not drugs.'

That explained Adrian. I remember the distinction at those places between the druggies and the alkies, especially in the expensive drying out clinics, a distinction that used to amuse me.

'My mother always came back with new friends after being in rehab for six weeks. She enjoyed a good social life there.'

Adrian nodded enthusiastically. 'You meet the best people there.' He excused his snobbery with a laugh. 'I mean they are nice people, the staff and everyone.'

I liked the way he guided me out the station and along the street. I didn't like the way Adrian rhymed with Vivien. I wiped rain from my forehead with the heel of my hand. 'Cold and rain again. Perfect weather for a funeral.'

'I hope we're not late. I was warned the ceremony doesn't last long.'

We had missed the religious service, if there was one. Monotone organ music played to the open rafters as we watched a coffin glide through red curtains, which drew together with a swish.

'If that's my mother that's a finale my mother would have appreciated.'

Adrian smiled into my eyes, making me smile. There were half a dozen people filing out, but no one I recognised. Not a mink coat among them. My mother sold the last of her mink coat collection years ago. As we walked slowly down the aisle, I got a pounding in my head like a warning of something, or was it a memory of walking down the aisle when I married Ed in a Roman Catholic ceremony? When we had gathered outside like some sort of meaningful group, someone suggested going to a pub which sounded like a good idea.

Busy ordering drinks, the crowd started to talk and the gloomy atmosphere lightened. There were only surface regrets, batches of conversation wafted my way.

'What a glamour girl she was, so thin and in fashion.'

'Could have been a model.'

'I'm sure she was in show business.'

'You're her daughter?' Almost an accusation from a matching raincoat and bonnet!

'Yes, but I haven't been in touch with her recently.' To immediately forestall their next question, I said hurriedly, 'I have no idea why she did it.'

I got tuts of sympathy but I was reticent, trying to stop them asking me why I wasn't more in touch with my mother. They knew little about her and soon began to talk of other things.

I missed Cleo and was disappointed she wasn't there, but then I remembered she had a ninety-year-old ailing mother. Was that why she was in England?

At the bar I ordered coffee for Adrian's sake while he stood by my side drinking soda water. When Adrian commented on my wish to be silent, I told him 'I'm never of much interest to curious onlookers. I was the sidekick, my mother the main dish. When I was a kid this made me want to steal her spotlight by becoming a famous ballerina. My ballet teacher was not encouraging because of my turn-out.' This made him laugh, which I didn't think appropriate so I added, 'Dreams of becoming rich and famous did not last long when I tried to earn a living in London. It was seeing the wealth around me which inspired me to join the Communist Party. It seemed a sane solution at the time.'

Adrian pretended to agree with my political confession by some furious nodding, an opinion I discounted because of his upper-class accent. He had about him a general desire to want to please everyone; a trait I had noticed in my mother, and which I mistrusted. We were about to leave the crowded pub when we were accosted by a small man with straight blonde hair.

'Hello, I'm Jason. I was the social worker assigned to Vivien's case.'

'Jason, of course, it was you who called me in Texas. Thank you for your help.'

'I feel guilty,' he confessed, edging us into a corner. 'I'm sure she wouldn't have done it if I was on hand.

If only I hadn't taken a couple of months' off to go to India. I left notes for her to be visited, but no one had time for my clients. Thatcherism! Terrible cuts are being made. They know more about efficiency in India.'

'Did she have any serious illness?'

'No, no. She was lonely. She'd be alive today if she'd been able to stay at the clinic, but we had to discharge her. She wasn't mentally unstable enough. I got her admitted to a respite house, but a wobble isn't a mental condition.'

'A wobble?'

'She was basically sane, as I'm sure you know. At the Priory she was the life and soul of the party. The staff loved her and she helped them do the tea trolley and clear up the art room.'

'My mother felt at home in institutions and clinics, perhaps because she was raised in an orphanage.'

Jason wanted to know more, but that was all I could tell him. 'I'm sure you did your best,' I assured him although I could see he felt responsible. 'How do we know it was suicide? Maybe it was murder. Would anyone want her dead?'

Jason looked shocked. 'I don't think so. She tried to slit her wrists in the bath and when that didn't work, she took sleeping pills.' He had tears in his eyes when he said this. 'It could have been left-over anxiety after the court case.'

I turned to Adrian, who shook his head to indicate he didn't know about any court case. Jason cleared his throat and took another sip of his larger. 'Your mother, Vivien, used to go drinking with a friend of hers, a Leo Martello. A couple of years ago, they got into an argument and she bashed him over the head with a bottle. The result was...' Jason drew a deep breath, as if uneasy about speaking ill of the dead. '... the result was, he lost an eye.'

'I never knew this.'

'She was charged with assault and had to wait a year or two for her case to come to court, but he didn't press charges. She was reprimanded and received a suspended sentence. When she began to drink again, I was assigned to her case.'

Ah, so the welfare system was allied to the criminal justice system. 'Leo Martello. I've heard that name, a name from the past. I think he was an old boyfriend.'

'A dodgy character.'

I'd forgotten the English fondness for that descriptive word. I wanted to hear more about Leo.

'He was on file at the police station. They were both drinking late into the night, but your mother blamed herself. She felt terribly guilty about it. Maybe that's why...'

'Were you the one who found her?'

'The postman. She'd invite him in for a cup of tea.'

'The postman and a cup of tea? Doesn't sound like her.'

'I think she laced it with vodka. I have joined them on occasion. When the postman noticed the coupons piling up he got worried.'

My chic mother collect coupons? I asked if Jason knew how she earned her living.

'Oh yes. We kept a dossier on her because she moved in elevated circles, but nothing in her file was incriminating. After the Profumo affair, MI5 were playing it safe, but Vivien was considered harmless and she was, except for the pub incident which was probably provoked.'

Jason was Vivien's champion. He passed me the keys to her flat which I took with obvious hesitation. Adrian offered to go to the flat with me, and I gratefully accepted.

CHAPTER FIVE

I have intermittent memories of David and Ed, but still cannot work out what happened to me. I remember meeting some man, or two men, one with blue eyes, one with long hair, but then I immediately get an image of Ed. This is not comforting, because there's something wrong with that Ed. He is not the man I married.

Adrian and I took a cab to a basement in Fulham; no longer the penthouse for my mother. We climbed carefully down wet concrete steps. When we opened the door, there it was. Not the smell of death, but a morbid deadness hanging in the air. No sign of dust or untidiness, and for once I was thankful for her obsessive cleanliness.

Someone had obviously been through her files. If they were looking for a will they would have been disappointed; my mother had nothing to leave anyone. On top of her papers was a newspaper article.

'Is that your mother in the Daily News?'

Her flattened face and large pensive eyes stared out at us.

'Yes, I remember that news story. Some guy bought her a Triumph sports car. The car's interior was leopard skin velvet. She must have looked a Hollywood picture when she took the roof off, because so many cars slowed down to look at her it caused a traffic accident.'

Adrian and I marvelled at the photo, which showed just the right amount of cleavage. The caption read, 'Vivien Langoni, photographer's model. A luscious blond. '

'She really did have friends who were photographers. She lived above their shop and modelled for them.'

Adrian had another prize. 'Is this you?' It was a photo of my mother and myself with one of her escorts at a nightclub.

'Yeah, my sixteenth birthday.'

'Is that your father?'

'How do I know? but I don't think so, because she gave that picture to Brenda, my foster mother, and if Brenda knew it was my father, I'm sure she would have told me.'

'Looks like someone important.'

'Maybe a diplomat or cabinet minister.' I tried to laugh.

'You look more Italian than your mother.'

'Blame my Italian grandfather. Whoever he was.'

In a tattered paper file we found my mother's birth certificate, I was reminded she had been christened Irene, Irene Langoni.

'She said she changed her name to Vivien at the orphanage, because there were three Irenes. But maybe she changed her name when she became a Party Girl.

It does make her sound more glamorous. Anyway, the name certainly worked for her.'

Adrian raised his eyebrows. 'Any chance of a cuppa?'

'Doubtful.'

Her kitchen was always clean and unused, nothing in the fridge except vodka and tonic.

I took a deep breath and ventured into the bedroom, and even more cautiously entered the bathroom. There was a pool of dry blood in the bottom of the tub. The sides were splattered with brown spots. The sign of the bloodied kitchen knife still in the bath sent me into an inferno of rage. There was no one in her life, no one to clean the mess except me. I was destined to clean up this last act of hers and I did it slowly and carefully, like it was some form of penance. I suppressed the desire to curse her for causing so much trouble. She was already drinking herself to death; wasn't that quick enough? I kept these uncharitable thoughts to myself. Adrian especially would not sympathise. I ran the taps to wash the tub clean.

'If the police were here, shouldn't they have taken that knife?'

Adrian came to the doorway.

'The knife didn't kill her. She took pills, didn't she? Look what I've found in the file.'

He held up a heavy coin, hanging on a multi-coloured ribbon. 'It's some kind of war medal. There's an iron cross on the back.'

'I've no idea what that is. Some man left it behind, I expect. 'Let's get out of here.'

Adrian was sensitive to my grim mood and helped me gently on with my coat. I had not even been aware of throwing it down. 'If you cannot bear to be here, I suggest we take the paperwork with us.'

I accepted the offer of dinner at his house. He meant the house of his parents because he still lived at home, a manse in Holland Park Road guarded by iron railings, a wrought iron gate and a Beware of Dogs sign. Two German Shepherds appeared and affectionately jumped on both of us. Adrian told me his dogs were his best friends. His drinking must have tested his friends' patience and left him, like my mother, with no friendships.

'You're welcome to stay the night. My parents are in Mozambique and we have nine bedrooms.'

'What are they doing here?'

'They're in copper. Don't ask.'

The size and opulence of the house told me more than I wanted to know. As the communists used to joke, all property (proper tea) is theft. In this case the theft of copper, I said to myself.

'Has my mother been here?'

'Oh, yes, often after we buddied up at AA. My parents liked her and used to invite her to our midsummer's eve parties.'

In midsummer the trees along the railings would be in full leaf. I imagined there would be a marquee on the wide expanse of a front lawn that was an amazing size for being in the middle of London. Plenty of booze to tempt the two of them! If Adrian's parents lived in this imperialist's mansion, they must wield a great deal of power in the financial district of London. I was shown the rest of the house. Royalty would have felt at home here. The bedrooms were period pieces, the bathrooms marble. Adrian's old room was lined with books and posters from his college days. His parents had left it untouched. I mused on the role of parents, the kind I had never had.

Dinner was served by a Spanish housekeeper who brought us heaped plates of spaghetti, fruit, salad, veal cutlets. We both made enthusiastic noises but ate little. When the housekeeper came to clear the plates, she watched me carefully as if I was going to steal the silver. I was submitting myself to this luxury for a reason. I wanted to quiz Adrian about my mother.

'Do you know if Vivien was seeing anyone special? Was she having an unhappy love affair with a married man, for instance?' Adrian shook his head.

'Have you always called your mother Vivien?'

'She wanted me to call her mum, but I couldn't. My foster mother was more my mother. So you have no idea why she was that depressed? No man in her life?'

'I remember Vivien going out with a stockbroker a few years ago. He wanted to marry her, but he had a heart attack.'

'You mean he had a heart attack when they were making love?'

'That may have been her last lover.'

I remembered she had suddenly advised Ed to buy gold. That must have been when she was dating the stockbroker. Buy gold, when we could hardly afford to pay the mortgage!

Adrian had turned his back on me and was inspecting the marble mantle shelf, moving the Lladró sculpture to one side. Talk of my mother may not have been wise. There was no bar or alcohol in sight, but he probably had a bottle hidden somewhere. The one time my mother visited us she hid a bottle under a bush in the garden.

To distract him from thinking about an after-dinner drink I suggested we go through the paperwork again. In a battered orange folder we found a birth certificate for an Ann Page Cuthbert.

'Who's that? Maybe a cousin or someone. What's the date of birth?'

When he told me, I was puzzled. 'But that's my birthday.'

'Then this is your birth certificate.'

'It can't be. That's not my name.'

'The mother's name is listed as Vivien's.'

'Then I must have a sister I don't know about.'

'Not with the same birth date. You have been going under a made-up name.'

'Hardly made up,' I protested. 'My mother wasn't married, so I took her name.'

'Your father seems to have registered your birth, and his name is...' Adrian waved the paper at me in triumph. I tried to grab it and he waved it higher.

'Don't keep me in suspense.'

'Hubert Edgar Cuthbert, listed as father. Your name is clearly written, Ann Page Cuthbert. I don't know how you ended up with Annabel Langoni.'

Even as Adrian asked the question, I knew how. My mother could dazzle her way through any government office to get what she wanted. If she changed her own name from Irene to Vivien, she could easily change mine.

'I wonder why my father disappeared from my life. Do you think he ended up in prison? And what's this MC after his name? Is it a degree?'

Adrian peered closer. 'I think that means Military Cross. He's won a military decoration. Hey, that's the medal I found, I showed it to you. What I don't understand is that it's a medal from World War One. It said so on the back of the medal. War for Civilization, that's what they called World War One. They didn't know there was going to be another of them.'

'You know more history than I do.'

'But that means your father must have been born before nineteen hundred. And if that's so, he was old when he fathered you. He must have been fifty or so.'

'Not so old,' I protested, remembering my own age. 'If, in fact, that is my father's medal.'

Adrian seemed convinced, 'At least he's a war hero. Cuthbert sounds like an old English name, but it's a name I haven't heard before.

'Me neither, Not many Cuthberts in Houston.'

'Sounds like Chaucer, or it could be an Elizabethan name.' Adrian took me upstairs to show me an Elizabethan portrait on the upper landing. I was not impressed. The more I saw of this soulless house, the more I wanted to redecorate. I began to see him as a potential client.

'I can't believe with nine bedrooms you're still in the same bedroom.'

'I was married briefly. Where do you want to sleep?'

I looked into his eyes. They wavered. Ed always looked straight at me. He put an arm around me. 'You're much prettier than Vivien.'

I gave him a wry look. He thought that was something I wanted to hear. I wonder how friendly he was with my mother. Good looks always tempted her, and although my mother expressed a taste for distinguished looking men, this did not mean she wasn't attracted to other forms of masculine beauty.

'If I'm staying the night, I need a bath.'

Even the guest bathroom was a grand affair with black and white tiles, and a standing bath on curved legs. With the warm water bubbling between my legs, I relaxed for the first time since I'd landed in England. Adrian did not join me in the bath, but he made a point of seeing me naked as he thoughtfully provided me with his pyjamas and an old-fashioned candle-wick dressing grown. He led me to a bedroom with twin beds stacked with designer pillows. He threw himself on one of them, feigning exhaustion. He just needed company and I knew why. If he went to bed alone, he would get out that bottle. Maybe loneliness is why anyone drinks. I understood because I was now more alone than I'd ever been. When I thought of that, I wanted more than company and reached out a hand to him. It was a clumsy attempt at seduction, and he did not notice.

****

A man is kissing my mother, kissing her in a loving and determined way. She instantly responds. As the second tick by, I want to stop dreaming this, but I also want to see more. I can only see the back of his head, and I find this very disturbing.

'I lost one of my black gloves,' she tells him. 'Oh, I'll have to buy you some more!'

I can see his hand slide up her tight skirt. 'But I'm glad you are wearing your best stockings.'

'It's Christmas!'

'Oh yes! Yes, it is!'

****

I woke up full of fear, not knowing exactly what I was afraid of. Adrian sat up in the other bed as if he had never been asleep.
'You were having a nightmare.'
'Sorry, I woke you up.'
I couldn't get back to sleep. I kept hearing Cleo singing the song, Annabel. My mother once boasted that the song might have been written for her; she was always implying that she was on friendly terms with the rich and famous. So my father was a war hero; maybe he was also rich and famous, a lord, a duke? Why didn't I insist on knowing more about him? I jumped out of bed.
'There must be something more about my father in my mother's things. We missed something, a photo, a letter. I should go through that stuff before the Salvation Army comes. My father can't have been a one-night stand if his name was on my birth certificate.'
'Definitely not'
'Why didn't I make her tell me? I hate not knowing who he is, who he was. Maybe he's a duke or something.'
Adrian generously insisted on coming with me, which meant we took a cab. While he was paying

the taxi driver, I ran down, and got caught in a wire stretched across the steps. I bounced backwards. An explosion burst my eardrums. I looked up to see chunks of concrete raining down on me. My hands went to protect my bare head and I just had time to think, *Ah, that's what happened!*

****

A shuffling in my hospital room alerts me to two tall policemen on either side of my bed. 'Don't think she's going to be much help. But they want to know what she was doing in that particular spot.' They exchange helpless looks and replace their comical helmets. What do they mean? Suddenly I remember going down my mother's basement steps and using my arms to protect my head. That's why the police are here. Am I going to be charged with something? In my bandaged state that's almost laughable. 'Too many head injuries. I'm afraid we're losing her.'

The anxiety in this voice amuses me. I'm not going to be lost. I'm leaving my hospital bed and leaving my damaged body behind.

****

Part II

CHAPTER SIX

'Annabel, you don't realise you've been influenced by other people your entire life. You never asked enough questions because you never wanted to know. You moaned about being kept in the dark, but you liked it. That's going to change.'

I hear this voice without understanding it, but I'm not confused. I know on some level I've escaped. Yes, this is what I've always been trying to do, ever since that day I tried to get out of that London taxi. I'm joyful at the thought of escape. When I open my eyes, I'm looking up at a bright blue sky. That means I'm still alive. When I struggle to my feet and look around, I see that I am in a severely damaged part of town. Has this devastation been caused by a bomb, my bomb? When I look more closely, I can see by the crumbling façades looming over me that this damage was caused some years ago. Is this where Vivien used to live? I can see no landmarks, except for one huge quarry in front of me, a hole at least a hundred feet deep. In the bottom of the pit there is a burnt-out shell of a London taxi.

What's happened? Was this caused by a hydrogen bomb? or an atomic bomb? I notice I'm not breathing. I don't seem to be breathing. Anxiety must have taken my breath away. A nuclear explosion of this size could have reached my family, even as far away as Texas. I fervently hope they are safe and not suffering from radiation. I must call Ed, but I already know there is no calling anyone from here. I yearn to hear his comforting voice. I see again the Houston skyscrapers from my window seat, the toy astrodome. Surprised, I'm thinking of Houston as home.

I glide down the streets of this ghost town dotted with skeletal structures that used to be houses, crumbling façades about to collapse; a tall Victorian house with its roof caved in stands out like an exclamation point. The next street is lined with houses that have had their walls blown away, revealing inner walls of peeling wallpaper, a washbasin hanging by its water pipes. I'm sure no one could have survived such destruction. Where am I? I walk through a row of concrete columns, still standing tall. They are leading me nowhere. Trying to make sense of the row of concrete columns behind me, I look back to discover I've been walking down the central aisle of what must have been a magnificent church. In front of me is a small gate of twisted iron, which must have led to the altar.

I turn away sickened and pick up a fallen road sign and brush it clean, 'Cripplegate'. I stare in amazement at this ominous sign, and look around for someone to ask directions. Across mounds of fallen masonry, I am thrilled to see a small group of people, They are all dressed in black or some dark colour that stands out against the ashy landscape. On the edge of the group a small girl is running up to the top of a heap of fallen stones. Dimly I hear her singing, 'I'm the king of the castle, you're the dirty rascal!' At first, I have an idea she is me. I have played that game, king of the castle on a pile of newly mown grass. A motherly figure chases her off and gives her head a mean cuff before pushing her toward the group. The mourners, if that's what they are, cautiously form a circle, making a forlorn attempt at cohesion. A priest walks past, heading a ragged procession of more people in black. He is resplendent in a robe of purple, gold and silver. He circles the group, swinging incense and chanting something in Latin. A young man steps awkwardly into the centre of the group, awkward because his left foot is encased in a heavy black boot. His dark hair is brushed back and gleaming with Brylcreem. Ah, that's a word I'd forgotten, a brand name from my English childhood. The man with a heavy boot on one foot must be symbolic, because the sign said Cripplegate. The symbolism makes me think I've wandered into a World War Two movie. If I'm in a film, that could be interesting. I edge closer to the group to hear what is going on.

'We will never forget this scene of destruction,' the young man with the booted foot shouts to his listeners. 'It will be commemorated every December. The innocent civilians who perished here will be remembered every year. We will not forget. We will swear today, a solemn oath, that they will not be forgotten. No one will forget the terrible number of people who died here.'

A couple of people in the crowd cheer him on.

'The Blitz will be remembered even if this part of London is rebuilt. The years 1940 to 1942 will be honoured forever.'

'Never forgotten!'

The little girl begins to cry, and some people are wiping their eyes.

'And God willing, we will gather here every year in the future to remember those poor souls who were burned to death or buried alive.'

Sobs are heard.

'In Spiritus Sancti.' The priest swings incense at the crowd.

A bulky woman steps out of the crowd. 'Hitler thought he could invade, but we are giving it back to him now! We'll give 'em hell, too!'

The crowd hoots and laughs at this comment. The priest, rather aggressively, swing his incense over them as if to silence such remarks. I look around to see if I can see hidden cameras.

'All those who have lost loved ones in this very place, step up and say their names.'

No one moves.

The priest confers with the heavy-booted young man and then approaches a well-tailored woman in severe black.

'Mrs. Walter, perhaps you and your niece would like to come up?'

Mrs. Walter shakes her head slowly as if overwhelmed by the request. The young girl turns away with a sneer.

The ground rumbles, and a few people cross themselves.

'Are the tunnels going to collapse?'

'They haven't yet.'

'Hey! That was a rat,' someone yells. 'A big rat ran by!'

'In those dreadful two years,' the priest intones as if he was singing a mass, 'there was a rain of fire many times greater than the famous London fire of 1666, but look at us; we are alive!' A louder cheer this time. As if this is the finale of the scene, the priest makes the sign of the cross and a few people impatiently detach themselves from the group. The news that these people remember the Blitz, which looks like it has just happened, makes some sort of sense because I'm obviously still in London. This is a comforting thought. So I am wrong in thinking this destruction was caused by a nuclear bomb. This is not a nuclear holocaust, or any future event, they are referring to the last war. If this isn't a movie set, I've gone back in time to the past. I do not believe this.

I try to remember which year World War Two ends, and I turn to my neighbour to ask him. The man ignores me.

'Hey, I'm talking to you. Please answer me.'

In spite of this shrill demand, he looks past me. I do a little dance in front of him and have to conclude that he cannot see me. I try rubbing my eyes, hoping it is just a nightmare, but the scene remains the same. Then I find my eyes can no longer blink. This frightens me because it feels like a sign of madness. A man in the distance captures my attention. He is making for our group and making long strides in spite of his limp. He bears an uncanny resemblance to the man I met in St. James's Park. What is he doing here? I must keep him in sight, my gentleman. His appearance comforts me. I am not in a fantasy of my own making. I'm not trapped in nightmarish past. I am in the middle of a movie, and the actors have been instructed to ignore me. Yes, this is an explanation I can live with. And if my gentleman is a movie star, that would account for his superior attitude towards me in the park. He is greeted by several people and is ushered into the middle of the circle. The priest steps forward. 'Welcome my good friend, Hugh. This man here deserves applause! This man worked day and night on the salvage crew.' My gentleman half smiles, and waves apologetically.

'Sorry I'm late. What about you, Ben?' He turns to the man with the booted foot. 'You saved a good many. How many people did you dig out of cellars?'

The crowd begins to clap, a pathetically soft sound in that abandoned place.

'There cannot be enough thanks for you, Ben!' The two men shake hands in a manly way.

My gentleman addresses the crowd. 'To those of us who remember this place as an inferno, we can only marvel at our survival. In commemorating this mass grave of so many people, we also have to look to the future. Better men than me have said this, but to reiterate, we must have faith that this country will, like the phoenix, rise from the ashes!'

Everyone cheers. The priest takes over as people kneel in front of him and he puts out a ringed hand to bless the tops of their heads.

'If we have survived', he intones, 'it is the Will of God. If we have survived it is to do God's Holy Work.'

My gentleman limps off, but I'm determined to catch up with him. He disappears down a narrow lane, and I run after him. I am beginning to have my doubts about him being an actor, but do not want to entertain any other explanation. If he really was my city gent in the park, he can explain what is happening.

I follow him with difficulty, cursing the alleyways and twittens that London is famous for. We reach Regent Street and I'm grateful to find its sturdy buildings still standing. The imposing fake Tudor building, which is the shop Liberty, looks the same as usual except for the surrounding sandbags. My eye catches some interesting fabric behind a window and a couple of shoppers are entering its wood-beamed interior. Most of the other shops and restaurants in Regent Street are boarded up. So everyone was expecting that bomb! Carnaby Street is strewn with litter and someone has made a shelter out of fallen bricks. On a raised counter on the corner, a burly man in an apron is selling drinks and sandwiches. He looms over his customers as if his mere presence is doing them an enormous favour. Maybe he is. I watch dispirited looking men and women come and go. I am sure now that I'm not dreaming, this is much too real. A tall young man joins me at the counter, but even he has to reach up to be heard. I like what he's wearing. He's in a beige uniform, and I'm sure that means he is American.

'Hey man! Can I buy a mug of tea here? No sugar!'

'No sugar, the man says!' the burly man barks out a laugh.

'No sugar, no SUGAR!' he shouts.

'No, thanks; no sugar.'

The American doesn't know why the burly man is so amused. I want to talk to this soldier and ask where he is from, but as I push myself in front of him, it is obvious he cannot see me. Another wave of insecurity: he is real, but I am not. I am about to despair when I see my gentleman go by. He is not stopping for a cup of tea, but I manage to catch up with him, convinced he will be able to see me. I throw myself in front of him and I am right. He can see me!

'I've been following you from Cripplegate.' He acknowledges this with a nod.

'I saw you at the ceremony. And we've met before, in the park. Don't you remember? You had a wavy green line round you, but you don't now.' It is clear he does not remember. 'You advised me to go to a hotel in Adelphi Square.'

'I'm on my way there now.' He says with surprising civility.

'Yes, that's what you said before.'

I follow him along the street, nimbly stepping over sandbags heaped along the curb. Some windows are crossed with tape, as if there was a tornado warning.

'What's happened here? Has a bomb dropped or something?'

'I'd say so.' He smiles, without meaning it.

'Are we at war again? Argentina? The Falklands?'

He frowns as if I am speaking another language. 'I would say we're at war, yes. I would say that! Where have you been?'

'Me? Houston, I suppose.'

He nods and walks on. I rack my brains for a suitable topic of conversation.

'I saw you at that commerative ceremony. The English love their history, don't they? They kept referring to the year 1940.

'Were you making a movie or being filmed for television?'

'Tele...what?'

We look at each other with mutual misunderstanding. He strides on towards Green Park, and I'm relieved to see that hasn't changed. A heavenly sound and two small boys, their faces scrubbed and shining, are playing the violin. We slow down to listen to some classical piece that soars right through me. Raised on rock and roll, I never bothered to listen to classical music, but I can suddenly hear rhythms and patterns I've never heard before. I turn to my companion.

'So young and playing like angels.' This comes out sounding more romantic than I intended. 'They ought to go far.

They must be from a local music school.'

He looks slightly disapproving and I regret my enthusiasm.

'I doubt there are music schools now.'

'Now?' I want to ask what he means by that, but I'm afraid of the answer. 'I've wanted to thank you for recommending Adelphi Square. My name's Mrs. Annabel Fuego.' I deliberately give him my married name. We are walking past shop windows that are not covered in tape. In the glass is reflected a tall, sombre man, but I see no reflection of myself. This is troubling, but there is so much to be troubled about. The newspaper vendors look like they're from another century and they selling newspapers dated December 1944. I refuse to think about this. 'Are you famous or something?'

'Hardly.'

'So why you won't tell me your name?'

'It's Hugh.'

'Do you work in the city? What kind of work do you do in the city?'

He screws up his face. 'Goodness me! You Americans are so forthright!'

'That proves we've met before. You know I'm American.'

'From your accent!'

In spite of his limp, he is putting some distance between us and I have to run to catch up.

'Don't worry, I'm not going to ask you how much money you make.'

'If you must know, I'm a tax inspector in His Majesty's Revenue Department.' He says this with menace, as if everyone should be wary of a tax inspector, but then his eyes twinkle and I fight down an attraction to him.

'Are you married?'

'As a matter of fact,' he must begin all his replies this way.

'We've just had a baby.'

'Congratulations.'

'A few months ago.'

We make our way down the wide thoroughfare that leads to Adelphi Square. I notice this time he uses his rolled up umbrella for a cane. We have now reached our destination, but I'm surprised to see the entry is no longer glass with automatic sliding doors. A large wooden door swings open. I look around confused.

'Where's the hotel?'

'There's no hotel here. Only residences.'

He crosses the lobby and goes to the metal mailboxes to unlock one. As he stands shuffling through envelopes, I read the name on the mailbox he has just opened, Hubert Edgar Cuthbert. Where have I seen that name before? Oh, that's right, on my birth certificate, the one I found in my mother's flat. It is my father's name.

'I thought you said your name was Hugh? Is your name Hugh or Hubert?'

'I call myself Hugh because well... because Hubert is old fashioned.'

'But that's my father's name. I've just read it on my birth certificate.'

'Excuse me?'

Of course, now it all makes sense. I have been guided here to meet him. This must be the only explanation.

'Don't you see? That's why I'm here. I'm here to meet you.'

He backs away from my excitement and reads his mail in an effort to discourage me, while I take a closer look at him. He is a tall man with tired lines round his blue eyes, a square handsome face but there is something negative about him, as if he's hiding something. 'Look,' I say consolingly, 'there could be another explanation. Maybe you have two daughters. Maybe I'm the result of a one-night stand. If you have any doubts, we could do a DNA test.'

He frowns in bewilderment, staring at the newspaper in his hand. It's *The Times*, and the front page looks much like it does in 1984, but when I look closer the date is December 17th, 1944. This time I have to accept the evidence. I am visiting my father not in real time, in dream time, or simply in the past. We stand motionless in the mailbox room on the edge of nowhere. This meeting which I've always hoped for, is now happening.

'I've come from the future.' I proudly announce. 'I am your future daughter. I'm your daughter who's visiting you from the future.'

Naturally he looks at me as if I was crazy. 'I'm sorry but you are sadly deluded. My daughter's upstairs with her mother, and I'm on my way up to see her.'

'Right, my mother's name is Vivien Langoni. She had an Italian father, which is all I know about my relatives.'

That last bit of information unsettles him. He is now afraid and escapes down the corridor.

I run after him.

'Let me tell you, I think you and this whole city, this whole era is a fantasy designed especially for me. I don't know what I'm doing here in the past unless it's to meet you. I am here because of you. Don't you see that? I've come back to the past because I have to meet you.'

'I don't appreciate... you're bothering me.'

'Yeah, well, you've bothered me a great deal. You weren't there. You disappeared. I didn't even know your name until yesterday, if it was yesterday.'

'I have to get back home.' He purposely leaps up the stairs, two at a time. He runs towards a door facing us, 101.

'I don't understand it either. You must be a ghost.'

'Me? You're a ghost by the look at you. And why are you claiming to be my daughter? You cannot be my daughter. She's only six months old.'

'Ok, that must be some other daughter. I'm 40. And you look old enough to have a 40-year-old daughter. You look 60.'

'I am 52. You could not possibly be my daughter.'

'I've just learned that my real name is not Annabel Langoni, it's Ann Page Cuthbert!'

An aggressive tremor goes through his body. 'I don't know where you got that information from, but please stop following me. My daughter is inside, with her mother.'

'Why don't you ask her, then? Ask Vivien.'

He reluctantly unlocks the door and we both enter a small, dull flat decorated with pictures of faded landscapes. One electric lamp gives the place a dusky dimness, which is pierced by the screams of an angry baby. He pushes open a bedroom door and there is a half-naked baby in a carrycot, red-faced from crying. 'Christ Almighty, she can't leave a baby alone like that!' He rushes out, leaving me to contemplate the baby. Could she be me? She looks at me with angry dark eyes, tears running down her cheeks. Why didn't he pick me up? Why leave in search of an errant mother? Then it dawns on me: this is another era, a time when men did not deal with a crying baby.

If this is 1944, this has to be me. I note with approval the satin quilt, but am upset by her unhappy face, although I know from experience that even well-loved babies are great protesters. I lean toward her and sniff, but I have no sense of smell. As a mother I know that babies always smell of milk. I put a hand to touch her, but although I can see my fingers reach her little arm there's no sensation. No sense of smell, no sensation of touch, and yet everything has the solid look of reality, from the shaded light to the bare walls.

A heated argument is going on between my parents as they return to the bedroom. 'She's all right!' My mother grabs me up in an unfriendly way. She does not react to my presence, so I have to conclude Vivien cannot see me, which gives me a chance to eye her. She is skinnier and more nervous than I have ever known her. Her large dark eyes look bigger than ever. My father is too angry to notice that my mother cannot see me.

'What if something happened to her? I can't believe you left her crying!'

'Nothing happened to her, and you were late. For all I knew a bomb got you and you weren't coming back.'

'If you went to Jack and Marian's, why didn't you take her?'

'She was crying. You can't visit them with a crying baby. She's still crying.'

My father waves a forefinger at my mother. 'You should have kept her quiet. You know I'm not supposed to have babies here.'

'You try stopping her.'

'We could be asked to leave.'

'I know! She's just a visitor, like I am.'

This barb from my mother makes him take a calmer more reasonable approach.

'Does she need feeding?'

'She's been fed three times today! I thought about giving her some of your whisky.' Does she say this to scandalise him? My mother takes me to the bathroom and runs water into the basin. 'She likes water,' she yells back at Hugh who is standing in the doorway.

'But now her nappy's all wet.'

After he leaves, my mother raises a vicious foot to kick the bathroom door closed. She's no right to take that attitude, he was only trying to help. Young mothers are always under pressure. My eye catches a tin pail of soiled linen and wonder if there's a washing machine somewhere. My mother flips water at the baby's face, which does not stop her crying. Then she scoops up some water and throws it down the baby's throat. '

Stop!' I cry out. 'Don't hurt me.' My mother hears nothing and when the baby spits the water out, she shakes me. The crying stops, but surely that's harsh treatment for a crying child. The baby looks away from her. Smart kid! I'm just about to accuse Vivien of child abuse when she covers the baby's face with kisses. The baby leans her head back and gives the world a faraway look.

My father must be in the kitchen because I hear my mother yell at him, 'Put the kettle on for her bottle!' She is now hugging the baby to her like the fondest of mothers. I tour the stuffy living room. A large cabinet radio suddenly beeps a few times, as if giving an alarm.

'In the 6 o'clock news today.' an unmistakable BBC voice announces, 'there are reported advances from Allied forces, although they have been repelled in certain areas. Casualties have been recorded as a result of massive German resistance, but the Belgian prime minister told MPs this afternoon that the situation is well in hand.'

The war! And if this is 1944, it must be World War Two. I take note of damage in the building opposite. Loss of two upper floors. I know the war will be won, but not sure when. I wish I'd paid more attention in history class. On top of the cabinet radio, which I remember was called a wireless, there is an array of almost empty liquor bottles and a soda siphon with a silver top. I haven't seen one of those in years. Every Christmas my foster father, Sidney Long, would bring out a soda siphon.

My real father appears at the door as if not pleased to see me.

'You still here?' he asks aggressively.

'Where else?' I say no more because I'm watching my mother collect the bottle and settle down to feed me. The force of her youth and beauty illuminates that dingy interior. I know she gave birth to me when she was nineteen, still a teenager, and now I've learned my father is fifty-two. That makes him thirty years older, which does not matter if they are in love.

My father is watching me, watching my mother. He looks away, as if embarrassed. 'Vivien cannot see you,' he whispers.

'I know,' I tell him 'That's upsetting me too. I don't understand why sometimes I'm invisible.'

'The whole thing's a joke!' My father clutches his head. 'You're not real. You're an hallucination.'

'I don't think so. For all I know, you are an hallucination and so is everything I see.'

'You're the ghost! And to prove it, your mother cannot see you!'

'Maybe she doesn't want to.'

'Then you're a figment of my imagination.'

I'm outraged by that casual dismissal. 'I could say the same of you.'

My father helps himself to a whisky and downs it quickly.

'I must be taking too many pills if I'm seeing ghosts.'

'What pills?'

'Barbiturates! Prescribed for my injury, an old war wound.'

'You've been fighting in the war?'

'Not this one, the one before. The war to end all wars!' Another of his ironic smiles. I'm getting to expect them. 'In this war,' he informs me, 'I've got a government job. In the last one, I was in the trenches.'

Although he says this quietly, he says it with pride. I want to hear more, but he sits down with a finality which silences me. Now he is watching Vivien.

'I may be drinking too much,' my father tells her. 'Or taking too many barbiturates. I'm seeing phantoms!'

My mother ignores him, and continues to nurse her baby, me, with a bottle. My father gazes at her attentively and there's a shift in the atmosphere. I remember Ed watching me feed David with a similar love-light in his eyes. When she rises with the sleeping baby and enters the bedroom, my father turns to me.

'Would you be so good as to leave now?'

I stand without knowing where I'm going. He empties a bound leather briefcase on the table. The boredom of paperwork surrounds him, but he seems determined to deal with it.

'Tell me about your work.'

'PAYE,' he replies. 'Pay As You Earn. A new system of taxation, but as with all these new schemes, they forgot something important; they forgot to include people's bank accounts. The MPs and the House of Lords didn't imagine ordinary wage earners had savings, taxable savings in their personal bank accounts. Now it's all got to be refigured.'

He doesn't want me here. I can hardly blame him, but that doesn't stop me feeling hurt. I search for the most hurtful thing I can say.

'I intend to go down to Brighton and visit Brenda and Sidney. At least the Longs will be glad to see me.'

'The Longs? You know about them?'

Ah, now I have some credibility. 'They raised me, didn't they?'

He nods slowly, beginning to take me seriously. 'For a phantom of my imagination you have a lot to say for yourself. Your mother's taking you down to Brighton tomorrow. The Longs can offer you a good home.'

He could be talking about a dog. 'But why?'

'The bombs. You're being evacuated to the country.'

He wants to get rid of me because he cannot have children here. I've seen documentaries about adopted children seeking their birth parents and how those children smiled and acted nicely and politely towards their parents. I'm now inclined to think those adopted children must have secretly wanted to stab them in the back for so lightly giving them away.

'I assure you...' my father begins.

'Who are you talking to?' my mother wants to know.

'No one.'

'What's that doing on the table? You're not going to work?'

'Afraid so.'

Suddenly this domestic scene is shaken by a tremendous sonic boom. They both freeze.

'No warning!' My father says quietly. They stand motionless a few seconds, as if the slightest movement would bring down the entire block. Then they throw themselves into a tight embrace. He kisses her protectively while they hug, but I can see they don't trust the silence.

'Sounds like a gas explosion.' Vivien says in a low voice.

'Right, only it's not.' My father's voice has an unassuming authority, like a teacher's. 'V2s. Unmanned rockets, that's what is in store for us now. They fly right under our radar, so we have no defence against them. The sooner we get the baby down to Brighton the better.'

My father turns to me as if he has said that for my benefit. 'That's why you have to go to Brighton, because of the danger here.'

Vivien looks at him as if he's crazy. 'Who are you talking to? You're right, you *are* going bonkers!' He looks from her to me and shakes his head.

'It's time I went.'

He does not disagree. I'm an unwelcome event, but I'm more upset about my mother not being able to see me. I have so much to ask her. I've always had so much to ask her. If I have come back to the past to meet my father, I am frustrated by seeing my young mother and not being able to ask her questions that have been troubling me all my life? Questions like what happened to my father, and why did she become a notorious lady of the night?

****

CHAPTER SEVEN

Ed sat at the kitchen table and traced numbers in the spilled salt. He was uneasy about Annabel going to London by herself, especially with an aggressive attitude. He felt guilty about her going to her mother's funeral alone, and wondered again about her mysterious father. He suspected Annabel of not knowing her own mind when it came to loving her mother. Surely Annabel had some love for her mother, who had never actually abandoned her. She had seen to it that Annabel was well taken care of by good foster parents. He understood how sad it was for Annabel that her foster parents, Sidney and Brenda, had gone to Australia but you could hardly blame them for that. They had naturally wanted to join their only son. People moved away, left, migrated. His grandfather had migrated, come for work, left his country and become American. It was the way of the new world, built on the ways of the old world.

Ed could cook, but he was inclined to make do with takeout food. He wanted to fend for himself while Annabel was away and not run to his mother's for dinner.

He thought his brothers ate there too often. When he showed up, he found himself competing with them for his father's attention as if none of them had grown up. It was better when they were out in the hills, hunting young whitetail deer. Rambling over the hills was the exercise Ed preferred. His doctor had recommended the gym, but Ed thought lifting weights unnecessary, and he saw nothing masculine about jogging about in an aerobics class with men whose shorts were too tight. He preferred open country and liked the ritual of gun cleaning in preparation for the hunt. There was a spirit of comradeship when he and his brothers met in the spare room where he kept the gun closet. A Mexican mat hung over the window, giving the tiny room a perpetually rosy glow.

Ed hoped David's church duties would not prevent him from joining the hunt this year, but David happily reported that he had been relieved of religious duties so that he could join them. He was needed on the hunt, being a much sharper shot than Ed's brothers, and he managed to keep up even while recovering from his hip injury. Before David's hip injury, Ed's family had dreams of David being a sports star, and Ed had been looking forward to a college scholarship. Those dreams ended on the Thanksgiving playing field. Waiting for news of David's surgery was the first time Ed had ever seen Annabel on the verge of hysteria. She shouted at the doctors and nurses and refused to leave David's side, but she did not cry. Ed had never seen Annabel cry. This confused Ed a little since his mother cried easily, even at birthday parties.

The night before they left for the hunt, Donna appeared at the door. Ed did not invite her in, because

David was home. David did not know about his involvement with Donna, and Ed had no intention of telling him.

'Going down to papa Zita's?'

'Already had dinner.'

Donna made a face and told him the story of the cheesecake. One of her dogs had jumped up on the table and wolfed it down. They started to laugh when she told him how the dog had been sick. Donna prolonged the laugh. They stood in silence for a moment and then she suggested they play tennis.

'You know I'm no good at tennis.'

'Neither am I.'

'Don't really like playing.'

She abruptly turned down the path, waving goodbye. In Ed's mind he had resolved the Donna problem.

****

'Now that you know your father better, what do you think of him? He's not going to help you, not that stuffy tax accountant. You can be glad he was never there to boss you around.'

There's an echoing voice of some female personality inside my head, which I'm ignoring because it is beyond my comprehension. I have enough challenges. My sense of time and place has shifted again and I don't understand why I'm in a white-tiled hall of what appears to be a Tube station full of quaintly dressed people climbing up the concrete steps. Déjà vu, because I've seen these people before but cannot remember where. Are they men and women in theatrical costume? Does that mean I am back in 1984? My hopes are dashed when I go outside and find a woman in a long skirt and shapely uniform jacket sweeping the entrance way. Another woman wrapped in a huge black cape is handing out tickets, her nose red with cold. I'm definitely not in 1984.

If the women are wearing long dresses, it must mean I am in another century. I've gone back in time, but how far back? In 1944 the people were hurrying as if their lives depended on it, but the people exiting the underground are not even walking fast. They move as if in slow motion. Is that the weight of their clothes or have they nowhere to go? Looking for clues to the exact date, I see a poster advertising 'A Season for Fresh Air and Room to Breathe'. This is a caption under a picture of a train pulling into a country station nestled among green hills. I head for the station bar, which looks familiar except there are no tables and chairs. Men are standing at the counter, gracefully tossing back drinks as if that is their only purpose in life. I need a newspaper. Ah, there's one, wrapped around a long wooden pole. It is a fragile copy of The Times, dated December 22nd, 1917. Why am I back here? I never wanted to go back in time, and certainly not this far back.

I head for natural light. Outside, a wide empty street is filled with traffic, horse-drawn carts and bicycles, hooded old roadsters and a rickety bus crammed full of passengers wearing hats, the women in bonnets and the men in bowlers or trilbies. The last word pops into my mind, although I haven't heard it since childhood. Sidney, my foster father, would wear a peaked cap to take his vegetables to the open market and a trilby when he spent his hard-earned cash at the racetrack. I wave as the open-top bus passes by, testing out my visibility. When no one reacts, I am again upset. All very well to have fun being invisible and spying on your parents, but now I realise I'm at a disadvantage. I'm lost in a strange time and place with no chance of asking anyone for directions.

At least it looks like I'm still in London, but surely 1917 was the time of World War One. I'm pleased to remember that much from my sketchy education. In the deserted street, an old man in a patched overcoat is sweeping up dead leaves. A purple-faced woman is leaning over a brazier of live coals. The colour of the flames cheers me, even if I am not experiencing any cold. She bends over to pick the roasting chestnuts out of the fire, discarding charcoal-burned ones. Her hands are half-mittened, her face spattered with moles. She reminds me of someone in a play I once saw, My Fair Lady. I give her a smile of encouragement, but she cannot see me.

'You're getting used to your surroundings and soon you'll have absorbed enough to make decisions and choose where you want to go.'

With a rising sense of panic and my head heavy with jumbled thoughts, I am at least soothed by familiar landmarks, Buckingham Palace, and Hyde Park on my left. I pass a colonial style house from which a doorman emerges, ceremoniously opening enormously gilded doors, decorated with crossed swords. A long black car creeps out with the royal coat of arms on its side. The same insignia as on my breakfast marmalade, the trademark of the reigning monarch. I approach Piccadilly Circus and find the usual crush of people, women with long skirts, men with whiskers. They appear to be shopping. Both men and women wear hats and fur collars and carry thin slices of umbrellas. They look smug and content and move with poise and grace as if they are listening to some music I cannot hear. Maybe they're all aristocrats or landed gentry. None of them have the subdued panic of the people in 1944. Maybe in December 1917 World War One is already over. Again, I regret my ignorance and the days spent at school, daydreaming through lessons. Why was I such a bad student? All I can remember is a keen desire to escape the classroom.

Trafalgar Square is a more awe-inspiring sight that in my era. As I approach the balustrade encircling the huge stone square commemorating Lord Nelson, I realise some of that square must have been hewn down to make room for our endless stream of traffic. There is a crowd gathered at the bottom of the imposing steps leading up to the four impressive black lions. Standing between those proud beasts is an equally proud old woman wearing a raincoat two sizes too big for her. She seems to be mid-sentence. The crowd waits while she thoughtfully strokes her chin. 'My Friends,' she shouts out, in a voice sharp enough to pierce the mist. 'Do you think you are superior to these people? You, sir, what about you? Do you feel superior to the people of India, that vast continent full of many tribes and languages?' The man questioned shakes his head.

'Not me!' he shouts back. 'I don't like being superior, sounds like snobbery. I refuse to be a cut above or below!'

This reply gets a laugh from the crowd. The woman sweeps the crowd with a practiced hand.

'We in England may think of ourselves as more important than other nations and peoples, but I have only to refer you to the war news for us to understand we may be more barbarous.' This is greeted with angry protests, but she is not afraid. 'No, my friends, we think we are superior, and yet, and yet...' She pauses dramatically. 'We are blind and deaf to the civilisations of other nations. In India, as I'm sure you know, they had religion and religious arts while we in England were half-clad and fighting off Romans. India has temples and shrines full of golden statues.' This woman seems enamoured of India.

'And can you deny them?' she remonstrates. 'These people who are certainly as civilised as we are, if not more so, can you deny them home rule?'

'No, no!' a red bearded man yells in support. 'Home rule for Ireland, home rule for India!'

'That is why we must give Mother India what her people want. We must give them independence.'

'Home rule for India, home rule for Ireland,' the bearded man repeats in an Irish accent, He is dressed in a pea green knitted jumpsuit, which emphasises his height and makes him look like an alien from outer space.

'The Irish can't rule themselves,' someone sneers. The Irish man in the pea green suit jumps forward.

The old woman puts up a hand to stop him. She will not give up the platform. Trying to get even closer, I step over a young man sitting on the curb. He looks up and smiles directly at me. Ah, the first person, besides my father, who can see me. Finally, there will be someone to talk to. I hope he's an Indian prince who will fly me to India. I've always wanted to go to the Taj Mahal.

As if he can read these worthless thoughts of mine, he shakes his thick black hair, which could mean he's read my mind and refused. When he tries to stand he bumps into a well-dressed gentleman. 'Get out the way, you blighter. You're in my way!' I expect the young man to protest, but he does not. He turns towards me and says in a soft voice. 'What are you doing here?' Proof that he can see me!

'I wish I knew. I'm so glad to have someone to talk to. I'm not sure whether I'm alive or dead, or halfway in between.'

'You don't have to worry about that!'

I then become aware of the people around us who think he's talking to himself. They start laughing and pushing and shoving each other. The disturbance has caught the eye of the speaker and she points to my young man.

'Come up, come up, Krishnaji. Come and join me.'

He moves towards her, but then turns dramatically back to whisper to me, 'Practise dying.' His words are clear enough, and in perfect English, but what a strange thing to say! I want to ask him to explain, but he's now the centre of attention.

'Come on up, Krishnamurti!'

He moves leisurely up the steps as the crowd parts for him. I watch with admiration the graceful way he moves. The old woman welcomes him to the top step.

'Let me introduce you to Krishnamurti. He is on the path of spiritual enlightenment and will soon be recognised and acclaimed for who he is, our new world teacher.'

The crowd stirs with interest and stares at the beautiful young man.

'He is here to speak to you.' She pushes him forward.

He clears his throat and seems to be waiting for inspiration. 'I'm a foreigner here,' he says in a soft charming voice. 'And you, dear sir,' he points to the man nearest to him. 'In my country, dear sir, *you* are the foreigner!'

He laughs as if he's made a joke. His joy is infectious and the crowd laughs with him.

'This man is my spiritual teacher,' the old woman is anxious to inform everyone.

The young man looks down at the ground, waiting until the crowd is silent. This takes a couple of minutes. Then he raises an authoritative hand, a gesture I've seen in pictures of Jesus. 'I do not believe in such things as spiritual leaders. I'm not here to be anyone's teacher.'

A wave of disappointment goes through the crowd, beginning with the old woman, although I don't understand why. Why should this young Indian presume to be any sort of teacher? The old woman shouts again at the crowd. 'He's been sent to us by the Masters in the mountains. We need a world leader. Western Civilisation is doomed if we don't follow Eastern religions.'

There is a confused murmur, the crowd is aware of conflicting thoughts being aired on the podium. The old woman and the young Indian are smiling at each other as if sharing an old controversy. He then turns to the crowd and says in an ordinary voice that few can hear, 'My dear friend, Annie Besant, is on a spiritual path like we all should be. But I'm not here to be anyone's guru.'

'Hear, hear!' There is a supportive shout from the crowd, but whatever is going to be said next is drowned by a threatening rumble from the sky. A shadow looms over us, which turns out to be a hunk of metal hanging in the sky in the shape of a plane. It lumbers slowly over our heads, threatening to fall out of the sky.

'It's them!'

'The Germans have come to bomb us.'

People run down the steps in terror, some people crossing themselves as they run. 'They've come to get us!'

'Watch out!'

The old woman in her commanding position does not look afraid. She takes the arm of the young Indian to support her. 'Stay, stay!' she yells. 'Don't be afraid! I can tell you the future is written, and we know this young man is destined for great things. He is fated to be a great teacher so he cannot die today, nor tomorrow. He has been chosen by the Masters. They came down from the Himalayas to lay their hands on him.'

The strange pea suited man, full of brash energy, runs up and grabs her by the arm. 'Why, in the name of the saints above, talk such rubbish? Paths and enlightenment! Don't bring your mystical Masters into politics!'

The old woman looks ready to scold him but thinks better of it, and addresses her protégée instead. 'I've told you about this Irishman, the very opinionated George Bernard Shaw.' The Irishman barely acknowledges this introduction.

'Time for us to get to safety.'

'There's no need to panic. I've told you that Krishnaji is going to fulfil his mission.'

'Excuse me if I don't have the slightest bit of faith in your fortune telling.'

She throws up her hands in despair and says, 'If you insist on us leaving, at least get us a taxi!'

'That's a complete waste of money.'

A vehicle with a black fabric roof drives by. It does not look sturdy enough to take these three enormous personalities, but they clamber in and drive off. If only I had been quick enough to join them! I want to question that young man. Why did he tell me to practise dying? Does that mean I'm already dead and I have to get used to it? Was his Indian inflection on the word practise or on the word dying? Maybe I'm able to access the past because I'm already dead.

Trafalgar Square is now empty of people and returns to looking like Nelson's tombstone. Suddenly I have a warm memory of sitting here with Ed, one New Year's Eve. After seeing the film Seven Brides for Seven Brothers, he asked me to come with him to Houston. I said yes, confusing Texas with the snow-capped mountains in the film. I didn't know then that Houston was flat or that even Hill Country was just that, small hills.

Then I know why I'm here because I see him, my father. He is young and vigorous and coming straight towards me at speed, limping and leaning on a cane. How different, how handsome he is. I wave hello, but he passes me by. I fall back, feeling rejected, but quickly calculate that he cannot see me. If we are in 1917, I'm not yet born. I begin to be afraid of my expanding consciousness. If I can access Time at any point in the past, where am I going to go next? I remember hearing my echo, that voice. Perhaps I'm becoming omnipotent, god-like. That makes me laugh. I'm having fun.

My young father heads towards Charing Cross, and I follow him. The lights of the railway station cut through the December darkness as he crosses the courtyard where a group of ragged boys are waiting. They put their hands out to beg. My father waves his stick at them and clutches his jacket more tightly until he reaches the safety of a crowded platform. A great many women are gathered here but they are standing in silence. They also wear hats, some with veils, or they are wrapped in shawls against the cold. My father finds a column to lean against, his face betraying anxiety as he bites his lower lip.

The noisy rattling steam train arrives slowly as if reluctant to unload its cargo. At soot-streaked window, solders peer out, their faces grim and gaunt. When the train stops, the men climb down the steep steps carefully, men as skinny as the beggar boys outside, men starving for the life that has been lived by the waiting women who now crowd forward almost hugging the train. Not one man leaps down gratefully or even ably. A path is made for nurses in blindingly white crisp aprons carrying stretchers for the disabled. Very little can be heard over the steam, but very little needs to be said.

My father leans against his column until he rushes towards an emaciated boy with a grimy face. The two embrace and that brief hug causes the soldier wipe his eyes with the back of his sleeve.

'I don't believe you're fucking here.'

My father takes his handkerchief and wipes away dirt on the soldier's face.

'I work at the Civil,' my father tells him. 'You can see lists of who's coming back.'

'It's a fucking miracle I'm here. I'm one of the lucky ones.' My father shakes his head. 'You must have lost three stone. I don't know what mater will say.'

Mater? Did my father really call his mother that? If this is his little brother, that would make him my uncle. But his accent sounds like he's from a different class?

'It's hard to believe you have any parents when you're being fucking shelled.'

My father stops walking at this remark. He looks down at his shaking right hand trying to grip his cane. Now it is my uncle who is the observer. They wait until my father's hand stops shaking and leave the platform with my father leaning hard on his cane for support. Their relief in each other's company is a circle of protection around them. Even the ragamuffin boys give way to them, almost respectfully.

'You know how much money they gave us on dismissal? Fucking sixpence! And there was nothing to eat on the train.'

'I know where we can get something.'

They catch an open-top tram outside the station and alight at a large stone archway. My uncle looks almost afraid of the entrance and groans. 'Not an officers' club!'

There is a stir in the dining room when they enter. Their arrival attracts attention. Everyone turns and then looks away. I am guessing this is because my father's brother is in a private's uniform, and this is an officer's club. The waiter glides up and they are seated at a table for two. I wish I had an appetite for food, but I get a vicarious kick out of seeing them order enthusiastically. A roast beef is wheeled up on a silver trolley. I try not to think of the hungry boys outside Charring Cross

Station. My uncle eats hungrily, although he looks around suspiciously.

'I'll bloody well kill somebody if they send me back.'

'You won't have to go back; it's almost over. Canadians and Australians are still enlisting. The French have just signed about a hundred thousand Africans from the Congo. The Germans don't have a chance.'

'You sound like one of the nobs.'

'I work in Whitehall. It rubs off.'

They say yes to the cheese plate and sip their wine like wine connoisseurs. Toward the end of the meal an agitated man of about eighty approaches them. I'm amused to see a sword swinging from his side. When I look back to the table he came from, I see every old man there has a sword hanging from the back of his chair. Very nineteenth century, I say to myself.

'General Briggs! Boer War!'

Having introduced himself, he begins. 'I for one have no objections, because I know what hell it is on the front.'

My father looks astonished at this interruption from a stranger.

The old boy clears his throat, and begins to blush. 'But standards, regulations, have to be kept up.'

'Let me introduce my brother, Charles.'

General Briggs looks slightly relieved but is not impressed. 'This man is a private.'

Charles immediately stands up. 'My brother's a decorated officer!' he shouts.

'I'm sure you all deserve to be decorated, but...'

'He won the Military Cross!'

My father stands up. The two of them form a united front. My father determinedly rings his glass with a fork. The luncheon clatter ceases.

'This is Charles Page Cuthbert, my brother, who's just today returned from the front.'

The General walks back mumbling, 'I was making a point about the rules. But rules can be stretched for a member of your family.'

Another old man with a pointed white beard, picks up his fork and echoes my father's ring as if not to be outdone.

'Attention, everyone. Let me introduce, I mean, we have dinning with us a holder of the Military Cross and his brother who is, this very day, back from the trenches.'

The whole room breaks into polite applause. For the first time I notice the complete absence of women. My father, still standing, is nervous and confident at the same time. He looks around and raises his wine glass.

'A toast! To infantry and tank!'

'Infantry and tank!' The words are reverently repeated through the room. I do not understand the references, but there is a pleased, if not smug, expression on their lined faces. A bearded old soldier leans to one side, an indication of how much he has drunk.

'I can only say,' he says with drunken authority, 'I can only say to the Germans...' He pauses and looks around the room and peers short sightedly at his audience. 'I can only say, say to the Prussians... we are not getting to love you more!'

A ripple of laughter at every table. men raise their glasses again.

'Superior old buggers,' Charles mumbles. 'Let them do our job and get paid as little for it. Have you got your medal on you?'

'Not on me, for heaven's sake.'

'Pity! We could pawn it!'

'Don't mention the wretched thing again.'

'At least it got you a good job. What the fuck am I going to do? Sing for my supper?'

When they leave the club, my father puts a hand round his brother's thin shoulder and guides him tenderly through romantically lit streets. There are signs of Christmas in the shop windows which are decorated with holly. I'm still in December, just a different year. They enter a rooming house and up the stairs to a one room bedsit. My father oversees his brother wash and shave and prepare for bed. After two glasses of beer they arrange themselves top to toe on the narrow bed. They are fully clothed, but I cannot tell if this is modesty or because of the cold. Charles twists and jerks under the blankets. After a couple of hours they are still awake.

'Did you get Jack Johnsons? Shit-black smoke choking you, did you get that?'

'No.'

'You never got fucking gas blowing back in your face? Your buttons didn't turn shit-green?'

'You've got to stop using foul language here. It won't do you any good. Try and get some sleep.'

'I can't,' Charles bursts out. 'I can't just fucking go to sleep. I haven't sleep for weeks.'

My father puts on the light. 'I'm not the world's best sleeper.'

The two of them squat on the floor of the small room with blankets round them. My father gets out a tin of tobacco and my uncle takes it off him.

'One thing learned from the war, how to make a fag.'

'And swear.'

'Two things, then.'

They smoke in a fever of impatience, as if they're stranded, not in London but the middle of France.

'You in pain still?'

My father sighs. 'Shrapnel's still there.'

'Can't they take it out?'

'They think it's sunk into the bone.'

'But can you still raise the mast?'

'Well, yes, thank God, yes I can.' My father rubs a finger under his nose, a gesture I've tried to cure myself of. Are gestures inherited? He clears his throat. 'What about French girls then?'

'Never saw any in the trenches. Not being a fucking officer!'

'I know where we can go for some female fun.'

'Yeah? 'My Uncle Charles smiles for the first time.

I watch them leave and I'm not sure whether to follow them or not. I have an inkling of where they are going and I'm embarrassed. They are so young and vulnerable. I am feeling maternal about my father; that's how time travel reverses our roles. He is not my father yet and I'm curious about him as a young man. I want to learn more about him and my uncle. Yes, I'm going to spy on them.

Outside the smog is a sickly yellow colour. Their footsteps barely sound. A girl with a plunging neckline runs up with a pronounced wiggle of her hips and when she is ignored, she moves up closer with her hand out. I'm reminded that not long ago, this was Jack the Ripper's killing ground. The two men walk quickly away. I cannot take my eyes off them, delighting in every curve of their almost hairless cheeks, their bowed shoulders, and how they walk so closely together. If only they could see me, if only I could make myself be seen. Trapped in the past I discover how lonely I am.

We are now in Soho, which does not look like the trendy place I know. The alleyways are littered with rotting cabbages and empty wooden crates. A heap of blankets is a family managing to sleep under a makeshift tent.

We stop at a three-storey tenement house with boarded up windows.

'I won't know what to say.' My uncle confesses.

'Say what you like, we're paying.'

'What about French letters?'

'They give you those. Don't kiss the girl. Bit dangerous, that.' A woman with rouged cheeks and ginger hair cracks open the door.

'Too late.' She seems glad to inform them.

'I know it's late, but my brother cannot sleep.'

'This isn't a hotel.'

'Come on, my brother's just come back from France.'

She tiredly motions them in. An African waiter with a silver tray takes money from my father before he ushers them into a smoky room. High above the mantle shelf a statue of the Virgin, in flowing blue robes, looks down at us. Red velvet ribbons hang from the picture rail, effectively drawing attention away from damp stains on the walls. The women are crowded round a coal fire. They are wearing short flouncy skirts of the

Moulin Rouge variety; some wear cloche hats, the kind worn at a garden party.

They are drinking out of cups like a bevy of maids after a hard day in the kitchen. My father and uncle sit on a moth eaten velvet bench. Two girls approach and sit either side of them.

'Where were you in action?' from a pert girl with a painted mole on her cheek.

'29th regiment of Foot,' my uncle politely replies.

My father shushes his brother at the question, indicating he should not have answered it truthfully. The girl gives up on him and another takes her place.

I hope they will choose their partners quickly, but they are accepting a bottle of beer. I am jealous of the way they slide their eyes over the women. Conflicting emotions. I feel like a disapproving aunt not wanting Charles to be indoctrinated into paying for sex and yet also aware that I'm being ridiculously possessive. My father smiles at a dark-haired woman with a wild look who approaches him confidently. My uncle takes this for encouragement and shakes the hand of a sweet looking girl at the fireplace. The others look amused at this gesture. My uncle only has eyes for her. My father suddenly brushes by, ushering his dark-haired woman up the stairs. As he passes his brother he whispers, 'Get a move on.'

'You chose quickly enough. Do you know her?'

My uncle goes back to his girl. She puts an arm through his and guides him toward a shiny brass machine.

'Got a penny for the concertina?'

Charles brings out a penny to insert into a prototype jukebox. The mechanical tune is so cheerful it sounds mournful. They hang over the cabinet and enjoy the mechanical music box song together. As they climb up the rickety stairs, my Uncle Charles is talking as if he is never going to stop.

I go upstairs looking for my father. I am too ashamed to go into their room, but I listen at the door. My father's voice is raised because he is reciting something. 'Who by severed limb? Who by shot or cannon? Who by hanging? Who by despair and grief?' Is he quoting his own or someone else's poetry? Did he write verse in the trenches? To give him some privacy I turn away in time to see my uncle enter a room with his arm round his girl. She is beaming up at him. When they enter the shoddy room and Charles sees the bed with torn covers, he is upset.

'This is a fucking awful place. What the fuck are they thinking of?'

The girl puts a hand over his mouth and leans up close to him. He stops and gazes mournfully at the mirror opposite the bed as if he's never seen his gaunt image before. The girl quickly puts herself between him and the mirror. I should leave them alone now, but I'm fascinated. I'm witnessing some ancient rite from biblical times. My uncle sits on the bed and dives in his pocket for a cigarette, but she waves it away.

'You see, I've never before...'

This is so obvious it makes her smile. Her smile is a blessing. My uncle feels it. I think he falls in love with her then. She takes off her blouse and gestures for my uncle to do the same. I can see his ribs and the bruises on his chest, and she traces her finger over them lovingly. This makes him shiver and sneeze and mutter, 'Sergeants... they love beating you up for fucking nothing!'

She is not shocked. She must have seen wounds and injuries before. An electric current of sympathy swirls between them. He bends on one knee like a romantic and covers her hands and knees in kisses. Working his way up like a practised lover on an inspired one, he finally falls on her mouth in a three minute kiss completely disregarding my father's advice. I'm sure he has forgotten he had paid for her and maybe she has too. He is mumbling endearments, running his fingers through her hair. Together they seem to achieve complete satisfaction. Maybe she is not being honest about this, but who am I to judge?

They cling to each other as if unwilling to end their love making, and I find myself staring at the crumpled skirt she has discarded, fluffed out with white tulle, like a ballet dancer's. There is also a ribbon-threaded bodice. My mother used to wear wire push up bras, which reminds me that I have always been conscious of the seamy side of the sex trade, but I have never seen it up this close. My handsome young father, who I saw paying for his brother, can hardly afford better but I am sad to see them here. No easy access to birth control, I tell myself. I think of my mother and her working-girl ethic. No matter how many diamond bracelets and mink coats she was given by the landed gentry, she would sympathise with these girls. Like them, she had that disturbing and innocent look in her eyes. Although the men are not blameless, they feel guilt-free. War has entitled them to this and opened the door to these places. If David had gone to Vietnam, he could have been assigned an R&R and found himself in a similar situation in Saigon or Japan. The whole business is intimately connected to war.

Eliza Wyatt

****

'You've forgotten that you come from a long line of reluctant warriors, some brave, some of them cowards, but men who liked fighting, even if they didn't believe what they were fighting for, which can be confusing to small minds.'

Waiting for my father and my uncle in such a place, I'm sorry that sleep is denied me in my altered state. I cannot even close my eyes and I can hear the muffled moans of women. I cannot determine whether they are the sounds of sex, or the moans of distressed women deeply asleep. I am happy to see my father and uncle clatter down the wooden staircase.

Charles gives Hugh's arm and expressive pinch.

'Let's have more fun like this tonight.'

My father shakes his head in a parental way. 'Don't get a taste for that kind of fun. I never did anything like this before the war. But in France I got the habit. Don't let it stop you thinking about getting a wife.'

'Not me.'

'Someone to darn your socks'

'Never getting fuckin' married.'

'If you swear like that no one will have you.'

'Bloody good thing!'

My father slaps him too hard on the back, making him cough. Charles looks at his phlegm.

'No blood!'

'You've got Trench Mouth, thanks to the bloody war.'

Charles ßslaps his brother back and they keep up this back slapping as they run along The Embankment.

It is low tide and the mighty Thames is reduced to silent puddles. A couple of rotting boats are caught in vast stretches of mud. Small dots in the mud turn out to be the heads of scruffy boys. Are they playing some sort of game?

'What the fuck are they doing?' Charles asks.

My father has seen them before. 'Mudlarks! They dig themselves into the mud to keep warm overnight. The mud is their bedroom for the night.'

'Blimming heck! Poor blighters!'

'Like us in the trenches.'

A uniformed man in a navy-blue cloak strides across the sinking mud and starts hitting the heads of the boys with his truncheon. They are quick to scatter, but some of them are sunk waist-deep in the mud. My uncle runs up to protest. 'That's enough of that!' The policeman ignores him.

'You do that again and you'll be sorry for it.' My father's voice is loud and determined.

My uncle tries to hit the policeman with his fists. The policeman jumps aside, and my father grabs him by the collar while my uncle whips away his truncheon. The policeman is outraged, but his heavy boots are sinking in the mud. He quickly moves to drier land. I wonder how they expect to interfere with a man of the law and get away with it.

Charles is excited. 'Get the fucker on the run.'

'Jolly well ought to report him.' My father flicks his eyes impatiently, still in action mode.

I have to admire their impulsive protest and remember experiencing a similar impulse in Nuevo Laredo. The sun was hot in Mexico, and I ran up to curse a man who was beating his horse. Ed did not approve of my action or my righteous temper. Ed always thought twice and usually decided against interfering. I'm more like these two young men who act before they think. Without warning, they are suddenly shaking each other by the hand.

'See you this evening after work. The Civil Service has taken over where the army left off.'

'Miserable sod!'

'It's a far cry from being a country schoolboy, isn't it?'

'I'm never going into harness again. But I'm going to report to the Army Depot, and they better pay up what they owe me. Ten fucking' shillings.'

My father, with a wry shake of his head, indicates he does not believe this is likely. I have to make a quick decision. I choose to follow my uncle, guessing my father's job will not be that exciting.

My uncle is now in a better mood, he jogs up and down the kerb and peers into expensive shop windows. When he arrives at what is advertised to be, Chelsea Barracks, hundreds of soldiers have formed a depressingly long line. This is going to take hours. Then I see a sight that I find difficult to believe. A group of African soldiers are loitering on the parade ground. Their outfits remind me of the latest craze for camouflage wear. Their accents sound Welsh or Indian which proves they are not Africans, but from the Caribbean. As I near them I see their shoulder insignias read, British West Indies Regiment. A man in an officer's uniform approaches them and one of the men steps up to him. He is not happy.

'They won't give us our dues. Sixpence a day for all of yous whites and whites from Bermuda, same as us, but they're whites. They get their sixpence but not us, even though we fought side by side. They won't give us the right to sixpence. Shame on you, shame, shame, shame on yous.'

The officer deliberates. 'Yes, I see your point but the trouble is you cannot lodge a protest in war time. It's considered mutiny, and for that... you know the penalty.'

'We's talkin' 'bout our rights.'

The way the English soldier shakes his heads makes it look unlikely these men will receive this payment, however well deserved. The words mutiny and rebellion are muttered in threatening tones.

'You can be hanged for talking like that!'

A sudden downpour of rain silences everyone. The six-pence deprived Caribbean men move off leaving the English men to wait for their sixpence, stoically soaking up the rain.

'Flanders all over again,' my Uncle Charles says to his neighbour.

I'm afraid that he will die of pneumonia in his weakened state. Is that why I never heard of an Uncle Charles? I put out a hand to see if I can touch the wet hair at the back of his neck. I'm more daring with him, because he is only my uncle, not my father. It may only be my imagination, but I can almost feel his skin. Unlike my father, he does not give any sign he can see me. I am missing my father and want to find him. My feet seem to know my feelings. They take me back to

Whitehall, which I remember is a maze of government offices. There I see my father nervously sitting in front of a mound of paperwork, in a cubby-hole of an office shared by two other men. All three are smoking and the air is hazy blue. I'm glad I have no sense of smell.

'Don't think you can get away with shoddy behaviour here, not in this office.' A gaunt skeleton head frowns in my father's direction. 'Coming in late and turning up to work in second-day shirts!'

'My brother came back from the trenches last night.'

There is a pause while the other man shuffles his feet under the desk. The older man makes a show of taking off his jacket and clearing his throat. My father does not look up.

'That's no excuse to leave work undone before you go home.'

'I do a good job in this office.'

'That's a matter of opinion. We went through your books.'

'None of your bloody business!'

A shocked silence. The older man stands, as if such insubordination cannot be dealt with in a sitting position. 'You will be fined for using a swear word. Take your things and go downstairs. There may be no point in you returning at all.'

My young father exits the room and grabs his coat as he goes out the door.

I almost lose sight of him as he jumps into a passing vehicle that proudly bears the sign 'For Hire'. I manage to jump in alongside him and we motor at about five miles an hour down Oxford Street. Many of the shops I know are there, looking new and spruce, some are being built.

My father climbs out at Marble Arch and begins to walk towards Queensway. His gait is compromised because he must have left his stick in the office, but he moves fast enough and reaches a narrow lane where he is confronted by wooden doors, big enough for a carriage and a pair of horses to pass through. The sign reads 'R.B. Taylor – Stable Mews'. My father knocks, but I can pass through expecting to find horses in this stable. No, it is a tailor's workshop. Rolls of material are stacked at the sides and compete for space with tailor's dummies. Pressed shirts hang overhead, hooked on a conveyance of pulleys strung across thick wooden beams holding up the loft space. Hidden among this ordered chaos, a white-haired man is eating something out of a paper bag. His attention is focused on a chess set, but there is no one else in the workshop. He is playing with himself. When the old man finally hears the knocking, he opens a small door hidden in one of the bigger ones. My father squeezes through. The old man is pleased to see him.

'Someone I never thought to see! Come in, I'm having lunch. Have you eaten?'

My father grins. 'I ate well yesterday.'

'Yesterday was yesterday!' The tailor goes to his paper bag and takes out a rolled pastry. 'Eat!'

My father offers him a cigarette in exchange. It is refused.

'How is it? And what brings the romantic here?'

'I've come to see you, and er... to talk to you about Gloria.'

'Oho! That's how it is! She's a grown woman and knows her own mind.'

'Her husband's now been declared missing, presumed dead.'

'Between you and me, boychik, Frank Cooper died over there three years ago, and the war office should have said so. What takes the government so long to make it official, I don't know. I suppose because he was only a private, not a decorated officer like you.'

My father brushes away this comment. 'It is official so she can marry again.'

The two men are silent for a minute and I feel they are in sympathy with each other. Gone is the young rebel.

'Where is she?'

'Feeding the ducks in Hyde Park with the kid. But before you go, I think it's time you had a custom-made shirt. You could be needing such an item in the near future. That is, if you have the honourable intentions.'

My father laughs. 'I am going to ask her to marry me, if that's all right with you.'

'Not until I've fitted you out.'

The tailor proceeds to slowly and carefully measure my father's arm, back and neck. When my father sees the old man has been playing chess by himself, he asks, 'Do you want a game of chess?'

'I have work to do. Go ask my daughter to marry you.'

I am upset to hear about my young father's desire to marry this man's daughter. I want him for Vivien and myself. I follow behind him to Hyde Park. A peaceful scene awaits us. Nannies are pushing gigantic prams while children cavort madly around them. The women are mostly grey-haired and look intensely respectable in their uniforms, all wearing the inevitable hat. My father rushes past them to approach a slim young woman in a green raincoat who is kneeling close to the water, urging a small boy to sail his boat. My father watches a while before he disturbs them.

They gaze into each other's eyes like lovers. My father gets out a handkerchief and blows his nose, which makes her laugh. Her mouth is wide and her even white teeth make her look more beautiful than she is.

'Don't mind me,' he says. 'I don't know why I'm crying.'

She makes no move to indicate she has heard him, but she takes off her scarf and shakes free her long brown hair. This intimate gesture prompts my young father to hug her.

'I've heard that there's been an official declaration of Frank's death. I've just come from seeing your father. I think you know why.'

Hearing those words, she pulls at the ring on her third finger and throws it into the water. 'It was only a fake ring.'

'Can you forget your Frank?'

She turns away impatiently. 'We've got to forget this awful war and everything about it.'

He is about to hug her again, but is halted by the child's dramatic sobs.

'What is it, Robbie? Oh, his boat, his boat has gone.'

My father wades into the pond immediately. My hero! I hope he is also Gloria's hero. In love with my father, I reprimand myself. In love, but not without a degree of bitterness. Gloria looks like a worthy wife, but I wish he were here with my mother, young Vivien. Then there'd be a chance he'd become my real father, young enough to lift me up on his shoulders like Ed used to lift David. I am angry that my father has had another love, and possibly a marriage before meeting my mother. Many fathers have more than one family, mothers too, and some of my school mates were miserably jealous of their 'steps'. I already feel possessive about my father, like I was with Ed, and even David when he was younger, before he was an annoying teenager. Possessive parents are the worse, but what about possessive partners? Possessiveness must be a natural emotion, certainly an emotion deep enough to cause a divorce, divided loyalties.

    A tremendous noise makes me look up and see an ugly shape in the sky. It is the same plane that flew over yesterday. It flies low enough for me to see an iron cross on its side. I suddenly remember my father's World War One medal and the words of a song. 'They too have God on their side'. A song from the seventies. When I look up, the bulging and unsightly plane is directly overhead, releasing bombs on warehouses edging the river.

CHAPTER EIGHT

1984

When Ed and David returned from Hill Country, they found the telephone answering machine flashing. There were several messages from the police in London, asking Ed to call back. It sounded like more news about Annabel's mother, but the bloody carcass of an old doe had to be delivered to the butchers. It was dripping blood from the roof of the Jeep. The Fuego brothers did not like the job of dis-embowelling deer and there were plenty of commercial butchers to chop the carcass up into family joints of meat.

When Ed finally phoned Jason he heard that Annabel had been in an explosion. He was thankful David was upstairs, which gave him a few moments to calm himself before he told David the news. 'Your mother's had an accident. She's alive but in the hospital, and in a coma.'

'Oh God! I knew it. I told her not to go. No one in this house listens to me.' David was angry. 'Has someone shot her?'

'An explosion of some sort.' Anger and sorrow made Ed more abrupt than usual. 'I'm going to England to get her.'

'Can I come?'

Ed did not have to tell David that the cost was prohibitive. They both tried to comfort each other with hugs but neither of them felt comforted. When Ed started packing, David hung over the bed rail, and with each item Ed put in the suitcase David got more and more upset and began throwing a baseball against the bedroom wall.

'You're packing like you're going to be gone for six months.'

'Don't know. Can't tell.'

Ed alerted his business partner and they agreed to close the office on Mendoza Road for the 'holidays'. Then he went to say goodbye to his mother. She told him not to blame himself, and Ed knew by her tart tone that his mother considered the explosion all Annabel's fault. When he visited Sunny Hills Country Club, they asked him to remove Annabel's possessions, if she was not returning to work any time soon. Ed understood this to mean Annabel was now out of a job, but it seemed the least of their worries. Clearing out her office, he found a teapot, a picture of an English seascape, and a paperweight with a thatched-roof cottage in a snowstorm. Tell-tale signs that Annabel had been homesick. Donna was outside the pro shop waiting for him. She gave him a brief hug.

'I hear you're going to England.' Ed did not reply.

'Don't worry about David. I'll go round with dinners for him.'

Ed felt that he could not refuse this kind offer. 'I appreciate that.'

'We Texans hang together, don't we?'

'David will be busy with the church over Christmas.'

Ed hoped this was the case, because he felt guilty about leaving David behind because of the costly flight. David came to the airport with him where they ate a silent meal.

Ed had dealt with David's silences through his teenage years, but he would have liked to make small talk about the new girlfriend Trudy or even the Church.

'My church is having a prayer meeting for my mother.'

Ed was not to be outdone. 'I expect my mother will have a mass said.'

David nodded. They both knew Annabel was not in the least religious. She often told them that in England, no one went to church, and no one believed in God.

The movie on the plane was a French black-and-white war movie, communicating a feeling of terror and despair. The American war movies were more cheerful and in colour. He remembered seeing war movies with Annabel, and now wondered what she thought of watching a movie about a war that was fought in her own country.

When the plane landed at Heathrow Airport, Ed had never felt so reluctant to exit. He did not want to be there, doing what he had to do. He stopped at the bar for a drink before finding the cheapest way into the city. He tried to get in touch with the feeling he had when he first landed in England, but it was useless. Gone was the delight of a twenty-two-year-old without responsibilities. Ed felt he had far too many responsibilities to ever be happy again, and that the last place he wanted to be was in London.

    He was not afraid of hospitals, but he was fearful of English ones. Ed feared that if they were free, they would be outdated and dirty, but he had to accept what was on offer. He had been impressed by the Houston hospital experience when David was injured and again when a cousin got shot in the leg by an irate friend. The hospital had allowed the family to gather round and provide the patients with their own rice and beans.

****

'Are you ready to claim your inheritance, even if that inheritance is a history of violence? You don't realise how lucky you are. Not everyone gets the chance to transcend daily life and discover what it's like to be all powerful.'

    I no longer trust this voice, and don't like what it says. It does not sound like me, although I'm not sure who I am in this netherworld. I regret how little I know about World War One and wonder what time zone I'm in as I walk down a tree-lined street which looks like South Kensington. The houses are intact and look as solid as they looked when I lived in the city, even if sandbags are piled up in doorways. I don't remember seeing sandbags until now, are they expecting a flood? This part of London is residential, calm with peaceful respectable-looking streets, air of prosperity about them. The graceful architecture that London is famous for gives me the impression that these solidly built neighbourhoods go on for miles and miles. Except that now that I've seen the London I was born into, I know many of these sedate residential neighbourhoods were blasted away in the Blitz.

I head towards Knightsbridge because I can see Harrods in the distance. Harrods is a landmark I know from when my mother used to eagerly push those swing doors. Now they are locked and shuttered. A sign in the window says, 'As part of the war effort, we are only open for regulation uniforms'. Very patriotic of them, but I still don't know which war they are referring to. I walk on past rows of shops that have nothing in the windows for sale. Further on I see a sign for 'Bistro', and when I peer through the partially shaded windows I have a shock, seeing my father at a table. But he is not the young man of 1917. Gone are his youthful looks, he is the slightly bowed gentleman that I first met in Green Park. His thick fair hair has faded and thinned, he is heavier and sadder. This means I'm no longer in 1917, I've probably returned to 1944 and World War Two.

My father's dining companion is a grey-haired woman. She looks familiar, and I wonder who she is. Is he having an affair while he's living with my mother? He reaches out across the table and takes the woman's hand. He must be having an affair, although she is an unlikely candidate as she looks older than him.

'You're right,' my father says. 'The news gets worse and worse.'

I hide so that he will not see me.

'The government knows everything.' The woman's voice is low and depressed. 'But no one is allowed to publish anything.'

My father replies, 'They're trying to keep the bad news to a minimum. Don't want the nation to lose heart.'

'What about the Americans? Are you trying to tell me the American people don't know? It's from Temple I hear all these things.'

My father appears to agree with her, but her question goes unanswered. He squeezes her hand again and she withdraws it.

'Gloria, you can't give way to despair.'

She laughs in his face. I edge forward for a closer look. Gloria? She must be the same woman he wanted to marry. Her grey hair is wiry and stiff and looks like a wig.

He leans forward confidingly. 'I've heard we are going to win the war.'

'Where have you heard that?' She twists in her chair and looks out the window. 'They say that every time Christmas comes around.'

'The Allies think Hitler's days are numbered.'

'You just told me there are terrible setbacks.'

'Well, yes. They're putting up a good defence and pushing us back. Calling it the Battle of the Bulge, but we're winning in Africa and Italy.'

'The world will never be the same again. Not for people like us. It will never ever be the same.'

The waitress delivers a steaming plate. 'Some potatoes?'

'People know about the camps. Word gets out from the synagogues. I don't see how they can pretend the camps are not happening?'

'They go by what they read in the newspapers.'
'That's what I mean. Nothing is reported. How can I eat?'

The waitress points to her plate of mashed potatoes.

'I know they're your favourite, Mrs. Cuthbert. Potatoes mashed with chicken fat. I know that's how you like them.' She waits until Gloria picks up her fork.

Mrs. Cuthbert? Then he did marry her, and I have to accept this is the same woman but how distressed she seems. I'm not sure which year it is, but if I have returned to the year of my birth, their marriage has got to be over. Gloria is my father's past, his claim to respectability because she is a conventional woman. Seeing the two of them together I realise there is not the excitement between them that is so evident between my parents. Gloria is a sad person and if England was invaded she could have been a holocaust victim. Her knowledge of that must make her fearful and despairing; she's living on the edge of disaster. My father's good fortune in finding someone to love, is not good news for her. I'm sure she doesn't know about me and even if she does know, would hardly be invited to my christening; which reminds me of my favorite fairy tale, Sleeping Beauty. Perhaps there is often someone purposely not invited to a christening, someone offended by the joyous event.

Gloria cannot eat.

My father takes her plate, 'Don't want to waste rations.'

'I have a headache. Do you have any aspirins?'

'Not aspirins, no. And you don't want my barbiturates. The building where all my service records were kept has been blown up and I have to apply directly to the War Office for my prescriptions. Let's hope the War Office doesn't get blown up or I'll be sunk.'

'I've begun to have bad headaches since my father died. I'm glad he died before this horrible war. I'm glad he died not knowing about the camps.'

My father makes an ugly face and, realising she has said too much, Gloria slowly begins to push a stale-looking roll into her mouth as if every mouthful is hateful.

'I could say the same thing about my father, I'm also glad he passed away before this war.'

'They knew the world was coming to an end, didn't they? That's why they died; they couldn't face it.'

'And what about your new house? I'm glad you're safe in the country. Do you like it?'

'Safer I suppose; but boring. The only sound we hear at night are the wailing cows. I didn't know they mooed and moaned so much.'

'It's the sound they make when their calves are taken from them.'

'You'd know that coming from Gloucestershire. I was brought up in Chelsea.'

'I suppose the price of being safe in the country is missing your friends in London. Have you met anyone there you can talk to?'

'I've been reading Freud, learning what the mind can do to you. Did you know that during the 30's in Germany, when their store fronts were being smashed back in the 30's, the rate of appendicitis in Jewish families went up three hundred percent.'

'I'm not surprised. But I hear Freud is safe in Hampstead,' my father's tone is hopeful. 'I hear Einstein escaped. He got to America in time.'

'Isn't escape just as hard to bear?'

She is not to be comforted, and my father clears his throat in an attention-seeking way.

'I have something to tell you.'

'You want a divorce.'

My father passes a hand over his furrowed forehead in a gentle caress.

'Let me tell you this, because it's important. I told you about Vivien. Now we've had a child, a girl.

I cannot bear to see the look of hurt on Gloria's face. 'Well, isn't that the last straw! So why are you telling me?'

'I didn't mean to upset you. I always think of Robert as my son, but he is my stepson. Talking of Robert, any news of him?'

Gloria shakes her head despondently as if the question's too burdensome. 'He came home for ten hours two weeks ago,' she says. 'He'd lost weight and won't talk about what he was doing. He was so happy to be drafted into the air force and not the army, but he's changed. He comes home and is unhappy.'

'His flying corps' still in London, they have been billeted at the Victoria and Albert Museum.'

'If you are able to see him, tell him to telephone me. And I have a letter here for him.' She digs into her bag.

'Will Robert be home for Christmas?'

'He says he will. He says he'll let you know because he'll come through London.'

My father sighs as if he is carrying the burden for them all. They are a sculpture of grief and despair as he says goodbye. I keep out of sight while they shake hands. I am about to reveal myself to my father when Gloria rushes back with an envelope in her hand.

'If you don't manage to see him, make sure you put it in the Armed Forces post.'

My father puts it reverently in his breast pocket watching Gloria walk away. When I reveal myself, he looks delighted to be distracted from his depressing luncheon. 'There you are! You vanished like a ghost and then appear like one.'

'I've been spying on you.'

'What did you overhear?'

'Looks like you're having an affair?'

I tell him my first impression, because I don't want to confess I spied on him in 1917.

'Gloria's my former wife.'

'And I have a brother?'

'No, no, not at all. Robert is not our child, he is Gloria's child by her first marriage, if she was ever married. Frank Cooper never came back from the trenches. I raised Robert like my own son but we never had any children. I was pretty shot up when I came back.'

'I'm sorry,' I say mechanically, like a paid-up member of the Sunny Hills Country Club.

'We separated a few years ago. Gloria's idea, but I wasn't sorry to be relieved of her melancholia; even though she has a perfect right, because of what was happening to her people in Germany.'

I like the way he tries to explain the end of his marriage. 'Your mother came to my rescue and has been the light of my life. She's had some hard knocks, but she never loses her *joie de vivre.*'

'She wasn't much of a mother.'

'I suppose she wasn't, if you say so.' He admits.

'What I really want to know is why you gave me up, why you couldn't care for me yourself?'

'I don't know what you're talking about. Naturally I cannot take care of you; I work. The Longs are just going to look after you until the war is over. Brenda knows your mother comes up a bit short on the maternal side. The answer will be to find a good boarding school.'

He has it all worked out.

'I'm glad,' I say giddily, smiling as much as I can. 'I'm happy to hear you always intended to take care of me. I've never been that close to Sidney; I love Brenda more than my foster father.'

'I don't know the Longs that well.'

I have given him a glimpse of a future without him, but again he doesn't want to know.

'Are you possessive?' I dare ask him. 'I am, and it may be a family trait.'

'It is! Nothing but! And family's are to blame for it. Have you ever been to the Victoria and Albert Museum?'

As if the country is not at war, we take a double-decker bus to Exhibition Road. When we arrive there is a long line of women waiting at the bus stop. My father winks at me.

'Fantail doves waiting for the men inside. You know what I mean by fantail doves?'

I don't tell him that my mother's career alerted me to many such names.

'An example of how morals go missing during wartime.'

This reminds me of a similar remark he made about his visit with his brother to a bordello. Above the museum are big black bags reaching up to the sky.

'What are those funny things?'

'Barrage balloons to stop the bombers. The balloons seem to work, although it may be luck. They've hidden the famous pictures from the National Gallery in country houses, but sculpture and furniture are not so easy to move.'

We enter the marble foyer and hear the clatter and chatter of a cafeteria. We make our way to a huge hall of men and women in uniform sitting at great long tables, looking like boarding school children at dinnertime. They look inquisitively at us, or rather my father. He signals for me to join a queue, and I think he's waiting for another meal, but it is a line of art lovers waiting to enter the museum's exhibition.

'Looks like Robert is not dining here to-day. Let's see the exhibits.'

We wait in line with a crowd straining to see Raphael's Cartoons.

'All very well,' he says cynically. 'Naked women drawn with a certain refinement. Fair enough!'

People seem to be enjoying the peace and calm of this church-like museum. I wonder if that's why we value art, as proof we can do other things besides bombing. My father stands in front of David, the enormous statue carved by Michelangelo.

'My son's name is David,' I inform him.

'That's right, you told me and I'd forgotten. Tell me more.'

'I don't know why I called him David. He's very like his father in looks and personality. He played

American football at school and is studying economics at college.'

'Sounds too good to be true,' my father says jealously, making me glad I have not mentioned David's recent baptism into a religious faith that my father will probably mock.

'And you live in America,' he says with a touch of hostility. '

Nothing for me in England. No family ties..'

'I can't believe you called him David,' he muses. 'Name of my favourite statue! Although the one here is not the original. Always wanted to go to Florence to see the original.' He sighs. 'This, apparently, is an exact replica. I'm not surprised it shocked the Florentines. I don't think England would allow a naked man that size in their High Street, even today.'

'They certainly wouldn't in the States.'

A guide pushes us along the line, down to a basement gallery. Here is a painting I recognise, a self-portrait by Rembrandt. 'Is that an original Rembrandt?'

'I suppose they think it's safe this far underground. Look at this, a picture of Lucretia and she looks like you. Her skin is as dark as yours.'

'You mean the famous poisoner?'

I take a closer look at this woman with a knife, a kitchen knife like the one in my mother's bathroom.

My father is reading the inscription. 'No, this is the original Lucretia from ancient Rome. She is the heroine who killed herself after being raped.'

'She killed herself like Vivien' I mumble.

I do not want to tell him this, but again he only half hears what I have said. Selective hearing.

'She doesn't look like Vivien. She looks like you.'

I take another look at Lucretia, killing herself after being raped. I don't consider suicide after being raped an act of heroism, but I live in another time and place and don't want to get into argument with him in case he doesn't agree with me.

'I brought you to the V&A to meet Robert. He's not here **or** he would have seen me enter the cafeteria. He must be out on some mission for the RAF, and that means top secret, even more so than the army. We never know where he is.'

'That must be upsetting Gloria.'

'Yes, it's dangerous to be flying over enemy territory. I must remember to post her letter to him.'

I hear both the fear and the pride in his voice, making me sorry not to be meeting Robert. This is more like the father I saw in 1917, a man who has a sense of personal responsibility as well as a man who is struggling with his country's problems. I'm growing a little fonder of this stranger now that I'm learning more about him. I must stop comparing him with his younger, more vibrant self, the kind of man I would have chosen as a soul mate.

Hugh Cuthbert, my father of fifty-odd years, defies any such romantic thoughts. Friendship with him may be possible.

'Are we friends now?'

He smiles in his off-hand way. 'I hope so.'

'Fathers and daughters can be friends.'

'And how do I know you're my real daughter? When I married Gloria, she told me she couldn't have any more children and God help me I was happy about that. Until I met Vivien I never thought… and there you are! Claiming to be my daughter, my real daughter! But any ghost could claim that!'

I'm glad he is making a joke. He waves a cheerful goodbye, and hops on a red double decker bus sweeping by. I wave back, feeling bereft and blank. I'm a phantom my father can leave behind. He is mid-life and mid-career in the Civil Service, a cog in the wheel of a tax department. I get out my book of comparisons and compare him with Sidney Long, my foster father who I was never very close to. My real father's work is very different from the work of market-gardening. He can easily abstract me from his thoughts when I am too much for him to think about.

****

CHAPTER NINE

1984

Ed had forgotten that London was nothing but traffic jams and that London taxis reminded him of hearses. The last time he was in England he was twenty. How easy it was to make friends at that age; how happy he'd been to escape Houston and the family. Now he was only glad to be familiar with cars being on the left and knew to be careful crossing roads. When Ed reached the hospital he was sent in the wrong direction, and then found he had to take three lifts and two staircases before he found the Intensive Care Unit. He thought he had prepared himself, but he was shocked by Annabel's appearance.

When the nurse pulled aside the curtains and he saw his wife's body on the bed, her legs and one arm encased in white bandages, her face barely visible under the tubes, he staggered backward and wanted to throw up. The nurse seemed to expect his nausea because she immediately handed him a metal bowl.

'That's not my wife.'

'Are you sure?'

'Her hair is white. My wife's hair is brown.'

'She was in an explosion.'

'But that wouldn't change the colour of her hair.'

'Unfortunately shock can do just that. Would you please have a closer look?'

Ed saw that it was Annabel. He was hoping it wasn't. 'There are a number of forms to be filled out. Do you have any sort of identification with you?'

Ed gave her a blank look. He was not sure he had the resources to cope with this situation. She exited with an almost playful glance at him. He was confused. Annabel looked dead. Another nurse appeared.

'Is there any hope?'

'There are always risks in a coma such as this. We have no optical reflex, but she has been seen to shudder from the shoulders down and that's good.'

Ed smiled sadly at the nurse's forced cheerfulness. He did not want to alienate this woman who was in control of his wife's well-being, but he wanted her to leave them alone.

At Annabel's bedside he felt a curious sense of being home. For hours he traced the outline of every tube attached to the forbidding equipment, perhaps keeping her alive or at least fed. He sat on the bed watching carefully for signs of life. He gradually put his feet on the bed, to lie down next to her, to keep her company.

'Excuse me, sir.'

Ed awoke to the gentle shake of an English policeman.

'If you don't mind, we have some questions to ask you.' Ed was about to object, but he did not want to argue with the police. He answered the usual policeman's questions about Annabel's date of birth, her place of birth, business in England, the date she had arrived. He was a little offended when asked whether he had any explanation for what happened.

'I'm pretty sure the explosion has nothing to do with my wife. We live in Houston.'

The policeman did not look swayed by this information. 'So she was visiting her mother's flat, then do you think her mother was the target.'

Ed shook his head. 'No, that doesn't sound right. Annabel came to England for her funeral. Her mother was already dead, she committed suicide.'

'Has suicide been officially proved?'

'She took an overdose.'

'It will need looking into.'

'I hope the explosion will be looked into.'

'As far as you're concerned, you cannot explain why there was a bomb in your mother-in-law's home?'

The policeman sat back in his chair and studied his notebook. Ed had nothing more to say. The silence lasted a few minutes until the policeman nodded a goodbye. Ed hated the intrusion, and hoped the enquiry was routine. He knew so little about Annabel's mother, except for her dubious profession involving almost-famous and almost-important people.

An overdose of sleeping pills was not a likely link to a bomb. Pills were evidence of desperation, and he was sure the police would agree with that conclusion. Given the tangled reality of Vivien Langoni, recently deceased, he hoped he wouldn't be asked any more questions. He could happily leave England without knowing further intimate details of his mother-in-law's life. He gazed at the Styrofoam ceiling, preparing himself for an uncomfortable night, or weeks of uncomfortable nights.

****

'London is the city you used to walk around at night, before you went away and came back pretending to be American; but you can change the destiny of this city. It's within your power to change not only your life and your family's future, but your country and the course of history.'

On hearing that voice I can't help wondering whether it sounds like my mother in a super sane incarnation, or whether it's my alter ego. I've been aimlessly roaming the streets of Pimlico without knowing where I want to go, but something is drawing me towards Victoria Station. The railway station is familiar to me because my mother and I took the train to and from Victoria station when she visited the Longs to take me out for a day in London.

I'm guessing I'm here to haunt my mother in some way, although she won't know she is being haunted if she cannot see me. I wonder what she will be wea–ring. I seem to have no sense of smell, so I won't be annoyed by the scent of her expensive perfume. I was not only annoyed, but embarrassed because her perfume used to penetrate the whole train carriage. I was such a reticent kid in her presence. No longer!

I'm eager to find her, spy on her. Yes, there she is, in front of me! Her clothes reflect war time fashion, an old fur jacket over a tweed skirt, but her shining dark hair contrasts with the dowdy scarves or hats worn by all the other worried-looking women.

When I overtake her, I'm surprised to see she's cradling a baby in her arms. This must be me! I'm all attention as she pushes open the door to Lyons' Tea Shop. She heads for a frumpy looking woman dressed in black. Oh, it is Brenda! She must have come up to London in order to meet Vivien. They are nodding hello to each other, and then they move their chairs closer together in a friendly way. They look very different from each other but I know that despite their rivalry over me, they got on well and almost liked each other. I never heard any overt disagreements between them during my childhood, which is surprising because my fostering, by today's standards, was a casual arrangement. Vivien would be asked for money on occasion and offer it on other occasions. The bond between them was contentious but strong. That is the baby me, who is about to be passed from one to the other. Suddenly I remember my mother's expensive dance dresses were also passed down to Brenda, who altered them to fit her short bulky frame. Although widely different in looks and dimensions, she somehow made those fancy dresses look right on her.

Brenda sits upright on the wooden chair looking uncomfortable and nervous. My mother places the white bundle in her arms and Brenda eagerly takes me, smiling happily. I cannot see my mother's face.

'We're only giving her up because of the bombing.'

I'm pleased to hear my mother say this, even if I don't believe it. I don't think she believes it either. Brenda screws her face to a pout.

'Terrible war! Never seems to end.'

'The poor kid hasn't been eating. She may be sickly or something. I don't know what's the matter with her.'

'Don't worry, she'll soon plump up.' Brenda rubs my cheek, and that protective gesture propels me back to a memory of being sick in bed and Brenda rubbing my chest with Vicks. Although I have no sense of smell in this strangely reduced state, the memory is so strong I want to sneeze.

'She's not the right weight for her age.'

Brenda shakes her head, but in a reassuring way. 'I'll take her to the doctor. He's a good sort, and he can prescribe a tonic for her. She'll soon put on weight. You won't recognise her.'

They walk out of the café together like a companionable couple, heading towards the platform. Vivien stops, like she has forgotten something.

'Wait here! I want to get you something for the train.'

Brenda frowns as my mother takes off, making me marvel at the awful responsibility of taking care of someone else's child. Me, the baby, begins to cry and Brenda jogs me up and down and puts me on her shoulder. When my mother returns, she hands Brenda a newspaper and a brown bag. This triggers a memory of my mother sitting opposite me on the train to and from Brighton; she always furnished us with chocolates and glossy magazines.

'Oh that's kind of you,' Brenda mumbles. My mother often redeemed herself with such acts of kindness. She would arrive with pet treats for the dogs and cats. A good memory of my mother is her red nails sunk in the fur of our golden retriever, and the way she would speak to him in an exchange of whines.

At the platform barrier, my two mothers huddle together as if they do not want to be separated. The baby, me, is securely clamped to Brenda's shoulder. I wonder if my mother has given me some whisky or whether she has given herself some whisky to counter the emotion of this separation. A whistle sounds, steam bellows out. Vivien bends forward to kiss me and Brenda rearranges my shawl protectively. The steam threatens to obscure them both, but my mother waits until the train slowly shunts out the station. She waves in a frantic way as if Brenda is a long-lost relative who will never be seen again, then turns and sways on her high heels through the station.

I run to catch with her, she is walking defiantly in the middle of the road as if she cares for nothing, but she wipes her eyes with the back of an impatient hand. I try to imagine giving David up. The thought blurs my vision and I have trouble following her, but my mother's vision is not troubling her. It was a quick simple transaction. It is deceptively easy to pass on a child to be taken care of by another, an act so unnatural it would never happen in the animal kingdom.

CHAPTER TEN

1984

Ed tried to make sense of the notes the surgeon had insisted he take during their interview. Lungs pierced by ribs, heart compromised, brain bleeding. Ed refrained from asking why these serious injuries had gone untreated for two days. He had doubts about the National Health treatment but was in no position to complain. Annabel's possession of the all-important NHS number meant there would be no bills to pay.

He forced himself to touch her cold hand and broke into a sweat. He watched the seconds go by on a large wall clock. He also worried about his work and thought about asking his mother to come to London and take his place. She was the most likely candidate, but she suffered from varicose veins, and they would trouble her on a long flight. He knew Annabel would not be happy about waking up and not seeing him, but the days of waiting tried his temper. He wanted to explode with anger at the delay in scheduling the operation, but the doctors insisted that they were monitoring her vital signs. Ed resigned himself to wandering the hospital corridors in search of coffee machines. He sat in the Outpatients lobby and watched television.

Then he stumbled into the Accident and Emergency department. Among the ragged and bleeding, he heard disturbing complaints about the National Health Service. He spoke little, afraid they would question his accent. He was the outsider and was becoming aware that he married into a culture without understanding it. He was not reassured when he overheard someone say in a loud voice, 'They keep you from getting any help in the hope that you'll get better by yourself. If you don't, it'll cut costs, because the NHS won't be paying for the funeral.' This remark was greeted with genuine laughter and repeated round the room to smiles and grins. Ed failed to find it humorous. He began to compare people here with people back home, remembering that he had been critical of Annabel doing this when she first arrived in the States. She did it so much that became a joke between them, this constant comparison between their two countries. He once called Annabel a split personality because she always saw both sides of every question and turned on a dime. Now he was seeing the world through two different cultures.

When they finally trundled Annabel onto a wheelie bed for her operation, Ed was grateful to be briefly relieved of his vigil. As he watched the crazy angle that the wheelie bed took round the corridor corners, he tried not to imagine someone slitting the skin of Annabel's chest and carving through her sternum, which they cruelly informed him would be the start of a lengthy operation where two surgeons would work in shifts.

When they reached the operating room, he was forced back by the brightness of the lights, and someone told him to wait in the lounge. The lounge was a sofa backing onto a plywood screen. He took a cup of bad coffee from the machine and tried not to think what he would do with his life without Annabel.

****

'You do not need your parents; you have outgrown them. You are in control of your life now. If you want, you can disappear without a trace, as if you were never here, or never lived on earth. You have had that option, which gives you power over others that you still don't know how to use.'

I am following my mother on her way out of Victoria station and hear a warning siren, which I cannot helping believing is the police coming for my mother because she has committed some sort of crime, handing me over like that with nobody to see or understand what she is doing. No, according to the mumbled relief of people around me, the siren is not a warning siren, it is an All Clear siren. Or maybe they're wrong and it is a siren telling people to go back to work. That would account for the lack of people and cars in the street. My mother does not notice. In spite of her high heels, she is almost running across Green Park. Then I see her get out a handkerchief to blow her nose. An unaccustomed gesture for my glamorous mother. She always had a ready cotton handkerchief for emergencies, but never suffered colds and flu. 'Pickled in alcohol,' she replied when I challenged her on her good health.

She approaches Piccadilly Circus and then disappears under the canopy of the Criterion Theatre. I follow her down the curved staircase into a lobby filled with well-dressed people. She is making her way through the crowd to greet two men waiting for her. She kisses them affectionately on both cheeks. The older of the two men is bullet-shaped with thinning hair, his face moulded in firm lines; the younger has an almost featureless face, framed by wavy blond hair. It's the longest hair I've seen in this era; the shape of hair to come. They hug her affectionately before inspecting her outfit.

'Darling, that coat, yes, but not the purple scarf. purple does not suit your skin tone. And look at the state of your hands!'

The older one holds both her hands in his and looks reproachfully at my mother.

'These hands have been working for a living.'

'I thought you worked in a lab.'

'I lost that job when I had the baby. Now it's washing up, and if I'm lucky they make me clean the toilets.'

'Take care of those hands. Although how does anyone have clean nails now! You know they won't let me do manicures during the war?'

'And he's done royalty.'

'Queens, anyway.'

I wonder how they all know each other. They look vaguely familiar and I'm trying to remember if I've met them. They join the crowd descending a great many steps to reach the underground theatre. The audience is intensely respectable, mostly grey-haired with a sprinkling of men in uniform, some of them American GIs. The two men give the G.Is. admiring looks, and I suddenly remember where I've met them. Their names are Fred and Michael, and they had the photography studio below my mother's London flat. She used to work for them occasionally and as a model. I sometimes saw her try and make their place as neat and tidy as her own.

'Why didn't Hugh come? We had a ticket for him.'

'He is so tired after the office.'

Fred makes a deprecating noise and Michael shushes him. There is the usual appreciative murmur of an audience before the curtain rises. It is all so normal that it is hard to believe England is fighting a bitter war above ground, and one that has lasted four years. The play is set back in the 1920s; a family comedy about a philandering husband, which of course makes me think of Ed.

The wife is vain and hypocritical, and the audience laughs at every opportunity, but I see nothing funny in such a shallow marriage.

When the audience has finished applauding, Vivien leads the way to the bar, her friends following discreetly behind. She positions herself on a stool, where her soulful brown eyes will attract the kindness of strangers. True to form, a balding man offers to buy her a pint. She chats with him for a while and then introduces her friends and asks her friends what they want to drink. She will not be paying. Her admirer seems to be someone connected with the production, because people come up to congratulate him.

'The show's amazing. A solid piece of writing.'

'If we can keep it up for a week, it will have a good run.'

He waves his hands in the air. 'We've papered the house.'

This comment does not please his admirers, and he extracts himself in order to return to my mother. 'Do you and your friends want to join us backstage?'

She nods eagerly and her friends look impressed. They follow a select group through a door marked, 'The Green Room'. It is a messy room stocked with two bottles of wine and two plates of sandwiches. Vivien attracts the usual attention, and with each admiring glance she grows more confident. She would always begin demurely at any gathering and then become the centre of attention without ever dominating the conversation. She was always willing to defer to others more educated and intelligent. 'I am in awe of London and Londoners,' she informs the room to the approval of everyone.

'Where are you from?'

Yes, where is this fabulous-looking creature from?

'Oxford.' Vivien does not add, by way of Dr. William Brown's orphanage.

Her friends come to the rescue.

'London and Vivien, Vivien and London, moth to the flame. And believe me, she's the flame.'

I approve of how generously her friends are promoting her. A distinguished older man approaches and takes my mother's hand possessively.

'Can you come with me a minute?'

She does not hesitate, but I am fearful for her. She's never had the usual feminine fears.

He leads her down a dusty passage to an office crammed with a large desk smothered in papers. She ignores him at first, reading the framed poster on the walls.

'I'm casting for the part of Joan. I'm talking about Bernard Shaw's *Joan of Arc*.' He hands her a booklet. 'You can read?'

She gives him a scornful look at this patronising question and bends her dark head over the script. Perhaps her dark eyes and hair makes him think she looks French.

'Joan of Arc was a farm girl who became a soldier and waged war on the English. This takes place after she is captured. She is imprisoned and awaiting her trial.'

My mother reads the passage out loud, slowly and carefully. He makes her read the speech three times. I can see that instead of becoming more involved in what Joan is talking about, my mother is becoming less and less interested. One free hand starts twisting her hair like a teenager; yes, she is still a teenager She once told me she wanted to get into the movies and almost got a part playing a Spanish dancer in a cowboy film but failed to get it because she did not look Spanish enough.

The impresario looks grimmer with each attempt and finally takes the book back with a shake of his head.

'You need to go deeper into how she is feeling. If you stay on the surface, so does your voice.'

'I'm sorry.'

She is close to tears, and that moves him to approach.

'You have magnificent eyes and a sympathetic face. You could be good in films I could get you into films.'

He leans into her as he says this and grabs a quick kiss. She does not act surprised, but I can tell from her face that she does not like him. Pinned to the wall, she does not move a muscle, which encourages the old lecher to lunge at her again and manoeuvre them both into the armchair, probably there for that purpose. Vivien's face is passive, empty. She's not there. She has the ability to absent herself at will even though she is usually intensely aware of her physical presence. Angry at the assault, I yearn to rescue her, and look down at my hands. They seem real, but they cannot touch or grasp anything. In this world I can only observe. I wonder whether, if I stay long enough in this incarnation, I will gain strength in these useless fingers. I want to take that chair and crash it down on his head. He is now grunting in frustration trying to hug the rag doll Vivien has become. He is shaking her, and I wonder if he's shaking her awake.

At this moment the door is thrown open with a loud bang. A young woman in a red suit stands there with a furious look on her face. He immediately releases Vivien, who almost falls on the floor. The young woman advances. 'Your wife will hear about this,' she shouts.

The old man goes to her and tries to kiss her, murmuring, 'Darling, darling, please don't misunderstand me! I was auditioning.'

Vivien escapes with a look of contempt at both of them. She joins her friends, who are covertly scraping crumbs from the sandwich plate.

'He says I should go into films,' she tosses at them.

Fred claps enthusiastically. 'Didn't I always say so?'

'No, you said she'd make a perfect model.'

'Because she's photogenic. She'll do wonders in film.'

Arguing affectionately, they climb the steep stairs to ground level where they are greeted by darkened streets and the boarded-up fountain in the middle of Piccadilly Circus. Here the world is still at war. There is a strangely grim silence and people bump into each other, confused about which street to take. They are not talking, they are listening to a faint thudding, almost like the beat of a drum.

'Stick bombing. Carpet bombing.'

'Nah, that's nothing. Hitler coughing.'

'I thought it was all over. We're in France!'

My mother's two companions turn to her. 'Maybe safer to go by Tube.' This does not appeal to me, but I follow them down the unmoving escalator to find an unexpected dance floor on the platform. Couples are jigging to a duo of double bass and trumpet, pumping out a jazzy swing tune. The dim light makes the dirty station look like a sleazy disco, the kind that was popular when Ed and I were dating. The music is little more than a staccato suggestion, but people are eager to dance. Men and women rub up against each other in pretend pleasure. Is this the beginning of dirty dancing?

'That's how I met Hugh, in the Underground,' my mother informs her friends. 'I love dancing.'

She jigs up and down as if to prove it. 'Come on, boys.'

The boys seem reluctant, but do join her in the dance. Michael is awkward in an effort to be fluid but Fred, in spite of his age, has a nervous energy and dances with his body weighted forward. Vivien's graceful body lightens the dirty station, and I remember that she received many accolades for her swishy dancing. Ballroom dancing was where and how she first made her mark. It was the early days of the BBC's television show, 'Come Dancing', which necessitated an endless supply of expensive dance dresses. I heard from Cleo, that my mother gave the privilege of paying for these dresses to the stage-boy Johnny of the moment. She always referred to men as 'boys' and once told me every important man was a stage-boy Johnny at heart.

A man in workman's overalls, with 'Home Guard' written across his back, tries to cut in and dance with my mother. 'My turn.' He says aggressively.

My mother edges closer to her friends, which annoys him.

'And wot you boys doing for the war effort?'

He gets no answer, which makes him even more aggressive. Pushing himself in front of my mother, he turns and repeats his question.

'They're hairdressers,' my mother explains.

'You mean pansies, don't you? Getting out of the draft that way.'

'I'm an air warden and we both do fire watch!'

This defiance does not go down well, and he pummels Fred in the shoulder. 'Why aren't you in uniform?'

Michael stops dancing and takes a stand.

'I am a photographer, and the government did not recognise my profession.'

'Not surprised Nancy boy!'

'The government ordered us to stay behind and be barbers, which is classed an essential service.'

'Oh sure, didn't want you Nancy boys in the army. That's a way of saving yer skins, if you sees wot I mean.'

This comment is received by cheers from the crowd and my mother panics. They run down a long staircase and reach an empty platform where Fred purposefully hugs Michael. Vivien looks round anxiously in case they are seen. I choose a seat opposite her in the Tube. I've never seen my mother take the Tube. When she could not afford taxis, she'd walk or take the bus. On her walks she invariably met someone she knew. London must have been much less populated then. 'I wanted to fight!' Fred whispers. 'They wouldn't have me.'

'They say war brings out the best in people; what about it bringing out the worst?'

'They were drunk.'

'How can they afford it?'

'Homemade gut rot!'

They tut-tut like puritanical Sunday school teachers. I'm beginning to see my mother from my father's point of view. Her beauty catches everyone's eye. She cannot be an ordinary girl. She is a would-be starlet waiting to be discovered. Her two men friends understand her and are comfortable with my mother's innocent enjoyment of life. She is more at ease with them than with my father. In their company the war is forgotten, while my more respectable father seems to be fighting on all fronts. Am I beginning to love my mother? How many times can you change your mind about a person? How many revolutions can a mind make? Now that I'm a ghost I can probably make my head turn 360 degrees, like the proverbial wise old owl. If my mother saw me do that she'd probably laugh.

Vivien suddenly screams and points to where I'm sitting.

Have I laughed out loud? Has she seen me?

'What's wrong?'

'Over there!' she shrieks. 'I saw my mother's ghost! The ghost of my dead mother!'

Fred and Michael look worried and fearful as if reminded of their mothers.

'Is she still there?'

Vivien shakes her head. I melt through the speeding carriage door in a spectacular exit no one witnesses. I have almost managed to appear to my mother, but I'm annoyed and disappointed. She often told me I looked like her mother, but I resented this and found it difficult to believe. According to my genetic calculations, my dark hair must surely make me look like her Italian father.

Part III

CHAPTER ELEVEN

'Reality passes quickly and soon becomes a fleeting memory; the more you understand this, the more powerful you will become. You have a lot to forget. But you also have a lot more to learn.'

My head is throbbing with the persistent refrain of a school hymn, one of my favourites: *Morning Has broken*. If only I had some say in where I'm going in the past. Before I can judge where I am, or in what time period, I cannot help hoping I'm going to be transported back to my school days. I have some good memories of giggling in class and swapping notes. I don't remember learning much; I was never interested in studying, but I liked being one of the class clowns.

I am in some sort of school, but I see it is not my elementary school in Warmdene Village. The teachers here are wearing a mustard-coloured uniform. I could be in a hospital, except that I recognise the morning assembly for prayers. I could be in some sort of prison. Perhaps they put children in prison back then. Back when? How far back have I gone this time? I tour rows of pale faces and open mouths singing with such sadness that I cannot bear to stay there. I walk out and cross a quadrangle of low-slung bungalows; living quarters that look like a prison. A massive stone house guards the exit, and a bronze statue of a man with folded arms. The plaque beneath informs me this is the famous benefactor, Dr. William Brown.

Then this is my mother's orphanage. I'm now inside the house, looking up at a high-domed entrance hall which leads to a winding staircase with a curved mahogany banister. Upstairs, on the long landing there are rows of glass cabinets full of leatherbound books. Then I hear a worrying sound, the barking grunt of a man. He sits with his back to the doorway, bouncing a thin girl sitting on his knees. I have a sudden and irrational fear that this skinny dark-haired girl is me, but of course I've never been in Dr. William Brown's home for orphans. It is my mother who is squirming in his grasp. The man is intent on enjoying his pleasure as his trousers bulge and look about to burst. Her long black hair is bouncing up and down with every grunt he makes. She looks up at the ceiling and I follow her gaze to a stationary wooden ceiling fan. Even so young, she is capable of absenting herself at this moment of abuse, like she did with the impresario. I'm glad to see that this bearded man, whoever he is, looks nothing like the statue of the stately Dr. William Brown, but I seethe with rage. I want to injure him in some way; but I'm in the same situation as with the impresario, I cannot save my mother.

Now he's giving her a piece of chocolate from his top pocket and holding a finger to his chubby lips as he sweeps her off his lap.

'Go back to assembly, and tell Theresa to come and see me,' he says solemnly. 'And hurry up or you'll miss prayers.'

She runs as if being chased by demons, down the stairs, and across the quadrangle. Disobeying his instructions, she runs past the singing assembly and disappears round a corner. When I catch up with her, she is crouching up against a rusty iron radiator. I try to work out how old she is, when the intensity of my gaze seems to affect her. She brushes the air between us as if warding off an evil spirit.

'Can you see me?' I ask with relief. She looks confused.

'Mama!'

This time I'm glad she thinks I'm her mother. I want to mother her.

'I saw what happened in there, and you mustn't let any man do that to you.'

I want to give her hope and support, I want to give her all the love she needs. 'You must protect yourself from men like that, and never be afraid of them, because I know you are going to be rich and beautiful and have a good life. Please believe me!'

She is now patting down her skirt and combing her fingers through her hair. I hope on some level she has heard me. Taking a deep breath, and twirling her long, dark but rather thin hair, she saunters slowly and gracefully away. I have a sudden insight as to why she became a blond.

CHAPTER TWELVE

Ed delayed calling David because he wanted to wait until there was good news. The good news was that Annabel had survived the operation, but somehow that was tainted with the fact that she was as comatose as before. Her lungs were cleared, her broken bones mended, but she was still hooked up to two machines. Ed tried not to be impatient. The surgeon said there was a good likelihood that Annabel would soon be returning to consciousness, but Ed could see no sign that her health was improving. The only hopeful sign, which he had reported to the surgeons, was that during his vigils he had seen Annabel's eyes move under her eyelids. Ed knew that in dogs that meant they were dreaming, which was a good sign. At least he could tell David that. He longed to hear the supreme confidence in David's youthful voice on the telephone and hear David's confidence in his prayers. Ed was still afraid to tell David that one side of Annabel's face had been badly damaged. He didn't want to admit to David his own fears that Annabel would be a different person looking so damaged, opening up the possibility that he would feel differently about her. When he managed to speak to David, Ed realised that David was not going to be as fearful as he was about the physical change in his mother. But when Ed came back to Annabel's sterile room, he was overcome with a sense of despair he had never known before. He was angry that no one caring for his wife had ever known her as a pretty and vivacious woman.

A friendly nurse, Lisa, liked to stop by for a chat. She said she liked hearing Ed's accent. Ed welcomed her visits because the day was long and boring. He did not welcome the visit from a plain clothed policeman who introduced himself as a detective. This meant the enquiry was going deeper.

'We've checked with the American Embassy and they've no record of a Mrs. Fuego.'

'We got married in Texas.' Ed's tone inferred that Texas was another country. 'And she is not an American citizen. When we got married, she got a Green Card which allowed her to work.'

'So, she must have used her British passport to gain entry here. Do you have any proof of your marriage?'

'Yes, but in Texas, and I can get it for you. We never bothered to register our marriage in England.'

The policeman frowned. 'You should have done that immediately. But at least the Embassy has found a record of you, Eduardo Fuego is on the Houston voting register; and according to them there is no criminal record of either of you.'

'Our marriage is registered in Texas.'

'We're checking on that.'

'Of course.' Ed felt it was best to be in enthusiastic agreement with him 'But there's no way Annabel or either of us could be connected to any bomb attack. She has led a blameless life in Houston as a wife and mother.'

The detective did not look convinced.

'For all I know, bombs like that often happen in England.' The policeman looked offended at this remark but refrained from asking any further questions. When he left, the friendly Lisa returned to chat, and to find out what the police wanted. This was unexpected, and Ed was suddenly afraid her attention was aimed at him. He was extra polite to her which in Houston would indicate he was not interested in her. He called her ma'am and hoped she got the message. He was nervous of Annabel waking up to see him flirting. He had some vague idea that even in a coma, she could sense him. He clung to that thought, because otherwise why was he there?

****

'Your ability to disconnect is growing, and that's what you have to do if you want to make a new life for yourself. You have to put that small self aside and expand your consciousness to include the universe. In that way you will have powers beyond anything you, with your little political allegiances can imagine. With your limited intelligence, you will have trouble accepting this, but you've made a start.'

I admit the voice is trying to inspire me in some way, but I cannot help distrusting it. Maybe because it's a woman's voice, maybe it's my other self but not a self I want to claim, or even recognise.

The London Underground has become my port of entry, or is it called a portal? This part of the station is empty, so I cannot read from the costumes of the crowds a clue as to where I am and in what year I find myself. The defunct escalator and the clock which says five o'clock, give me no clue. I have to find a news stand and read unsold newspapers. The headlines are about as large as they can be. The date is December 15th, 1941 and the report is about the bombing of Pearl Harbor. I suppose it was an important event here in England. I have some memory that the disaster meant the United States joined the war effort. According to the giant typeface of the newspaper, Japan has declared war on both England and America. The thought of tiny Japan doing this amuses me for a minute, until I remember Hiroshima.

Outside in the street people hurry silently by, looking as if they have suffered the ultimate shock, and then I remember from the memorial service that this was the year I of the Blitz. A shimmer of heat ripples the air, which makes me look down at the pavement. I do not feel the heat, but I'm surrounded by cinders smouldering under the fallen brickwork. Blocking the path is a hunk of twisted metal that must have been an office chair. I'm beginning to think being in the past must have some message for me, but I cannot think what that message is.

I'm having déjà vu. A young girl is picking her way through the rubble, long black hair bobbing off her heart-shaped face. Then I recognise my young mother, the teenage Vivien, a few years older than when I saw her at the orphanage. She looks like a young housemaid with flashing black eyes and a tightfitting coat. She is carrying a heavy book under her arm, which amazes me because I've never seen my mother read any book like that. I work out her age. She must be about seventeen and my heart cries out to her. If only she could see me! She looks around as if lost. When she sees the familiar sign for the Underground she runs towards it and I cannot help but follow her, drawn by the speed and lightness of her step. I'm curious to see what she is doing this early in the morning.

At the Tube entrance people are surging past me, clutching blankets and squinting at the daylight. They give my mother a distrustful look because she is going in the opposite direction, down instead of up. She pushes her way onto a platform, where a feeble light bulb illuminates heaps of bedding and cardboard boxes. Out of these boxes, dishevelled people are stirring like bemused night creatures unwilling to be disturbed from a comfortable cave. My mother picks her way through them and chooses to hover near a well-dressed man sitting on an army cot. He is bent over a crossword puzzle, balanced on top of his briefcase.

'Nearly finished?' she asks, with a perkiness I seldom saw in her.

He barely acknowledges her words, but her continued gaze forces him to look up, and I recognise my father. Does she already know him, or am I witnessing the exact time and place they met?

'Aren't you going to be late for work?'

He does not reply but takes a closer look at this young girl who dares to ask him this.

'What are you reading?' There's respect in his voice, seeing the book in her lap. He reads the title and makes an impressive grimace by turning down the corners of his mouth.

She laughs. 'Not my book!'

They both frown and laugh at the same time.

'I was sent to fetch it from the University Library for professor... um... you see, my professor...' Her eyes fill with tears. 'Sent me to get this book yesterday, and when I get back there, the house... gone... everyone... gone.' the last word is a whisper, but he hears it.

'Your family?'

'I was working for them, but now I have nowhere to go. And no clothes, nothing.'

My father immediately understands her predicament. 'You mean their house was bombed in the raid last night? If so, there are emergency government stores where you can get some clothes and rations. They'll fit you out. Even get you another job.'

'I'm lucky to be alive.'

He smiles. 'That's the right way to think.'

He looks her up and down. Although dressed in unflattering black, it enhances her dark eyes and her complexion is youthful, she has perfectly curved lips in a perfectly shaped face.

'Come with me, I'll show you where it is.'

It makes sense that my father knows about government departments. I wonder when he will take her to his bachelor flat in Adelphi Square. He has a detached air of indignation about her precarious situation that makes him look dignified and trustworthy. When they stand up, I can see my mother has not yet grown to her full height. If I remember from first seeing them together in Adelphi Square, she will grow slightly taller than he is. She looks up at him now as if comforted by his interest, and I notice that she manages to wiggle ever so slightly when he ushers her in front of him.

When we reach ground level, he buys a paper and I look for the name of that Tube station where my parents met; but the entrance sign is under rubble. My father walks in a dignified manner beside Vivien as if taking a fatherly interest in her, and I can see she enjoys falling into step beside him. I'm sure these two people will convince themselves they are in love. Why am I being so cynical? Am I jealous? I do some calculations. They are going to have a couple of years to get to know each other before my arrival. Time enough to love each other. When I saw them in Adelphi Square they were acting like a married couple and dealing with a noisy baby who is me. The unwelcome visitor.

****

CHAPTER THIRTEEN

1984

The next time Ed called, David could not understand why his mother was still unconscious and drew sorrowful conclusions. Ed could not think of anything comforting to say and when Ed suggested prayer, he hoped David would not think he was being ironic. It was difficult to sound sincere on the phone. He promised David he would spend as much time as possible at Annabel's bedside, and his son had to be satisfied with that.

Lisa had arranged for a TV to be rented and Ed was absorbed in *EastEnders* when Adrian arrived, almost obscured by red roses. His appearance was a surprise, but after two weeks Ed was becoming accustomed to being part of the hospital community even if this meant he had to accept that every conversation was public knowledge.

'You must be Ed. The police have just interrogated me. I was with Annabel when the explosion happened. I was a friend of Vivien's, Annabel's mother. Annabel and I met at her funeral. I was there when the explosion happened, paying off the taxi. Jolly good thing I was there, because I immediately called an ambulance. How is she?'

'No way of knowing. She's in a coma.'

'I'm sure she's in good hands.'

Ed was not so sure but nodded his head. This young man, who wore a silver-threaded jacket and long hair, was not someone Ed understood. 'I'm Adrian Woodard.' He announced.

They shook hands and Ed thought his handshake pitiful. To counter his discomfort Ed took the remote and started pressing buttons. 'I've heard from the nurses that coma patients sometimes respond to music.'

Adrian tapped his foot in agreement. 'Everyone likes the Beatles.'

'Their music is okay, sure. But they can't sing.'

Adrian hooted with derision, which prevented Ed from justifying his taste in music by adding that his music featured tenors and bassos, Tejano music. He also wanted to say that those millionaire Beatles looked like lost boys to him, but then he realised Adrian looked lost. Maybe a lot of Englishmen looked that way. Adrian slapped Ed on the back which Ed took for a gesture of friendship from this untidy looking man who was a fan of the Beatles.

'They say she'll be okay.'

'That's good to hear.'

'When she revives, they will do reconstructive work on that side of her face.'

'Let me know if you need anything. Are you staying at Vivien's?'

'No, why would I be?'

'It's empty. You may as well use it rather than a hotel.'

Ed was embarrassed by the implication that he needed somewhere to stay. He had been told the address of the accident, but now it seemed he could use the place. He decided to consult Adrian about another problem. 'Is there any way we can find out whether Vivien had any relations? We know she was raised in an orphanage, but even orphans have parents. You see, they would be Annabel's relations, and I'd like to know if any of them are around.'

Adrian got out a packet of cigarettes and twirled them in one hand. He made Ed regret putting on weight. Annabel would have liked Adrian. He was beginning to wonder why they were together when the bomb went off.

'You can always go to Missing Persons. I seem to remember Vivien telling me she made up the name Langoni so you may not have any luck.'

'I'll make a start with Missing Persons.'

'Start with them. There must be something about them in Records. This country keeps ample records of births and deaths.' Adrian did not feel like telling Ed about finding a completely different surname on Annabel's birth certificate.

Ed was glad to see him leave. He tried to imagine Adrian and Annabel together, but his imagination was not that good. There was always his worry that his happy marriage had been destroyed by Donna. He wondered if Annabel was going to be changed by this medical ordeal and whether she would still want to be married to him when she recovered. Sitting alone on a hard chair, Ed wondered how long he was going to sit by her bedside. If only there was some movement from that frozen form under the sheets.

****

'The more you learn about the past, the easier it will be to change it. For once you'll be able to choose. Yes, you! Everyone has the power to change the future, but only a few people experience that power enough to make a difference. You could be one of a select few.'

I'm beginning to feel that I'm not being guided by this voice, but that I'm being mocked because I'm certainly not in control.

I'm stumbling down a street in Soho. The sky is ringed with fire, which silhouettes the burning roofs. A woman in front of me trips over white hoses crisscrossing the street. Fire wardens in tin hats are spraying the bonfire of burning houses, and then turn the hose on their helmets. Watching this spectacle, a bunch of kids are whooping with delight as if it is firework night, and a thin man in a dressing gown throws up his arms. I don't know whether he is praying to the heavens or hailing the fire. I catch a glimpse of a child's bicycle under the rubble. Were children killed in this inferno? David's voice rings out, 'My mountain bike, they've stolen my mountain bike!' An echo from the past.

The Tyneside Bank of Scotland is guarded by a man with a rifle. They must be expecting looters. I drift in and find a dozen men in long black coats leaning anxiously over the table. Ah, that's why I'm here: to see my father at work. He is sitting with the bank's account books in front of him. He speaks little and with reserve. His clients, or perhaps his suspects, hang over him as if the weight of their presence will justify whatever's lacking in their ink-lined and underlined account books. He looks up and smiles at me.

'Glad to see you appear from nowhere.'

The bank clerks look confused, but he is not embarrassed to be seen talking to the walls.

'Come to see grown men despair?'

'Have you caught them cooking the books?' I ask.

He turns to his audience. 'See that it is in order next time.' They half bow with consenting nods. He shoves a sheaf of papers into his briefcase and makes for the stairs. Once outside he looks nervously up at the sky and says, 'I don't feel safe in this part of London. It's not Adelphi Square.'

'Why would they rather bomb here?'

He gives me a sly look. Is he trying to tell me the rich and powerful in the West End are more secure? Or maybe it's the proximity to the Houses of Parliament. He holds up his briefcase triumphantly. 'I've got the bastards on the run. They've broken too many rules. With a hefty fine, they'll end up owing the government a thousand or two. I only hope this doesn't involve lengthy investigations which reveal criminal intent.'

I don't like to hear this, because the *Miss Marple* in me alerts me to the fact that he may have been murdered because he knew too much about crooked finances.

'I promised to stop in on the local Servicemen's Club.'

The entire area looks like a construction site, which is probably why he has to ask directions. As directed, we pass a precarious wooden scaffold, and my father shouts up to a figure climbing down. The man waves back and in spite of his bulk, makes a graceful descent.

'John McPherson!' This is said for my benefit and he wants to tell me more. 'At least some of my friends are able to make a living in wartime. He'll become a millionaire if we live to see the day.'

John McPherson reminds me of John Wayne. He thumps my father on the back and they walk a few blocks to reach a pub that has escaped bomb damage, although it has seen better days. They go to the bar and my dad is furnished with a whisky. The barman's hand shakes as he is pouring the drinks and when he hands them over, his face goes into a spasm. John McPherson, turns with a sad look, and whispers, 'These days you can't tell which war to blame for shell shock.'

'He's not old enough to be a veteran from the trenches.'

'This war then. Blanket bombing.'

After clinking glasses, the two friends join an assortment of older men in an inner sanctum. They are busily pinning paper flags on a wall map. I learn from their mumbled remarks that blue indicates the advance, white flags the Allie's retreat. The white flags make a wavy line along an expanse of green on the map, indicating the French countryside. This odd assortment of elderly men contemplating the map behave as if they are vital commanders and generals. I wonder if their information is accurate. The talk is about setbacks, push backs, retreats.

One of them doffs his hat to my father. 'What's the word from Whitehall?'

'Reason to hope!' my father quickly replies, looking at me. 'The Eighth Army is in charge of the bombing and Hitler's running out of fuel.'

'Don't believe it! They've accessed Middle East oil fields through Turkey.'

'Haven't seen you for a while George!'

A white-haired and bearded man taps the map with a stick. The men crowd round him with exaggerated respect.

'A smart man,' my father whispers to me. 'We were friends at Cambridge. I had to leave after one year for lack of funds, but he stayed on and taught. War ministry saw fit to send him to a razor factory. His beard is a protest.'

George has overheard my father say this. 'I'm engaged heart, mind and body in keeping the men of England clean-shaven. Or what would become of them? The Government sees fit to condemn a factory full of women to making razor blades in wartime, so what is there to say?'

'I'm sure you will have your say, George.'

'You have no idea of the deafening noise. I'll be deaf before this war is over, and so will those women.'

'You still a commie, George?'

I want to hear what he replies to this, and edge closer. My father notices and gives me a questioning look which I ignore. 'Are you still afraid of us?' George asks. 'That's how Hitler got Germany's elite to back him, fear of the workers.'

'Doesn't Hitler appeal directly to the masses?'

'They're afraid of communists too.'

George's upper-class accent makes me doubt his politics, and it seems I'm not the only one.

'I don't know how you run a factory with that accent, matey.'

'Yer think I dunno 'ow to talk like one of the workers?'

His cockney accent raises a laugh, but it makes me take George more seriously. Lenin advised his followers to go in disguise.

This attempt at comedy is cheered by the bartender polishing glasses. George is encouraged. 'Land nationalization, that's what this country needs. We have to take back the land from those chinless wonders who stole it back in them awful Olden Days.'

'Maybe land nationalisation is enough. We don't need total communism.'

I look at my father in amazement at the suggestion of all the land in England being nationalized, but George nods and grins as if he is looking forward to this possibility.

'Pre-fabricated housing! Prefabs!' McPherson shouts out in a defensive tone. 'That's going to replace our slums, and a good job too. I've seen slums in the East End that aren't fit for Englishman. We are going to rebuild. The Germans have done us a favour.'

'Yeah, we should thank them!'

'Do you mind if we don't thank them?'

My father's gentle banter reminds me of the humour I heard when he was a young officer.

'Whoosh bang, revolution.' George threatens again.

'It won't happen!' I yell, but only my father can hear me, and he is putting on his coat to leave. Before he reaches the door, someone pulls his sleeve.

'You never gave us the latest from Whitehall.' The room is quiet as they wait for his reply.

'We are not the only ones suffering from retreat. Horror stories in the Ardennes of German soldiers, killing and pillaging, I suppose in revenge because they're injured and hungry; burning a whole congregation in a church and shooting those who tried to escape!'

'War is inhuman, or this war at any rate. The Germans were civilised in the last one.'

'Using mustard gas on soldiers?'

'We used mustard gas! And worse, too.'

They edge closer as if trying to shield each other from bad memories as well as bad news. For a moment there is an eerie silence, and then they go back to familiar toasts, health and happiness. McPherson slaps my father on the back, and says, 'Happy Christmas!'

'To you and yours.' My father replies.

The men's talk of politics has made me think of my allegiance to the communist ideal. I want my father to know that I, too, was drawn towards an equal division of wealth, and powerfully driven by my meagre circumstances to believe in Marxism. When I try to explain he is unpleasantly surprised.

'So, you're interested in politics?'

'I was. I wanted wealth to be shared and an end to the class system.'

'But it sounds as if you've changed your mind.'

'I'll tell you one thing about Marx that holds up. He said people who put their labour into a product have a right to own it. That's the essence as I understood it from my evening classes in the theory of Marx and Engels. And you see I had first-hand knowledge of that. Brenda brought me up, she raised me. Not Vivien.'

He frowns as if I've said something hurtful. This could be the signal that he is beginning to take what I say seriously.

I press on. 'Because it was Brenda who took care of me, I think of her as my real mother. I feel allegiance to her, and that I belong to her, exactly like Marx said.'

My father looks shocked. 'But you are not a product, you are a person.'

'Same difference!'

For some reason I use David's teenage expression. It is not the moment to lecture him on the doctrine of materialism that includes people. Not even sure I am correct after my rote learning.

'I gave up politics when I got married and went to America.'

My father smiles. He's happy about this.

'I toyed with the idea of joining up with the Socialist Party of America, but never did. I became a feminist instead.'

'What's that?' He is puzzled, but I don't try to give him a précis of feminist history. He needs more personal information.

'Your mother wasn't around when you were growing up?'

'Not much. You were conspicuous by your absence.' This is a lot for him to imagine, and I can see he is afraid to ask any more questions. Strange how willing he is to blank out the future.

'Vivian never referred to you, so who knows where you were.'

'Expect I got killed in France. They're calling up the over fifties now. That's how short of manpower they are. I won't escape that, even with my job at Whitehall.

Service in the Great War and disability is no longer to be taken into account. Can you imagine all those old men at the pub in uniform for the final push? More like the ultimate in humiliation.'

'I keep telling you, it won't come to that.'

He looks sceptical. I try and see the war from his point of view. I still have trouble believing Hitler is alive and living not that many miles away. As if to underline the fact there is an enormous explosion in front of us. A black cloud of dust billows down the street toward us, and my father falls to the ground to escape falling debris. When the smoke clears, he is on all fours trying to stand.

'Do you want to go back and find out if the Servicemen's Club was hit?'

'No, no. I will find out soon enough. I'm alive, that's all I know. War makes a mockery of our morals. You have no idea what it was like in the Blitz. You prayed for them to hit your neighbours.'

I bow my head. He's right. I have no idea.

'Why should I worry?' He continues. 'I must become a bomb victim if, according to you, I'm about to die.'

'I don't know whether or not you die. You disappear. For all I know, you marry a missionary and go and live in China.'

'Okay, then I die there of swamp fever.'

We both laugh at this. For the first time, I feel we are on an even footing. But that may not be true, because I'm beginning to love him.

****

CHAPTER FOURTEEN

'You're beginning to appreciate your unique perspective, aren't you? You, who dreamed of having ordinary parents, a father who came home from the office to find your mother has cooked dinner. A childish fantasy, not worthy of you. You know more about the world now.'

I've been haunting familiar streets in Soho looking for my favourite coffee shops. Most of the shops are boarded up. I am following two women who look like mother and daughter. The younger is tottering ahead on too high heels, as if to escape her mother.

'All Clear! That was the All Clear!'

'Come back! You can't go! I forbid it!' The mother is short of breath, but her angry shouts propel her forward.

'Go tell it to the Marines,' the girl replies. She has dyed red hair that curls down her back.

'I forbid it, you stupid bitch! You don't have no morals to go spreading your legs!'

This annoys the girl who stops and turns. 'I'm doing my bit for the war effort! You're jealous because you're too old!' The three of us are now in front of a fanciful building. It is The Café Royal, which has so far escaped bomb damage. The sturdy edifice encourages me to enter. There is an old sedan chair at the entrance, reminding us of a yet more distant era when men carried their 'betters' through the filthy streets of the city. This richly carpeted room is hung with crystal chandeliers, the walls are green silk shot with gold thread. War is far away from this old pleasure palace. Strains of '40s dance music lead me through a marble foyer to a ballroom where, under a ribbed dome and a ceiling decorated with filigree gold cornices, men and women in uniform are dancing to a live band.

There is my father sitting at a table with another darkhaired young woman. He certainly likes brunettes.

'Ah ha, there you are, ghost!' He waves his beer glass at me. 'Come and join us. Do you know your Aunt Lilli?'

I approach, but Lilli does not see or hear me.

'Who is my Aunt Lilli? I never knew I had any aunts.'

'One of your mother's twin sisters.'

'She never told me about twin sisters.'

'Can't help that. Lilli's down from Middlesbrough, that's where your mother was born apparently. In Yorkshire.'

Aunt Lilly has what they call in Texas a 'homely' face. Her dark hair matches my mother's, but besides that there is little resemblance. She is short like I am, and her hair grows far down on her forehead like mine does. I'm disappointed that she does not see me.

'Come and join us for a knees-up.' My father sounds drunk.

'Is the war over?' I ask cynically.

'If you're any sort of ghost you should know, and if you remember I made a point of telling you that the war, at the moment, is far from over. The latest news is the Germans are pushing us back with heavy losses. It's a cold winter for the poor devils over in France, like it was for us in the trenches.' He shivers and drags on his cigarette.

'So, if this is one twin, where's the other?'

'She's still up in Middlesbrough. Her name's Lizzi. Lilli's twin sister. Lilly and Lizzi.'

The names amuse him, and I am a little embarrassed trying to adjust to being a niece. For all I know, I have cousins I don't know about. This makes me feel bitter. My father ignores my mixed reaction to the aunt information and wants to talk about more serious things.

'You may be wrong about who wins this war. I have it on good authority that the Germans have designed a terrible new bomb, powerful enough to smash the whole of Europe to smithereens. The War Office doesn't want anyone to know.'

Lilli nods in agreement, thinking he is talking to her.

'No one tell us nothin'. We's always the last to know.'

'I have it on good, but secret authority.' He replies to Lili winking at me and continuing as if for my benefit. 'A Czech scientist told me, someone who escaped the Nazis.' He is revelling in his news, and perhaps his pessimism. My mother arrives from the dance floor, still swirling her pleated skirt. I'm afraid this time she will be able to see me and become frightened again, but no, I'm still invisible which gives me a slight edge, although I'm disappointed. I still yearn to talk to her. She touches Lilli lightly on the shoulder as if anxious to claim her, or simply because she is a sister. I wonder why my mother never mentioned her sisters or contacted them. As far as I know, she died without seeing them.

'Isn't this grand?' she says to everyone. It is obvious she is having a good time and I'm happy the way she deliberately avoids the eyes of passing soldiers. She bends closer to Lilli, who is reverently lighting up a cigarette.

'Lilli, go and dance.'

'Oh, flower, yer're not getting me up on that floor.'

Lilli's accent is northern, setting her apart from my parents; she has obviously been raised in a different part of the country. She looks uncomfortable here and may be despising the whole event by the way she sniffs and slyly moves her eyes around the room. Dance music bursts out louder than before; four shining trumpets are intent on blasting us. People are swinging each other round as if there is no tomorrow.

The red-haired girl I saw in the street is surrounded by a group of GIs. Her mother is nowhere to be seen. Reflecting on the fact that I could consider myself a war baby, I can understand her mother's warnings. This young girl looks oblivious of the danger of an unwanted pregnancy. My mother, although only nineteen, looks more worldly. She has my father to protect her and she edges her chair close to him, but this tactic isn't enough to repel a young man in a sharply tailored suit. He clicks his heels together in such a German manner I want to laugh.

'Let me introduce myself.' This is said with a strong accent. 'Albert Schweitzer at your service.'

'Not *the* Albert Schweitzer?' My father laughs at the idea. The man clicks his heels again. 'Not *the* Albert Schweitzer, no. But he is my father.'

My father raises an unbelieving eyebrow.

Lilli turns to whisper to my mother. 'Oh, flower, you must have heard of him. He's been on the news!' My mother claps excitedly. She has no defence against fame. She would excitedly point out well-known personalities on her little black-and-white television, and claim she'd seen them in this or that night-club. Albert Schweitzer's son kisses both my mother's hands while Lilli laughs at this old-fashioned gesture.

'For all I know, you are a German spy.'

'Sir! I hope you joke, sir! I am Swiss.'

My father says, 'Oh yes, they're neutral, aren't they?'

Albert Schweitzer does not respond to my father's sneering tone; he takes my mother's hand and leads her to the dance floor. My father waves the two of them away, and in his face I read the fear of an older man trying to keep up with a younger woman. My happiness at how my parents met evaporates. Have they had a quarrel? Have I missed a vital piece of information about what is going to happen next? My father is looking around the dance hall like a single man, and stares at the red-haired girl.

I can see he's seduced by her casual defiance, which is even bolder than Vivien's *joie de vivre*. I approve of him liking bold women, but surely he should not be ogling this redhead? My father doesn't notice that my dancing mother is giving him a warning frown. Are my parents about to go their separate ways after a quarrel on this dance floor? I presume he has forgotten about me, but I'm wrong.

'Come to the bar.'

He is sure his orders will be obeyed, and he is right. I'm eager to join him, to please him like a dutiful daughter. The barman defers to my father. He is more polite to him than to the callow youths arguing about who is going to only buy beer. My father must be a chain smoker. He gets out a cigarette and blows smoke rings before he turns to me. 'You don't know about your aunts? Vivien wants them to look after you.'

'Tell me what you know about them.'

'I don't know much. They were sent to a Catholic convent while your mother went to the Dr. William Brown orphanage. According to your Aunt Lilli, your mother got the best deal by going there. They suffered under the strict rule of the nuns in that place.'

I wonder if I dare tell my father that Vivien was sexually abused at her orphanage. I want to tell him, but something holds me back. I will tell him, but not while he's drinking his whisky. Strict rules of a convent may be something to complain about, but my aunts probably never suffered the abuse I saw my mother suffer.

'My aunts can complain all they want,' I tell him. 'But they were twins. They had each other, didn't they? My mother was alone at the orphanage.'

He doesn't know how unusual it is for me to be standing up for my mother.

'You are right! But look at Vivien now. I've never heard her complain about being an orphan, and at least in that orphanage she learned to speak the King's English.'

I am painfully conscious that he is a snob. If Vivien had her sister's northern accent, he may not have befriended her. Those were the bad old days when you were treated according to your accent; you had to sound cultured if you wanted to go up in the world. We watch

Vivien doing dynamic spins on the dance floor now that she no longer has to watch out for Hugh.

'Why do you want one of my aunts to look after me?' I ask him.

My father leans close to me to whisper. 'The story is, one of your twin aunts was unlucky enough to be assigned to the munitions factory up in Middlesbrough. Tough work for women. Lilli has been telling me about it; a sixty-hour-week, and that's work on their feet; only a day and half off a month. Lilli and Lizzi, because they are twins, share the shifts between them. No one catches on because they're identical.'

The barman has been listening to my father's whisper. 'So right you are, guv! Wot are we doing to them young women?'

Of course, the barman sees a man talking to himself, bemoaning the state of the country.

'I still don't understand why you think they can look after a baby.'

'That's your mother's idea. She thinks you should be looked after by relatives and they are the only relatives she has. Also, it's better to think of two on the job rather than one.'

'I hope you're not going to agree to that?'

'I don't want to. That's why I think you should go up north and find your other aunt, and then report back on what you find up there. You see, all I have to go on is hearsay.'

'You want me to spy on them?'

'For your own good! Surely a ghost can do that? In my opinion, you'll be better off down in Brighton. Middlesbrough is a port and could easily be targeted.'

'Is that why Lilli is here?'

'Yes, I sent her money to come down for an interview before I agreed to anything. She impresses me as a capable sort.'

'Look, it won't happen. The Longs will take care of me my whole childhood. I told you.'

He ignores the certainty of my futuristic knowledge. 'Your aunts are family. Or that's what Vivien says.'

I find it hard to believe my mother ever said such a thing. I'm sure the word 'family' never crossed her lips. But I could be misjudging the Vivien of today and confusing her with the Vivien who was the life of every party. I wish I dared ask him what plans he has for the two of them. If my parents are quarrelling, is he getting ready to leave Vivien? It doesn't look like he's getting ready to marry her. Is it possible that in war time it is futile to make plans to marry? Or does he not consider Vivien a worthy marriage partner?

'Do you want to dance?'

I give him a fake smile but cannot resist his offer. 'Didn't they say this was a two-step?' I object. 'I can't manage that.'

'We can wait for a waltz.'

Miraculously the next dance is a waltz, and my mother and Mr. Albert Schweitzer Jr. are pounding the floor with their version of a waltz by making it into a polka.

My father is an average dancer, but I have never been so light on my feet. I savour every sensation I ought to be having, hanging my head back to relish the sweep of his turns, and at the same time trying to feel connected to the person who is responsible for my existence. If he had been killed in the trenches in World War One, I would not have been born. 'We could be dancing at my wedding. Ed's family made up a large and noise party at my wedding. I was missing Brenda and Sidney and my friends in England.'

'I can't believe you got married and I wasn't there. What university did you go?'

'Me? There was no money for education.'

'Then I must have died. I would have made you to study.'

'I don't know what happened to you, but I'm determined to find out.'

He assumes a fated look. 'I had plans to send you up to Cambridge. I went there after the war, but with my groin inflamed from the shrapnel, I couldn't study. I had to take pills to kill the pain. Tried to read History, then Mathematics, but gave it up and got a job in the Civil Service. I still can't believe I have a daughter who lives in America.'

'Nothing for me in England!'

My father stumbles back to his seat. His resigned smile does not fool me. I know he is feeling emotional, but I don't know whether that's because of what I've been saying or because my mother is dancing with another man.

Albert returns my mother to her table with additional heel clicking.

'Are you so drunk you're dancing by yourself?' my mother asks my father. He gives me a conspiratorial wink as our attention is taken by a commotion at the door. A group of American soldiers are surging forward with loud words and lots of arm waving. Their creamy beige suits soon blend in with the khaki uniforms. Next to our table a man stands in protest and yells to get people's attention.

'Here they come! Overpaid, oversexed and over here!'

I hear someone applauding this resentful remark, but my father tells him to shut up. My heart lifts at the sight of these fresh faced boys whose energy and enthusiasm shows in every muscle. My mother, always sensitive to atmosphere and the mood of crowds, gives them hospitable looks and forgets to avert her eyes.

Two GIs approach our table. 'Can we dance with the girls, Daddio?'

My father pales. I'm sure the GI does not mean to insult him, but how can my father know that American expression? He waves them away and as he does so, the red-headed girl throws herself in his lap.

'Whoopsy daisy! Do you mind?'

'I don't. You can't get rid of me that easily.'

Unexpectedly she drags him onto the dance floor while my mother turns away and taps her foot. Lilli puts a hand on her shoulder.

'Don't fuss yourself, flower.'

'She must have been lying in wait for him.'

'He's a nice-looking gent.'

Both sisters watch while my father does a slow shuffle with the redhaired girl. My mother squirms in her seat. 'He's showing me up, behaving like that.'

'Let 'im have it when he comes back.'

Lilli is angry on Vivien's behalf. I am also shaken with waves of anger and resentment that have nothing to do with my father dancing with someone else. I am jealous of their family solidarity which makes me realise what I have been missing not knowing anything about these aunts I never met. Why did my mother keep their existence a secret? What family quarrel could these sisters have had that was so final?

When my father returns, wiping lipstick off his face, my mother is furious but says nothing.

'Do you want to dance now?'

My mother proudly shakes her head.

'Then let's go.'

My mother opens her mouth to say something, but then turns her back on him. My father sounds tense. He may be her saviour, but he still has to earn her love. I remember her once saying in her vague way, *'Your father wasn't that important to me, really.'* I remember replying *'He must have been, because of me.'* Once on the street, my father strides ahead as if he knows the way home and she doesn't. I think it's time to insist on telling him something about their future, but I must ask his permission. I'm aware that what I'm offering is somewhat unnatural. 'Do you want to know anything about Vivien's life after you left?'

My father gives me a warning look and I have to conclude he does not want to hear because he can tell from my warning tone, that it is not a happy story. My mother, unaware of our conversation, is leaning on Lilli's shoulder in the dependent way of a younger sister, even though she is a good four inches taller.

'I want you to take care of Annabel. You and Lizzi can manage her between you.'

'You mean, Anne?' My father turns back to protest.

My mother does not reply. 'He will insist on calling her that. Not my choice, to me she's Annabel. Hugh says he'll pay you both five pounds a week. That's a lot of money.'

'Bloody hell, it is too! And we'll do a proper good job as well.'

'I can't have her looked after by those people in Warmdene. I don't trust them to give her back. You and Lizzi must promise to give her back when the war's over?'

'Don't you worry about that, flower,' Lilli replies. 'I've got a young man of me own, and he won't be wanting to raise your bairn.'

My father turns back.

'Lilli, I didn't know about this. You have a fiancé?'

'I do. He just don't know it yet.' The sisters hold each other's eyes, sharing the joke.

'Is he in the army?'

'No, he's running his father's newsagence.'

My father moves ahead of them, so that he can whisper to me.

'I didn't know about this fiancé. Go and find out what you can about this other sister, and report back to me.'

'With pleasure. I want to meet my other aunt and see if there's any more of my mother's family there.'

By this time my mother had caught up with Hugh and linked an arm through his. They had survived the dance hall and joined forces again to become a couple.

CHAPTER FIFTEEN

1984

Contrary to her doctors' expectations, Annabel had not returned to consciousness. Two tweed-jacketed doctors jostled for space, bringing with them a strong smell of tobacco. Ed flattened himself against the wall.

'We cannot be certain of anything at this stage. The cerebrospinal fluid glucose level is as low as it could be in a living person.'

'But she came to.'

'Briefly.'

'You spoke to her?'

'We tried. Deep comas are still something of a mystery.' The doctor hummed and looked at the ceiling for inspiration.

'Her verbal skills may have been affected, a temporal prefrontal issue, an impairment to the prefrontal cortex. Integration can be blocked, and impairment linked to unknown factors.'

Ed was given time to absorb this. 'Was it too much anaesthetic?'

The two doctors determinedly shook their heads. When they left, Ed put his head in his hands and covered his face. He hated being inactive, but there was nothing he could do. He secretly despaired of ever speaking to Annabel again, which left him feeling bitter and punished. He also tried to stop thinking that if he had come to England with her, if he hadn't been unfaithful, none of this would have happened. Maybe they should have had marital therapy like so many couples. Neither of them wanted this, although Ed knew that was partly the expense.

When he walked the cold streets, he clung to the image of a vibrant Annabel who was gracious hostess in the foyer of the Country Club, who whipped up cheesecake in the kitchen. Never still, Annabel was always a graceful person. He wondered whether that grace was gone forever. He remembered pressing against her in their first dance. She was so slim he could barely feel her shape; he liked her trim waist. He never expected to marry her. She was to be his guide through the club scene, a dance partner. Things changed between them that night they saw *Seven Brides for Seven Brothers*. They were both sighing for wild, open spaces after seeing that movie, despairing of the dirt and dust and pigeons of Trafalgar Square, and this made him invite her back to the States. Ed thought she would enjoy Texas, and he was right. It was not an offer of marriage; it was a shared adventure with an attractive young woman, until it gradually became more than that.

ANNABEL LANGONI

****

I'm happy to be accompanying my Aunt Lilli on a train heading north. In Houston I never took trains. Houston, Texas, the whole American continent, is no longer real to me. If I imagine myself there, it's as a ghost floating over other people's lives.

I'm beginning to feel I belong here, in this war-torn era. The train is crowded, and I have to disturb Lilli's aura by squeezing next to her, but she doesn't notice. She has an intact dignity that reminds me of my foster parents. My sophisticated father and playful mother don't seem to have kept their dignity intact, maybe that's because they live in war-torn London and don't work the rich dark earth to make a living. The famous English countryside is glistening with snow. The heating does not work. I don't feel the cold, but my aunt shivers in her thin coat. She counters the cold by smoking. I saw my father give her money, and before boarding the train she bought two miniature packets of cigarettes labelled Woodbines. I remember these from my childhood, but they have since disappeared. A workman with a peaked hat eyes her cigarettes, smiles and tries to talk to her, but she rebuffs him. She gives the right impression of being an unavailable young woman, her behaviour a stark contrast to my mother's. When the compartment empties a little, she brings out her knitting; her dark head bobs up and down as she counts the stitches under her breath.

At Middlesbrough, Lilli stumbles out and looks down at her feet. her shoes are covered in snow. She starts off, crunching stoically over the snow until we reach a boarding house: 'For Young Ladies.' The sign outside is more respectable than the lobby, which is cramped by too many tables and chairs and littered with Do Not notices. She climbs up to the third floor and enters an attic with two dishevelled beds. She bangs down her case and blows her nose violently, and the noise stirs the bedclothes on one bed. An old man's head appears.

'Where you go?' he whispers.

'None of your business.'

There is no mistaking the dislike in her voice, and his presence in her room puzzles me. Is he a lodger who shares the rent? Wartime and poverty must result in some strange bedfellows. He turns his back on her and Lilli goes to the mirror where she carefully applies lipstick. Without bothering to change her wet clothes, she takes another coat out of the closet and slams the door behind her. I follow her down the wide streets of Middlesbrough, a town I've never heard of before. The shops are mostly shut, but Lilli is advancing towards the lighted window of a tobacco shop and newsagent. My thoughts immediately go to when my mother visited me. It was always on a Sunday, and only the newsagents and sweet shops were open. She would astonish everyone by telling me to buy anything I wanted.

The bell jangles invitingly and a young man appears in the doorway. He is dark haired and looks Italian. If he is Lilli's boyfriend, he does not look pleased to see her. He fills the doorway, barring her entrance.

'We're closed,' he says.

This does not stop Lilli; she pushes her way into the shop.

'You've no business being closed this time of the day.'

'Had a good time in London, then?'

'I didn't go for a good time. I went for a job and I got it. Yes, and there's money in it. Looking after the baby.'

'What baby?'

'I told you! Me younger sister's kid, that she had a baby without being married.'

'Don't think it's a good idea.'

'Only 'til the war's over.'

'Ha ha! When's that then?'

'Who knows? London's bombed worse than here.' A noise out the back stops this conversation, and they turn to see a young woman whose face and hair closely resemble Lilli's. This must be Lizzi, her twin.

'What you doin' here? Lilli's voice is high and aggressive. She looks like she hates her sister.

Lizzi does not want to reply to this, but her sister stares her down. 'He needs extra help at Christmas.'

Lili is almost snarling. 'I said, what are you doin' here with him? Goin' behind my back with him?'

Lizzi puts herself close up to her sister. There is little more than inch between their noses. 'He doesn't want to be engaged to you anymore. You forget that him and me, we was going out together before yous.'

The young man feels he should support this. 'Yeah, you remember that Lilli? Before you and me.'

Lilli hits out at her sister at this comment and the young man pushes Lizzi into the back and slams the door shut. Lilli pounds on it with a force I'd never have guessed.

'Come out here. You can't have 'im. He's mine!' 'Go away!'

'We was already engaged!'

The young man appears at the doorway. 'Go away!' I am puzzled by their quarrel. Is he the only young man in Middlesbrough, or are the twins using him as an excuse for sibling rivalry?

Lizzi now confronts her sister. 'Leave us be, Lilli!'

'He's going to marry me!'

The young man pushes Lili back. ' I was going to marry you, but if you remember I liked Lizzi first. '

'You only want him 'cos he's mine.' Lilli yells.

'What if he likes me best?'

Lilli cannot tolerate this question and lunges for Lizzi, getting a good grip on her head and giving it a yank. Lizzi grabs her neck. They look like they are used to fighting each other, but the young man is appalled. 'Stop it, stop it! I'm not going to marry either one of yous.'

The two sisters ignore him. I am not that bothered because I have seen sisters fight before. Sidney's daughters by his first marriage would often quarrel on their visits to Warmdene. Once they threw knives at each other. For some reason, my aunts' ability to fight and scratch each other has a calming effect on me.

Lizzi is the victor of their scrap, pinning Lilli to the floor by standing on her hair,

'You've got the devil in you.'

Lilli writhes away and launches herself at the young man.

'You told me we was engaged. Everyone knows you and me is engaged!'

'Yeah... but...'

He retreats to the back room, and Lizzi is triumphant. 'You see! he likes me better.'

Lilli sinks back to the floor, and sobs into her hands. But not for long. In her despair, she suddenly senses something and turns to look in my direction, peering at me short sightedly. 'Can I help you?'

Lilli can see me? 'Can you see me? I'm so glad!'

Lilli is now looking at me more closely and is scared by what she sees. She slowly backs away and crosses herself, murmuring, 'I believe in God the Father, Mary Mother of God, and the Saints above.'

I cannot help smiling, but I have to convince her I'm no vampire. 'I'm a ghost from the future. In fact, I'm that baby you're taking about.'

Lilli looks aghast, and I cannot say I blame her. 'I'm that baby, your niece, the one you were supposed to look after. Well, I am now an adult and I've come to visit you from the future.' She crouches in fear and continues whispered prayers.

'Don't be afraid.' I say, beginning to sound like the Angel Gabriel. 'And don't try and look after me as a baby. I'll be happy down with the Longs, and I'll stay with them right through my childhood until I grow up and get married.'

She starts a Hail Mary. I decide to trouble her no more. 'I'm going back to London now. Let's hope the trains are still running. And I hope you make up your quarrel with your sister.' I thought this last attempt at normality would steady her, but it seems to have the opposite effect. She wobbles back down on her knees, biting the back of her hand. Sadly, I go out through the driving snow, back to the train station, where the train is inevitably delayed. In the waiting room, I'm met by another strange sight thanks to wartime England: sitting cross-legged on the hard concrete platform are a group of preschool children, frozen with either fear or cold. Round their necks are slung huge boxes that some part of me knows are gas masks. Where are they going? On closer inspection I see name tags also hung round their necks. Are they orphans from bombed-out families in London? A teacher or leader is counting the children and filling in some sort of form.

'Now children,' she yells over the noise of steam. 'Don't be afraid. Your new families are probably delayed because of the snow, but they're on the way.'

One or two of the older children wipe tears from their eyes. The teacher continues. 'I know you're cold, but soon you'll be in the warm. Your new families can't wait to see you. And you'll only be with them for a little while. You'll soon go back home.'

I wait with them as darkness descends. An old man comes up to the toddlers, and out of a cloth shopping bag he magically produces a glass jar filled with lemon sherbets. I remember this candy. The trick is to suck until the sherbet inside is released. The old man carefully doles out a lemon sherbet to each child. Although he does not gaze into their upturned faces, I know he is thrilled by each acceptance. He only has two refusals.

An agitated face looms in front of me. Lilli has followed me to the station.

'I've been thinking 'bout what you said. Makes no sense. No sense.'

She is giving me another chance to explain. I'd like to hug her in relief, but quickly stop myself.

'I'm your niece from the future. I know it's hard to believe.'

Rose nods, 'I do believe you. I'm having a vision, like Bernadette?'

'No, I'm your niece.'

'And that's why you look like that?'

'How do I look?'

I'd like an objective answer to this question, but Lilli just shivers in her wet clothes.

'Don't stand there catching your death.'

I hope by showing ordinary concern, this will help her accept me, but she continues to look awestruck. We are both distracted by the harmonic wail of a mouth organ. It is the old man, who gave the children candy. He has started to entertain them by playing a tune for them.

'Look at that darling old man,' I say, trying again to appear normal. 'He's been giving the kiddies lemon sherbets.'

My Aunt Lilli follows my pointed finger and I hear her cursing.

'Do you know him?' I ask.

'I know him, but he don't want to know me. Refuses to claim his own flesh and blood, that's him! His own children!'

'What do you mean?'

'He don't admit it, don't admit he's our father.'

I am surprised. 'You mean that's your father? Then he must be my mother's father, which makes him my grandfather!'

The old man is stuffing his mouth organ into his shopping bag and is already halfway out the station. 'Let's catch up with him. I'd like to speak to him.'

'Don't believe a word he says.'

I head off in pursuit and she follows. Suddenly the stationmaster appears ahead of us and jumps on my poor grandfather as he tries to board a bus. The stationmaster takes great pride in yanking him by his fraying collar.

'I knows who you are. You're an Itie! Whatcha you stolen from this young lady?'

Lilli hoots with laughter at this accusation. 'Tell him, tell him! He's stolen everything from me; he's stolen my life, that old man has! Says he ain't my dad. He denies it!'

'Some kind of family quarrel?' The stationmaster's hold is relaxed, as he looks in puzzlement from father to daughter.

'Ask him if he knows his own daughter.'

'I don't know this young woman.'

'See!' Lilli screams! 'Did you hear him deny it? The beast sent us away to that rotten convent.' The two men look like she is a crazy woman but I see that it is the little girl Lilli who is screaming, the little girl who was sent away.

The old man turns to the stationmaster and makes a show of tapping his head as if Lilli is mentally deranged. The stationmaster does not know what to do next.

'If you're an Itie, why aren't you with Mussolini then? Or if you're with us, why aren't you in uniform?'

'I was a soldier in Italy! We fight the Austrians in the war before. The same as now.'

The stationmaster scratches his head. 'I don't know anything about that.'

He gets out his book, and my grandfather runs off between the cars. The stationmaster watches him escape his jurisdiction.

I hear a whistle which means my train has arrived. 'Don't worry about looking after me as a baby,' I tell Lilli again. 'I'll be fine. But I'm sorry you had to go to a convent, and my mother to her orphanage. I mean, sorry there were no other relatives.'

'It was the Depression, that's why, my love; the Depression!'

I wish I could hug my Aunt Lilli goodbye. Then I compare my reaction to her, versus my reaction to my mother. I never wanted to hug my mother. My train arrives with a thundering hiss of steam. I run towards it gratefully and leap aboard. Lilli comes up to tap on the window.

'If you're from the future, tell me what's going to happen!'

'We win the war.'

'Will I get married and have a son, like I want to?'

'I don't know, I'm sorry.'

'You're from the future,' she scoffs. 'And you don't know what happens!'

The one person who wants to know the future, and I cannot answer her. 'I'm sorry,' I shout from the departing train. 'I don't know. I never knew you existed. My mum never told me.' Lilli shrinks into a small dot as the train speeds up. I am in shock, and not only because of everything that's happened in Middlesbrough, but because for the very first time I have just called my mother, Mum. In spite of the fact that she signed her cards and letters mum, I always called her Viv. I spend the journey wondering about my Middlesbrough family, and my Italian grandfather. Why did he come to England, never to return to Italy?

Was he a refugee, a deserter or fleeing another family back in Italy He didn't look like a dark-haired Italian. He referred to fighting the Austrians. Does that mean he's from the North of Italy? What was the Italian Austrian war all about? Was that World War One? How little it matters now which side he was on.

CHAPTER SIXTEEN

'You are getting some perspective, some idea of your family's story, which is not that different from other poor families. Your future does not have to include them, or any of your families. You are an individual who can stand alone.'

As I'm doing the mathematics of family relationships, I realize my aunts may still be alive and living in Middlesbrough. I may have cousins. If I ever get back to 1984, I intend to find them. At first, I don't notice the train picking up speed but we going too fast for an old steam engine. My windows are fogged up, my vision blurs and I brace myself for another time shift.

****

I'm walking on hard waves. When I look down, I see I'm standing on the frozen furrows of a ploughed field. For the first time in my travels, I'm afraid without knowing why. There is ice on the puddles. Brenda used to tell me tales of scraping the frost off their cows when they ran the farm. They gave up the rigours of farming for market gardening, and in this winter landscape I have an idea of their stark, uncompromising toil. I listen but hear nothing, not even birds. The field is edged by scarecrow trees lifting their imploring branches to a cloudy sky. I experience a dreadful fear, a horror of being transported to the trenches of World War One, of seeing maimed and bloodied bodies of boys David's age, fighting and dying in that war.

Looking upwards to a gentle sloping hill, I am relieved to see two women and some children making their way towards me. The two little boys arrive first, one pushing the other on top of a wheelbarrow full of branches. The women are determinedly collecting every bit of wood in sight while a little girl is running behind, trying her best to keep up with them. I join the group to find out what they are saying, but they are too busy foraging in the bushes. They are all dark haired and ragged; the taller of the two women has a hemp-like sack for a skirt while the other, shorter one has a torn tight-fitting bodice, and a torn but flouncy short skirt.

'Let's stop a few minutes.'

I'm pleased to hear they are speaking English.

They flop down on the side of the road and the boys abandon the wheelbarrow to fight in the ditch. The little girl climbs on top of the sticks in the wheelbarrow.

'Shocking,' the taller woman is saying in an aggrieved tone. 'You mean you can't even be buried next to your husband of thirty years? The Church has got a lot to answer for.'

'They won't have it because of her name.'

'What's wrong with Mam's name, for heaven's sake?'

'Her. surname, before she married. I never bothered with it but they tell me she were Rachel Abraham that means she was Jewish and can't be buried in a Christian cemetery. No one knew but she was born Jewish, yer see. She acted like a Christian.'

'She's every right to be buried in that church next to her husband. But wait a minute, does that mean we're Jewish too?'

'Don't go on about it. We got better things to think about. Main thing is she left us the house, so they gave me some money when it was sold. At least we got some money out of it.'

The woman with the short skirt digs in the satchel across her chest. She brings out a ring and shows her sister. 'Mam's ring!

Do you want it?'

'You keep it.'

'Won't be doing me no good. Too late for me.'

'Don't talk like that. You're gonna get better now. You got money for medicine.'

'The doctor says six months at most. Six months before I'm dead.'

The older woman hangs her head as if this medical news shames her. Who are these two women who are not sure whether or not they are Jewish, and how are they related to me?

'Watch out for Renée!'

The baby has fallen out of the wheelbarrow and is screaming because her knee is scratched. She is caught up in loving arms and is kissed until she stops crying.

'Such a beauty!'

'Oh yes, Renée won't have to worry none. She stops people in the street with those eyes. Look at them, size of saucers!'

Renée? Who could that be? I must have some intimate connection with these two women, but they aren't my aunts. This seems to be another family altogether. What is Renée short for? Could it be Irene? If so, she must be my mother? With a shock of recognition, I know that I am right. This toddler is my mother. She cannot be more than three or four. I do a quick calculation. Then I must be back in 1929. If that is so, then the pert one who says she is dying and who little Renée is clinging to, must be my grandmother. I am curious about her dying because she looks young and slim and healthy with rosy cheeks, maybe too rosy.

The women march grimly on while I listen to their complaints about the recent funeral, and about what the priest said and how he turned his nose up at them. I understand now why Vivien thought I looked like *her* mother, who is a dark pretty brunette. I get my dark looks from her, not from my Italian grandfather.

As if she hears me the younger sister says, 'anyway, I can tell you Mr. Alberto Langoni's not getting one penny of me Mam's money. That's why he married me, I'm sure of it.'

The taller sister considers this as they walk on. 'Wasn't it you who asked him to marry because you was pregnant?'

'Yeah, but 'e didn't 'ave to accept. There were plenty of others who were keen.'

'Oh, but you was that taken with him!'

'More fool me.'

The two boys trundle the wheelbarrow on ahead and we follow them until we reach a picturesque farmyard with chickens roaming free and an iron pump next to a water trough. They unload logs from the wheelbarrow and take off the kindling they've been carrying on their backs. The taller sister goes to the iron pump with a pail. She pumps water with a kind of reverence for this ritual task and then enters the stone cottage. The one room has a loft and a curtained off area. The central feature is a stone hearth, which is clean and empty. My grandmother pushes twigs into a long metal incinerator and lights the fire with a foot-long matchstick. Her sister puts a pot on the perforated metal top which serves as a stove. Renée is asleep, tucked inside my grandmother's coat. The hungry boys creep closer to the pot. The floor is made of trodden-down dirt, which makes me think of the expression 'dirt-poor.'

A well-built man in overalls appears at the door and gives everyone a guarded, questioning look as if my grandmother came to share their last crust.

'Me sister's come with me Mam's money,' the taller woman says immediately.

The man almost manages a smile at this news as he tiredly throws himself into the only armchair.

'Is that the barley soup we had for breakfast?' the man complains as his wife spoons the soup into bowls.

Either his remark or his presence has cowed the two little boys, who crawl under the table and spoon their soup determinedly. Renée gurgles with pleasure as she chews a piece of bread. There is respectful silence for this man in his work clothes, except for the two boys under the table slurping their soup and then scratching their heads.

'What they up to?' the man demands. 'Scratching again? Come out of there and stop scratching.'

'Nits,' his wife explains to her sister. 'They get 'em at school.'

'I'll delouse them, see if I don't.'

The boys hoot with laughter at this impossibility. My grandmother puts her head under the table. 'I'll give you a farthing for every ten nits you can show me.'

This is an offer not to be refused and they immediately come out their hiding place and start digging into their thick black hair, only to receive a cuff from their father.

'Not while we're eating,' he bellows, giving honour to their sparse meal. Tired of being supervised, the children run to a curtained area, which contains nothing but a lumpy mattress. Being children, they have to jump on it before pulling the covers up and cuddling to keep each other warm. The three adults finish the evening by pouring themselves a drink of beer from a large metal jug. My grandmother draws a bundle of notes from her satchel and slowly gives them to the man, who counts them carefully.

'What you gonna do with all the money then?'

'Go to town and get a better job."

'You mean you don't like cleaning out the cowshed? You getting ideas above your station? You think you're too good for them cows?'

This attempt at humour gets a laugh from all three. They finish the rest of the beer, repeating the joke in various guises. My grandmother's voice is strong and loud. 'Do you mean your man don't like shovelling manure?'

'Why, of course he does. He dreams of doing nothing but! Aren't you just the farmhand, love?' The love in question barks out a laugh.

My grandmother picks up Renée and crawls into bed with the little boys. No wonder she wanted to delouse their heads. The husband and wife settle down on the lumpy sofa by the dying embers of the incinerator fire. I spend the night watching my mother as a baby, peacefully asleep in her mother's arms, despite my grandmother's constant coughing.

It is still dark when there's a rumble on the cobblestones outside. A horse-drawn milk cart has arrived. They all run to the door and greet what appears to be their taxi! Tearful farewells are taking place between the two women.

'What are you going to do?'

'About dying?'

'About your kiddies?'

'Too young for the workhouse.'

'Why can't Alberto care for them?'

'He's a man who can't take care of himself. I'll send them to the convent orphanage. Now that I've got me mam's money, I can pay those old nuns. They said they'd take them for a fee. But I don't think they'll take the baby.

'I can't believe I'll never see you again.'

The two sisters are crying, but the milk boy is impatiently waiting.

'Don't cry about me,' my grandmother tells her sister in a warning voice. 'I'm gonna take the rest of that money and go to London for some fun until I'm dead and buried.'

'Oh my, what a thing to say!' Her sister is distraught.

My jaunty grandmother jumps up on the cart and squeezes herself in front of milk urns. Her sister hands her little Renée, and so begins a long, slow journey of about three miles, going slowly uphill, quicker downhill to the rhythmic sound of the horses' hooves. When the woods give way to streets a sign welcomes us to Middlesbrough. The cart stops and my grandmother climbs down, but not before giving the young farm boy a kiss on the cheek. He blushes, and I presume that is his only thanks for giving them a ride.

She trudges on and has to carry Renée most of the way, even though there are heavy logs in the canvas bag on her back. She stops every now and then to cough. The town looks newly built in the London style, boasting gracious municipal buildings. She finally stops at a row of terraced houses. Some of them look cared-for, but my grandmother enters the shabbiest looking doorway. She pushes through the unlocked door, and I see a man rise from the sofa, crinkling as he does so because his jacket is stuffed with newspaper. Hardly greeting her, he seizes the logs from my grandmother's back and sets to making a fire. Inside, the place looks less like a home than her sister's mud-floor cottage. 'What you doing home? Lose your job?' The fear in my grandmother's voice sets the baby Renée crying.

The man does not want to reply, but also knows the question will not go away. 'They gave my job to a Jordie.'

'You lost your job!'

My grandmother throws herself on the sofa in a state of exhaustion and coughing. But she immediately springs up, restlessly. 'When I'm dead and buried you'll have to find a job, won't you? Good-for-nothing!' Her words are spat out like venom, and it is quite clear that if she had the energy, she would take a stick and beat him. Instead, she picks up a piece of wood and throws it on the fire. He dives into the flames to rescue it.

'Stop, that's mine!' He brushes the cinders away and I see he has been carving a mouth organ out of a piece of wood. He holds it up accusingly. 'I can sell this.'

At this point, two girls of about seven or eight years of age clatter down the wooden stairs, 'Mam, mam!' They hurl themselves at their mother. Now that I've been introduced to my grandmother, I know these must be my twin aunts, Lizzi and Lilli. They cling to their mother with frightened faces.

'Don't ever leave us again!'

'Dad says you're going to leave us forever and ever.'

'You can't, you can't!'

My grandmother takes a difficult breath. 'I may have to go to the hospital!'

'No!'

She tosses her head. 'Or I may just go to London and have some fun for once!' When she says this, she comes up close to her husband and repeats it for his benefit. 'Just try and stop me; see if you can stop me

from having the time of my life!'

'Dad says we're going to a 'home'.

'What's wrong with that? The convent school, where all nice girls go.'

They refuse to be calmed. 'We won't go!'

'Hush, now; hush now! We'll see.'

The twins begin to chant. 'We won't go. We won't go. You can't send us!'

One twin bops the other one on the head. My grandmother then bops her and both girls start screaming.

Albert is opening a small tin of sardines with a knife and a hammer. My grandmother gives Alberto a few coins from her pocket and as soon as he pockets them, he picks up her coat to wear it himself.

'Get us a large chips.'

He looks down at the sleeve, 'Is that blood?'

My grandmother is silent and sweeps up the flounces in her skirt as if she's about to do the can-can. Her hands are never still, and the twin girls follow her round the room clinging to her skirt. They could be two angels trying to save her, their fresh young faces running with tears.

'They're not even washed. Why don't you help? You'll have to do something about them when I'm dead and gone!' My grandmother's unhappiness makes her yell. 'Can you get that into your thick head? You will have to look after them!'

'How can I?'

'You better, because I'm going to my grave!'

The twins start bawling and Alberto wipes his eyes with the back of his hand as if he could wipe the whole scene away.

'You're a snivelling excuse for a man.'

While I admire her talent for dramatising a bad situation in an attempt to make it more bearable, the pain in that house cannot be ignored. My grandfather's miserable face is no different from my grandmother's, but they are far from comforting each other. He runs out.

I look round for the toddler Renée, my future mother. She is at the bottom of the stairs. Her baby cheeks are wet with tears although she can't possibly understand what her sisters are yelling about. One baby hand clutches the banister. She is alone, like she will be for the rest of her life.

****

CHAPTER SEVENTEEN

1984

Ed lost track of time and date. In an effort to will her back to the land of the living, he tried to get inside Annabel's head. What was it like to live life as Annabel? He felt uncomfortable enough in England and he knew she had a difficult time adjusting and feeling at home in Texas. Perhaps she never felt at home in her adopted country. But people do that: move, change countries, migrate! Ed's grandfather had walked from Mexico. he remembered that in his grandfather's wooden house in Kerrville there were a pair of shoes. They were kept on the windowsill on the porch, the porch where everyone sat round on rusty chairs. They were the shoes with which Ed's grandfather walked into America. As a kid, his grandmother had batted him away when he tried to play with them.

Ed had often suspected that Annabel had come to the States without being sure she loved him. Later he guessed she left England to escape her bad relationship with her mother. But so what? Wasn't that the reason everyone come to America, because things got bad at home? Didn't they come in search of a better life? Weren't all immigrants on the run, and at the same time in grief for their homeland, for the past? He remembered the love light in Annabel's eyes when they eventually married. No mistaking that. Then again, when David was born, she told him 'You two are my whole existence.' Then what happened? Annabel was not happy with her job at Sunny Hills Country Club, but Ed felt that was not the root of the problem. He thought that went back to childhood.

When the cosmetic surgeon approached him, the usual depression he felt when he thought of Annabel deepened into an unbearable anxiety. The surgeon wanted Ed's permission to reconstruct Annabel's face.

'The team feels that we should take advantage of the fact that she is still in a coma. It'll save distressing her further with another anaesthetic. We think she's got a good chance of coming out of this coma, and she'll have a reconstructed face.'

At first Ed resisted entering into this discussion. Ed felt they were simply taking advantage of both of them being in a strange and painful situation, but he did not dare alienate any of her surgeons; or go against decisions taken by the team. He was told the skin would come from her backside and the surgeon told him her cheeks would be soft as a baby's bottom. Ed wasn't sure whether this was a joke or the truth. He wanted to throw up at being hassled about such a thing, but the nurses lobbied on the surgeon's behalf and Lisa told Ed that he was refusing the best cosmetic surgeon in the country.

'If she hates it,' Lisa reasoned, 'they can do another op. But after all, no one wants to look like they've been in an explosion.' Ed understood that they were all thinking of Annabel's future, but he wasn't sure whether Annabel would want cosmetic surgery. Eventually the surgeon gave up and left the consent form on the bedside table. In the middle of the night, Ed took a deep breath and signed it.

****

'Now you're speeding ahead, expanding your universe. Can you believe you can change the past? Do you know that will mean you will change the future? Are you aware you can do that? Or, with your small mind, is that too much for you to believe?'

Despite its shrill dictatorial tone, I'm beginning to trust this voice. It may be keeping me sane. It's not easy being totally unable to control time and place. My own time and place have become unreal to me, I'm forgetting who I was or when I was.

A muffled announcement informs me the train is heading for Marylebone station. Although this means I will arrive in London this was not the scheduled destination, but I am ready to accept this. Others are not; this latest disruption has the effect of making neighbours turn and complain to each other as if they were old friends.

'How am I going to get to Clapham?'
'Awful bomb damage in Clapham.'
'I know, me ears will never recover!'

'Big banger came down yesterday. Eating plaster, I was.

Plaster in me porridge, big bits of it!'

'I had dust in me toilet! Won't flush, it won't.'

The anxious look on their faces is relieved by their camaraderie, which I cannot share. I want to give up my obsession with finding out what happened to my father and simply enjoy his company without encountering any more bomb damage or frightened people rushing home in the dark. The memory of my mother as a toddler, with fear and sadness in her dark eyes, makes me think I am similarly friendless and alone. I walk the sandbagged streets, beginning to feel I'm being punished for not understanding my mother, for not caring for her enough. A red post box reminds me that Ed and I sent her a cheque for Christmas. It was larger than usual because she was going through a rough time. She wrote back a nice letter saying she 'jumped for joy' when she saw the amount, but this letter was quickly followed by another. 'The bank wouldn't accept the cheque because you altered the date. I don't know why the banks have got so high and mighty,' she wrote. 'I don't know what the world's coming to. They want thirty pounds for a box of chocolates!'

I tried to imagine her frustration, her humiliation at having to ask me for money, and then not being able to access it. I quickly wrote another cheque, but I didn't call her. I was in a hurry to finish the tartan walls of the Sunny Hills Country Club and upset about Ed and Donna.

Coming out of the Underground I catch sight of my father walking toward me.

'Howdy, Ghost!'

He is trying out an American accent for my benefit.

We pass a handsome row of houses spared by the bombing. My eyes greedily seize on a piece of earth, a flower bed sprouting bare twigs of carefully pruned roses. 'I planted roses when we first moved to our house in Houston,' I tell my father. 'But they always needed so much water.'

There is an explosion in the next street. We look up to see a chimney in the air and my father runs down the steps of a basement. I'm glad to see he's trying to protect himself. Ambulances rush past driven by women in green tin hats. We watch some schoolboys climbing on fallen walls. My father turns away and I wonder if he is thinking about those boys in 1917, the Mudlarks. His hands shakes as he wipes his forehead. I wait for him to recover, and weave a fantasy around taking him to Texas, making introductions to Ed in my kitchen while David forks pancakes into his mouth. My family in one time and place.

He climbs up the basement steps like an old man. 'So much for the war hero!'

'You are a war hero. You won the Military Cross.'

'How do you know that?'

'Saw your medal in Vivien's things. You can be proud of that.'

'Proud of surviving the horror of it all.'

'What did you do? Save someone's life?'

'It was for carrying out a raid and ambushing the enemy. It was a suicidal thing to do and normally I wouldn't have done it. I'd just lost a friend. I saw him shot down going over the top.'

His voice breaks there, and I do not want to press him further. I don't want to think about World War One when I'm still trying to understand World War Two, but he suddenly wants to talk about it.

'I don't know how we, well I mean the government, took country lads off their bicycles and made them into soldiers, which meant lining them up to be shot at and blasted by canons. Enough to drive any man, or animal for that matter, crazy.'

The memory of this distorts his face, but his war injuries have not distorted his mind. I wonder how many years he is going to live. If my father had not disappeared from my life, I could have cared for him as he aged. I imagine how I'd stay with him until the end of his days. But then I realise in 1984 he'd probably already be dead. That gives me a shock. When I get back, I will do my best find him, but he will be in his nineties, if he's still alive.

Adelphi Square looms ahead, solid and familiar. 'When the war's over I'm going to live in the country,' he says. 'Perhaps somewhere near Brighton.'

'But that doesn't happen.' He doesn't hear me say this.

'I'd like you to take lessons in the piano or violin.'

I like this idea, but he doesn't elaborate. I have a feeling my spectral self is becoming less real to him. I don't know whether that is because my force as a ghost is fading, or whether his mind is busy with too many other things. When we reach Adelphi Square, the woman behind in the reception area gives him a strange look.

'You have a friend visiting,' she warns him.

My father goes to the wall of square metal letter boxes and opens one with a small key. He flips the metal flap and hangs his head, depressed.

'What is it?'

'I expected Robert to write and tell me whether he'll be home for Christmas. No word, so he's got no Leave.'

I have forgotten that he is worried about his stepson. He loves Robert and I'm sorry that he's not coming home for Christmas. I'd like to meet him. When we enter the flat, a domestic scene greets us. My mother and her hairdresser friend, Michael, are huddled on the sofa. He is filing her nails. They both look up and shift in their seats, but neither of them notices my father's ashen face. He does not mention he's survived a bombing and goes into the kitchen. My mother looks like a young woman without a care in the world.

'I hope you are both coming to our party?' Michael says as he reaches for his coat.

There is a grunt from the kitchen.

My mother repeats the party invitation. 'Don't forget, Hugh. I promised the boys we will go to their party on Boxing Day.'

My father pops his head round the door. 'Thank you, and we will come, unless Hitler is planning another sort of party for us.'

'We're not doing anything else Boxing Day,' Vivien tells Michael. 'None of Hugh's friends invite us, even though some of them know about me.'

'I know the feeling,' Michael commiserates. 'We avoid families this time of year; stick together on Sundays and holidays. Orphans' Christmas, we call it. On Christmas, Fred's not always nice to me. I love him of course, but he can be mean and I don't have to stand for that. I have them waiting in the wings.'

'Of course you do!' My mother gushes.

Vivien and Michael link arms as she walks him to the door. Hugh calls out to her. 'I hope you remember I've got to see my mother on Christmas Eve.'

My mother rolls her eyes pointedly at Michael as she calls back to my father, 'I haven't forgotten.'

'I suppose you want to come?'

I know he's addressing me but my mother mistakenly thinks he's asking her.

'Me?' She looks surprised. 'You said she doesn't know anything about me.'

My father stands accused and feels he has to explain himself to me, and maybe also to her. 'I've tried to tell her, but she refuses to listen and keeps asking about Gloria. Don't forget she's not been herself since losing my father.' He ducks back into the kitchen while my mind is whirling. If my grandmother has been shielded from knowing about Vivien, she won't know about me.

Michael seems disturbed as he protests my father's behaviour. 'Is he never going to tell his mother about you?'

'Oh I'm not his class and much too young!'

'We can do something about that!'

Michael grabs her bag and starts to over-powder her face. Then he takes her eye mascara and smudges it under her eyes. She grabs a shawl to wrap round her head like an old woman.

My father, sensing something is up, makes another entrance. Michael waves a hand in front of his face, as if it's a magic trick. 'What do you think? Is she old enough for you?'

My mother bends her back like an old woman. Michael's laugh is high and silly. They wait for my father's reaction, but although he half smiles, he looks annoyed. Michael promptly kisses my mother and says goodbye.

My father gently removes the scarf and wipes the smudges away from under her eyes. They kiss, and I hover near the door, ready to make an exit. My mother goes to the sofa and lifts a cushion to take out a tinsel wrapped parcel.

'I want to give you your present.'

'Not yet, it's not even Christmas Eve.'

'I want you to have it before you go to your mother's.' He takes the present, and she hangs over him until he agrees to open it.

'I'm used to waiting until Christmas Day.'

'You can't. Not in wartime. Open it, please.'

He pulls out a tie, with two coloured stripes. 'Ah, thank you!' He fingers the tie thoughtfully. 'Where did you buy it?'

His subdued words set my mind racing. There's something odd about his reaction.

'What have you got for me?' Vivien asks, kissing his lips. 'Lots of coupons, I hope.'

He puts the tie back in its wrapping and unlocks his desk drawer to bring out a carefully wrapped package. It does not look like coupons. 'Not to be opened until Christmas Day. I mean it!'

'Oh I don't want to wait.'

'That's what Christmas is all about.' He was raised to respect restraint. My mother always wanted everything at once.

'I hate waiting for things.'

'When the war's over, we'll have a good time, everything you ever wanted. We'll travel to Paris together, and bring Annabel back from Brighton!'

He kisses her face in a consoling way, and she instantly responds. They are soon locked in an affectionate embrace and then a hungry kiss. As the seconds tick by I reluctantly prepare to leave.

'I lost one of my black gloves,' she says.

He makes a long face. 'Oh, I'll have to buy you some more.' He slides a practised hand up her tight skirt. 'But I'm glad you are wearing your best stockings.'

'It's Christmas!'

'Oh yes! Yes, it is!'

She is desirable and dependent and is enjoying being both those things. Although there is nothing unusual about my parents' sexual desire, I'm reassured they are still in love. The sight of them together gives me a warm secure feeling and makes me feel that I have a right to exist. I absent myself and exit into the hall, but not without feeling a little rejected. I am jealous of their love. I try not to think of what is happening in the bedroom.

With no possibility of sleep, I begin to contrast my parents with the Longs. The Longs' love for each other was different and as a kid I mistakenly thought it revolved around bringing cups of tea up the stairs. I was innocent enough until Paul invited me to watch through a crack in the door. We saw a pile of blankets move in a slow and, to us, sinister rhythm. Paul told me he'd seen sheep do the same thing. My mind is so invaded by the past, that I have trouble remembering where the Longs are now. Oh that's right. They left for Australia.

It's true they did not leave England until I was living in Texas, but that did not stop me feeling abandoned and resentful. I started a piggy bank collection to save towards the fare to Australia, but when David was injured, I used the money to buy him presents.

The next morning my father appears very much the city gent, suited and coated. He actually smiles at me. 'Ready to meet your grandmother?'

'I never had a grandmother, now I have two.'

'How very unusual!' he says sardonically, putting out a hand towards me, but thinking again he rubs his neck.

'What did you get Vivien for Christmas?'

'Perfume.'

'Why didn't you like the tie she gave you?'

'Ah, you noticed that. It's a regimental tie, but not my regiment. She doesn't understand that schools and universities, and certainly regiments, all have specially designed ties.'

'Why didn't you tell her?'

'No good pointing out our differences.' He does not want to talk about their differences which may mean he has tried before, or it may mean that their relationship is not important enough to explore.

We take a taxi to Victoria Station. The trains are crowded. Soldiers are being transported to and from their barracks. They squeeze into overcrowded compartments in order to spend a day or two at home over Christmas.

'Hugh! Over here, over here!'

My father is being hailed by a thin distinguished-looking man, leaning his head out of a first-class carriage. My father automatically waves back, but hurries away.

'Anywhere but near him,' he whispers, choosing a second-class carriage, even though I saw him buy a first-class ticket. There are no seats left in second class so we stand in the corridor.

'That man's a very dubious solicitor, Stanley Page, and he claims to be related to my mother just because Page is my mother's maiden name, but she's never heard of him and Page is a common enough name. He's definitely no relation of hers, which is a good thing. He's under surveillance for crooked practices.'

I'm glad my father would rather stand in the second-class carriage corridor than sit next to him.

'What's this Stanley Page done?'

'I can't pin anything on him. Too clever a cove! A solicitor who makes a point of learning who's bombed out, who's missing, presumed dead. He's the proud owner of three houses that have been blown up with no one left to claim them, but my friend McPherson says the land is worth a mint. I suspect he forges wills for people.'

'A carpetbagger!' I'm proud to know the right American word, but he is not interested.

'I can't be seen speaking to him.' The tax inspector walks a solitary path, because his job makes him a kind of detective. I'm pleased to think my father is on the side of law and order. It goes with his personality.

'I was surprised to find Page was one of the names on my birth certificate. I never knew anyone called Page. I've been going under the name of Annabel Langoni.'

'I named you after my mother. Her name was Anne Page Cuthbert and that's what I put on your birth certificate.'

The train stops at every station, but the crowd eventually thins out. My father makes a point of facing the engine. I like watching the Sussex countryside steam away from me. I've always liked the sensation of leaving the past behind me. I laugh at the thought now that I'm back in the past with no wish to leave. A memory surfaces. When I got up to mischief as a kid and Sidney would complain about me, Brenda's habitual retort was that she didn't have eyes in the back of her head. But this resulted in some bad dreams, dreaming I was awake I'd open my eyes and see not what was in front, but what was behind me. Literally seeing out the back of my head.

When the train pulls into Brighton station, I'm curious. 'But I grew up in Warmdene Village, which isn't far from here. I can't believe your mother lives in Brighton so close to where I grew up.'

'Like many others she moved down from London the first year of the war, after the bombing started.'

At Brighton station, we hang back to avoid meeting Stanley Page. My father says, 'I wonder what he's doing down here.'

I volunteer to spy on him, and my father laughs like a conspirator, but gives me permission. 'As long as you come along soon after.' I love him for saying that, and promptly begin my mission.

Stanley Page heads for the nearest pub, The Nightingale. I cannot imagine why that name, unless it refers back to a time before they built roads and a busy train station. At the bar, Mr. Page buys a single pint, and nods a greeting to a buxom woman whose bleached hair lifts her peaked cap. I wonder about the uniform but read on the armband that she is an ambulance driver. She beams a welcome at Stanley. 'Flying bombs in London, I hear.'

Stanley nods. 'More damage to come, I'm afraid.'

Is it my imagination, or do I hear him cackle?

'Got any news for that's interesting?'

'I've got a list of recent bomb damage.' The ambulance driver pulls an envelope from her top pocket. They bend their heads over it. This must be why they are meeting, and why does a solicitor need to know these details unless to profit by them? I have seen enough to confirm my father's suspicions that Stanley Page is up to no good. When I catch up with him, he is panting from the steep climb up Dyke Road. He smokes too many cigarettes. When I give him my report about Stanley Page, he curses him again. 'He's a crook. He knocked on my mother's door and asked her if she knew who was selling because he wanted to move down from London. For all I know, he read my father's obituary and knows she's a widow. That was before I came on the scene. He claimed they were related because my mother's maiden name was Page. I had to convince my mother that was all part of his scam. I hate to think the liberties he would have taken, if I hadn't emerged from the front room.'

'Will your brother be there for Christmas?'

'How do you know about my brother?'

I don't want to tell him about my visit to 1917 so I think up a lie. 'Vivien told me you had a brother.'

'She shouldn't have mentioned that.' He sounds angry. 'My brother's dead.'

I want to know more about his brother's death, but I'm afraid to ask him What was his name, Charles? Maybe now is not the time to ask for more details. A rhyme comes into my head, words written above a shanty bar on Brighton's seafront. 'The Rewards of War are plain: a wooden leg and a golden chain.'

He looks bemused as I chant the lines out loud.

'It's true. You've got a leg injury, haven't you?'

'Twists in my groin every time I move. That's the reason I take sleeping pills.'

I don't want to feel sorry for him. I want him to be my hero.

My grandmother's house on Tivoli Road is a villa of white stucco, a symbol of an ordered life and relative security.

'By the way,' my father says at the door. 'In the unlikely case my mother does see you and hear you, I haven't told her that Charles is no longer with us.'

'Don't you think she has a right to know?'

'I want to wait 'til the war's over.'

Is my father a coward about grief, or is that a wartime thing? Why tell anyone bad news when there may be worse to come? Why waste time on grief when the next day could be your last? The woman who opens the door is a tall woman with hollowed cheeks. He embraces her delicately, as if she might break. She cannot see me, which is no surprise.

'You didn't bring Gloria?'

'Mother, she left me. We've been separated four years.'

'When are you getting back together again?'

Hugh makes a noisy sigh and stands in the doorway, as if he's not welcome. His mother stands aside for him to enter. Before he agrees to do this, he faces her deliberately. 'I'm with someone else now, I told you. Vivien.'

'You wrote me you were in love.'

She sounds incredulous, and my father picks up on that. 'As much as anyone can love under constant bomb attacks.'

His mother feels sorry for him. 'Close the door, you're making the house cold.'

'Freezing on the train coming down, the only warmth to be had was from people breathing down your neck.'

She 'ums' at this and he 'ums' back. I sense they are exchanging a kind of Cuthbert humour. They go into the kitchen, giving me a chance to look round the living room; a very ordinary room lined with bookcases. The only book I ever saw Brenda read was a pocket size red leather dictionary. My grandmother's house has a bourgeois elegance, but when I see two large vases of artificial flowers I have to laugh. Brenda hated artificial flowers and wouldn't have them in the house. There is no tv. Of course, tv has not yet arrived.

'What do you want to drink? I made ginger wine that's almost alcoholic.'

'I'll shut my eyes and pretend then.'

'You better shut your eyes, because it says 'Liver Tonic' on the bottle. Sit down. And tell me, have you heard from Charles?'

'No,' my father lies smoothly and does not elaborate.

'I've heard nothing, which is odd. I don't know why the post doesn't get through from America. Care packages sometimes get through.'

'Oh, care packages might; not letters, though. At least he's safe in America.' My father is making an excuse here.

I cannot help but be critical of my father not wanting to inform her that Charles is dead. Not the American way! I take the opportunity of my grandmother's exit to the kitchen to prod him into telling his mother that she has a granddaughter, me. 'I haven't been able to get her to meet Vivien yet, so how can I tell her we have a baby? But I will.'

I hope I'm not like this grandmother. She is a forbidding elder of a woman; I cannot imagine her being a devoted grandmother. Even in the wedding photo on the sideboard, she is not smiling. The other pictures are of two small boys. Seeing these pictures makes me sad. The two small boys look out so eagerly and confidently. Then I recognise a picture of my father in his officer's uniform. He peers out from under his peaked cap, looking as if he wants to be anonymous, and succeeding.

My father and his mother sit down to dinner, with an air of formality.

'Sorry about the meat,' she comments as they chew their way through lamb chops. 'I tried to get fresh fish but who can expect fish when the seas are full of land mines. Not to mention noise of the bombardment.'

'That's right. If you want fish, you have to go to Scotland or Ireland. I hear there's good fishing there.'

'I wonder how long that will last.'

'Are you enjoying the bigger house?'

'I will when the war's over. When Charles is de-mobbed I hope he comes to live in Brighton. He says he wants to work in the theatre, and there's theatre work down here. There are two piers, and before the war there were five theatres to choose from.' My father is silent, and I sympathise that he cannot honestly reply. His mother begins again. 'If you and Gloria move down, I can have my family together in one town.'

'I've told you, I've met someone who makes me forget the pain in my groin. And sometimes even the war.'

'I don't want to hear that nonsense, especially on Christmas Eve. Charles knows better than to talk to me about his lady friends. I don't really understand why he hasn't written. Films, theatre, I wish he'd do something useful for a living.'

'He's the bon vivant,' my father says with a sigh.

'He's devil-may-care,' she agrees indulgently. 'Not at all like you. Couldn't have had two more different sons, and I thank the Good Lord for them both.'

'I'm getting to be more like him,' my father ventures.

'You're nothing like him. He's a ladies' man,' She puts up a hand to ward off his reply. 'I'm sure you and Gloria will make up your quarrel. Bring her next time!' She clears the plates and sweeps out to the kitchen to bring in dessert.

'Nice house,' I comment. 'In America we call this a Colonial: four up, four down.'

'Glad you like the house.' My father's first attempt to please me. 'One day, it'll be yours.'

He does not know that if I had inherited this house my life would have been different. I would have been able to go to college, although I have no idea what I would choose to study.

My grandmother returns with coffee and launches into neighbourhood gossip, chatting away as if she hasn't spoken to anyone for months.

'A couple of streets away from here, this couple locked themselves away in one room and had milk and groceries delivered on credit, mostly potatoes. That's all they ate for three years. They were afraid the next knock on the door was going to be the Nazis.'

'Who found them out?'

'The grocer, of course. They didn't bother to pay the grocery bill. Apparently, a lot of people are hiding out like that, fearing the worst. Tragedy is, if they're too frightened to leave their homes, they may not know when the war is over.'

'It will be over soon.'

She gives him a trusting look.

'I hope so. Are you coming with me to Midnight Mass?'

'Have you become religious since Dad died?'

'Not really, but I've got more lonely.'

The radio is switched on and we listen to Christmas carols until it is time for my father and my grandmother to muffle up. They walk in silence down the hill to a flint stone church with a cracked and clumsily repaired spire. The congregation is singing 'Oh Little Town of Bethlehem, how sweet I see thee lie, above thy deep and dreamless sleep, the silent stars go by.'

Religion does not impress my father, and after ten minutes he exits for a smoke.

'My groin's bothering me,' he tells me. 'All this walking up and down hills. Wretched town.'

He reaches in his pocket for a box of pills and throws a couple down his throat. I'm beginning to think he's addicted to painkillers.

During the night I take the opportunity to tour the house in true detective fashion. I don't know what I'm looking for, but I want to learn more about my grandparents. In the hall are two teaching certificates;

apparently both my grandfather and grandmother were teachers. If they were both teachers, that accounts for the bookcases. The only book in my foster parents' house was a gold-covered commemorative picture book with photographs of the Royal Family. I was the first in the house to join the local library. Nothing of interest in my grandmother's bedroom. She has few toiletries. The picture book on her bedside table is 'The Napoleonic Wars'. On the bureau is a wedding photograph. The black and white wedding photo in a silver frame makes my grandfather look like a kindly man. My grandmother looks like the brittle woman she has become, a woman about to snap in two. I go to the attic and see a love letter from my grandfather, ornately framed. He wrote flowery phrases, comparing his love to a rose in bloom. And here are old class photos. That must be my grandfather in the centre of a series of photos for each different school year. My grandfather, in the earliest year is clean shaven, and as the years go by he grows a black moustache, which turns into a white moustache while his hair thins and disappears. In the last year, 1931, he's stooping forward, clean shaven, his oblong-shaped head looking too heavy for his neck, bowed by his continual toil in education. The children, his pupils, remain the same age, looking more and more defiantly out at the camera.

Breakfast is a mournful meal. My grandmother has tears in her eyes.

'I never know when I'm going to see you again. Have you seen any of these terrible gas explosions?'

'They're V2 unmanned rockets. Flying bombs. But we're going to win the war, don't forget.'

'It may be a pyrrhic victory,' is her taut reply.

I do not understand what she means, but my father nods wisely. His mother gives him a shake of her hand and *'ums,'* and again he *'ums'* back.

'And how is Robert doing in the RAF?' She speaks of Robert fondly. She probably likes and approves of my father's stepson. 'Heard that he'd passed the exams. Will he get leave for Christmas or the New Year?'

'Doubtful.'

At the very last minute, at the front door, they exchange gifts. He gives her a sealed envelope.

'Don't give me your coupons,' she protests.

'They're for meat or fish. You've lost weight since I last saw you.'

'When you get older you lose your appetite.'

'Take them!' It sounds like an order.

She then presses something unwrapped into his hand. 'I bought them for your father, but he never liked them. Too flashy for him. Good for London.'

He opens the box and thanks her for the gold cufflinks. They kiss quickly to cover up some confusion or embarrassment and we are in the street. It's snowing. Unlike my foster mother, she does not stand in the doorway and wave, and I have no regrets leaving that sad house.

'You haven't told me what happened to Uncle Charles. How did he die?'

My father folds his face into lines of grief and gets out a packet of cigarettes at which he stares, as if his brother smoked the same brand.

'Players,' he indicates, when he shows me the picture of a bearded sailor.

'Does he look like my uncle?'

'No, Charlie was clean shaven, good-looking. But you see, these cigarettes are called Players and he called himself a player, a theatre person if you will. After the trenches he escaped into the fantasy of the theatre world. But to him it was real, his chosen reality, and I suppose he had something of career. Several false starts before he got work as a theatre director and talked of Broadway and Hollywood. When I learned there was going to be another war, I told him to take a boat across the Atlantic and escape the carnage.

'He wanted me to go with him, but I had a responsible job and wanted to do my bit for England. Anyway, he went to America to be safe and I breathed a sigh of relief. So much for that.'

'He died in America?'

'He got killed in an air crash as he was trying to come back. Coming back to enlist.'

The sombre way my father says this stops me asking any more questions, but he senses I need to know more.

'He was coming back to England to help us fight. The passenger plane was attacked by the Luftwaffe. They were already torpedoing passenger boats.'

He lights a cigarette.

'I see,' I say, trying to think of something positive to say. 'He came back to do his duty.'

'Yes, after he got away safe and sound. On account of Noël Coward. He'd heard Coward speak in New York City. You may not know the name, but he was the toast of London town for years, actor, playwright and *bon vivant*. When the war broke out Coward was too old to serve, so he went to America to recruit English expatriates and American soldiers for the war. My brother heard him speak and felt guilty about deserting his country.'

'How do you know all this if he died in a plane crash?'

'I didn't at first. I waited three days for him to be identified while they searched the wreckage. It was only when the Eighth Army came over and America was really in the war that the American post finally came through. I got a couple of letters from him. My brother wrote that he wanted to come back and fight for England. He deserves a medal more than I do. And he hasn't even had a funeral, because I can't face telling my mother.'

I look around and find we are not walking to the station. We're heading for open country, climbing to the top of the Downs, which is what we call the hills that surround Brighton.

'Shouldn't we be getting back to Adelphi Square? It's Christmas Day!'

'Vivien and I have no plans for Christmas Day, just the evening. We're going to the annual festive meal in the evening. Your mother could never cook a Christmas dinner. But before we go back to London, I want to visit the Longs.'

'The Longs? My foster family?'

'That's right. I wasn't impressed with the report of your Aunts, so we decided to keep you with the Longs. Your mother has already taken you down there, and apparently you are putting on weight.'

'Do you realise your mother lived close by me then? Warmdene Village is only a mile away. Was she living that close to the Longs all the time I was growing up? And I didn't know anything about her!'

My father ignores the anger in my voice.

CHAPTER EIGHTEEN

1984

Ed did not enjoy staying in Vivien's abandoned apartment, but he tried to think of it as camping out. He'd been told there was a housing shortage in England, and he was lucky to have a roof over his head. Jason had wangled the keys out of the landlord and negotiated with him on Ed's behalf. Ed tried not to notice the peeling paint, the noise from upstairs, the odd scratchings at night. He had slept in worse places as a student. He had to enter through the front hall of the converted town house because the basement entrance was still covered in fallen masonry. There was always a smell of tenants' cooking in the hall. At least the flat was clean. He took the mattress off the bed and moved it into the sitting room. Back from the hospital, he got into the habit of drinking a glass of brandy before climbing into damp and unappetizing sheets. He often thought of his extended family and it irked him Annabel had no relatives to help him out in this situation. Then he felt guilty. For him it was a minor annoyance, but for Annabel this uncomfortable feeling of having no family support had been the story of her life.

****

Despite my righteous anger that I had been kept in the dark about my grandmother living so close to where I grew up, I am looking forward to going back to the much-loved home of my childhood. The memory of the leafy-green streets of Warmdene village is immediately challenged. It is a cloudy day in midwinter. I look for the cobbler's shop, which is shut for the holidays, but I cannot help telling my father that behind the counter a man in a leather apron expertly used his stump of an arm as a tool on which to hang the shoe he was repairing. My father is not interested in the cobbler; but looks up when I point out my red brick school.

'What was your favourite subject?'

'None of them. I learned next to nothing there; but I did enjoy being in the school play. I was Jessica in The Merchant of Venice because of my dark hair.' I did not mention my discovery of my Jewish roots.

'Maybe you should have become an actress. Your mother had that ambition.'

'I think she wanted me to.' I did not add that was a good enough reason for me never to darken the door of a theatre.

As we approach Warmdene I mourn the loss of that large tract of fertile earth where the Longs grew fruit and vegetables. When they moved to Australia and sold up, the dilapidated house was torn down and rows of brick council housing built on the land. I find it peculiar to be arriving with my father at Christmas time when it was my mother who visited every Christmas.

'My mother would arrive with a hamper of goodies, crackers, bottles of liquor, velvet dresses for me and presents for everyone. I don't know if my foster parents enjoyed her visits, but when you foster a child, I guess you run the risk of fostering the mother too.'

'So, I must have disappeared early on in your life.'

My father is at last saddened by this thought, but I want him to know I was happy here and to share with him the joy of my childhood and its surroundings. I point out the evergreen privet hedge that smells so deliciously in summer; and tell him how Brenda insisted on growing hollyhocks and roses as well as vegetables. We go up the twisted path, flanked on each side by mountain ash trees. They're bare of leaves, but when I look up, I notice birds' nests in the top branches. I'd forgotten how Paul and I used to pick up broken bird's eggs from the rock garden. I show my father the patch of earth near the potting shed where I was allowed to grow primroses. I tell him about the strawberry field, which in summer would be covered with a black mesh net.

'It was my job to crawl under it and pick the strawberries. And there's the chicken coop so we always had fresh eggs. I used to put the baby chicks in my doll's pram. More fun than china dolls.'

My father says nothing.

'I used to have nightmares of seeing Nazis on that lawn.' My father nods, as if that was something he understood. I cannot help thinking that if the Germans had invaded, my mother and I could have been rounded up for the furnaces, or would we have escaped with our Italian name? I'm sure Vivien never mentioned her Jewish roots to the Longs, but that could have been because she never knew about them. I am waiting for the right moment to tell my father that Vivien is part Jewish. He may be amused since his first wife was also Jewish.

My foster brother Paul answers the door and like the eleven-year-old boy he is, does not immediately invite my father in. I never knew Paul in short trousers, and he does not look tall for his age. He was a teenager when he first swam into my consciousness, but his grin is the same.

'Welcome, Mister Hugh. Did you see the new door? They took our garden gate because it was made of iron.' This is said in a proud and defiant tone. 'War Effort! The next day they came and took the good gardening tools and gave us rotten old wood ones.'

'Who's here?' I ask, but I can guess; three grownup daughters, who are a female force. Paul calls them Aunts. They are Sidney's children from his first marriage gathered in the living room to greet my father, a gent from London. He politely shakes the hand of Sidney's youngest daughter Pat, a fiery redhead and beefy Land Army girl, then greets tall thin Betty who drives a bus. He shakes her hand respectfully. The eldest daughter is Simone. She is the one who will die first, but I don't want to remember that today. Sidney proudly informs my father that his twin sons, Raymond and Everard, are fighting on the Front. My upright foster father gives a good impression of being proud of his children, but I don't remember him being that interested in them. It could be that he never liked or wanted children, or he may have resisted Brenda's constant infatuation with them. There is no sign of me, the baby.

A dog bursts into the room! Penny, my cocker spaniel, whose passing was one of my childhood's sorrows. Here she is only a puppy, tugging at my father's trouser leg. Seeing my dog is a painful joy. I want to prolong the image of her soft brown eyes even if I cannot feel her sensitive floppy ears.

Sidney leads my father into the lounge and brings out a dusty bottle of port. They sit companionably in front of the coal fire roasting their shins, which is the only way to keep warm in an unheated house.

Mr. Hugh goes to speak, clearing his throat as if to make a significant communication, but all he says is 'Good port!'

'South end of the vineyard,' Sidney replies.

This room is furnished just as I remember: a modernistic Bakelite coffee table where contentious games of cards were played, a faded pink silk divan in the bay window. On the shelves are pots of Brenda's collection of miniature cacti, the only exotic touch in the whole house.

Betty, more socially aware than the other two sisters, goes to the wooden gramophone cabinet to wind it up. She puts on a huge black disc. A deep man's voice sings a vigorous Italian folk song that makes them tap their feet.

'We'll have music for a while,' Sidney allows. 'But then we'll put on the wireless. Don't want to miss the King's speech.'

'We listened to the radio a lot,' I tell my father, who looks a little bored. 'My favourite was the detective thriller Dick Barton. I loved being afraid every time the theme music was played.'

'You say you spent your entire childhood here?'

'Vivien came and visited me at Christmas. She had no family to go to during the holidays. She borrowed my foster family, and I'm sure they felt sorry for her, even though they prejudiced me against her.'

There is a disturbance when Brenda walks through the door, carrying me in her arms, and puts me down on the sofa. My father shifts the shawl to see me better.

'When are you going to take her back?' Simone always manages to say something hostile, given the opportunity.

My father takes a while to reply. 'When the war is over; children are still being evacuated out of London because of the flying bombs. They fly so low our wonderful radar system is useless against them.'

Sidney stands in front of the fire to warm his backside, always depriving the rest of the family. 'We have to do our bit for the war effort.'

He glares at Simone, whose fair skin reddens. An emotional woman!

'Don't mind Simone,' I tell my father. 'She's in perpetual disgrace, because her husband won't fight in the war. He is a Quaker and serving a prison sentence.'

'Where's Brenda?' Sidney would not ask unless he wanted her to fetch something.

'In the kitchen.'

Betty turns to Mr. Hugh for support. 'She's slaving away in the kitchen. Christmas is a nightmare for her because Dad insists on having a fresh turkey, that she has to pluck.'

She is right, Brenda spent hours before Christmas in the outside toilet plucking the chicken or turkey, surrounded like an angel by a cloud of white feathers. I wonder why her step-daughters did not offer to help her 'pluck the bird.' I suppose they didn't feel like this was really their home. It belonged to Paul and me. But I like Betty for sympathising with her step-mum. Yes, there is Brenda is in the kitchen frowning over the gravy.

'Gravy was a ritual fraught with failure before gravy granules.' I cannot help saying this out loud, even if no one hears me and my father looks puzzled. Brenda looks up briefly but then bends over the stove again. I'm disappointed. I had hoped she would see me.

'I won't be staying for dinner.' My father is saying.

'Nonsense! Of course, you'll stay.' Brenda insists.

My father bows his head. 'If you insist.' He goes towards the baby, me, and I think he wants to pick me up but does not dare. He opens his briefcase and takes out a white rabbit made of pure sheep's wool.

'I recognise that!' I'm pleased to tell him. 'It was one of my favourite toys. I called it Bunny.'

He props it against the back of the sofa, but I am too busy kicking my legs in the air to notice.

'Look what I got.' Eager to be the centre of attention, Paul bursts into the room with a zooming noise, sweeping a wooden replica of a Spitfire through the air. It is only two pieces of interlocking wood, carefully painted. My father smiles and nods but does not join in Paul's game. Does he not know how to play with children? Paul then takes my father to the Christmas tree where he generously hands out small parcels of clear plastic, tied with white ribbon, hanging on the fir tree branches.

'We pooled our sugar rations and Mum iced some raisins.' 'Delicious!'

My father eats one and puts the rest on the mantelshelf.

The quiet is shattered by a healthy cry of protest from me, the baby. Pat goes to the kitchen and returns with a bottle and lodges it on a pillow. I presume feeding me is usually Brenda's job. Looking down at my trusting happily guzzling self, I'm overcome with an unexpected urge to sweep her up in my arms. She has now lost the bottle and is looking around for it. No one notices. The baby looks up at me. A smile hovers on her lips and her eyes give me a look which makes me imagine she can see me, which prompts me to speak.

'You will grow up strong and healthy and have a son of your own and you will be proud of him.' I am not sure why I say this, and I'm surprised that it expresses an approval of my life as an adult.

'I need some help!' Brenda yells from the kitchen, and her step-daughters troop out.

My foster father toasts his absent sons. 'To Raymond and Everard, and don't ask where they are. Loose lips sink ships.' Now that he has everyone's attention again, he takes centre stage and addresses my father with a hint of sardonic humour. 'You're used to better grub in London, I hear. London's the hub of the black market, I've heard. Champagne flowing from the Swiss Embassy, or is it the Swedish? You'll be having a fine dinner somewhere, I bet.'

'I was invited to join the Royals at Balmoral,' my father takes up the satire. 'But they were having haggis.'

Everyone laughs at this attempt at humour, and he goes over to the sofa as if he wants to say hello to me, the baby.

'She can laugh, look.' Paul comes over and makes a funny face. My father rumples Paul's hair.

Oh, it is heaven being here, seeing these loved ones. The memory of my childhood Christmases infuses me with as much warmth as a ghost can expect. I revel in the glint of crystal wine glasses and the starched white lace tablecloth, which was only used once a year.

'Take Mr. Hugh up to the baby's room.' Sidney instructs Paul, who grabs my father by the arm.

'Come and see the bedroom she'll be in when the air raids have stopped.'

We climb the worn blue carpeted stairs, secured with shiny brass poles.

My room, as I will know it in the future, is small and shabby. My father nods an acceptance, not sure what he's being sold here. When we return to the dining room, things are hotting up. Pat is loading the table with vegetables from the garden. The family atmosphere is in marked contrast to both his mother's house and his one-bedroom at Adelphi Square. Sidney is pleased to be toasting Mr. Hugh again. 'Here's to the End in Sight. We're finishing them off, if you ask me. ' He says with an unbelieving gruff laugh.

'Or it'll be the War of the Worlds.' There is some fear in my father's voice.

'No doubt about it, we'll finish 'em off,' Sidney promises. He does not want bad news. 'And what about your regiment? Mechanised transport, I hear?'

'Yes, they've taken away our horses.'

'And I don't want to hear what they did with them. No horse meat is going to end up on my plate.' Sidney's indignation makes him almost inarticulate. Sidney considered horses superior to dogs in affection and intelligence and spent his spare time at Brighton's famous racecourse. From him, I learned how they 'came home,' or more often 'let me down badly.'

'When the war's over, we'll get her a horse.'

'Oh, really?' My father's querulous tone reassures me that he has no intention of leaving me here forever, but maybe that's just wishful thinking.

'Surely dinner must be ready!' Sidney complains.

His daughters obediently arrange themselves round the table and Sidney takes his customary place as head of the table in the tall, carved oak chair. If anyone sat in Sidney's chair, I think his world would end. They are awaiting the entrance of the bird, and here is my beloved Brenda at the door, carrying a properly glazed roasted turkey. She smiles hello at my father and then the smile freezes on her face. She looks straight at me and, thrilled, I immediately smile back. She has seen me! But my appearance must be a shock to her. She staggers back and almost falls while the loaded plate cascades onto the floor with a splintering crack. The sisters run to save their dinner.

'Are you all right?' Sidney reluctantly asks. He is used to being the centre of attention.

'Dad won't eat that,' Paul chants.

My foster father is filling his plate with vegetables. 'He is right.'

Betty and Pat are busy scraping away bits of china from the turkey.

'Oh, go ahead, it's not the first time you've been served food from the floor.'

Sidney fixes everyone with an angry look, and then pours himself another drink of port.

Pat dumps the bird on the table. 'All the more for us.'

My father goes to Brenda's aid, taking her arm and leading her towards the door.

'Don't be afraid!' I whisper to Brenda.

'Saints preserve us, saints preserve us,' she mumbles to herself.

The family does not understand what is happening. My father, quick at thinking on his feet, takes command. 'Let's go into the front lounge. I've something to explain.'

Brenda follows him with her mouth open, still not taking her eyes off me. When the three of us are in the front room, I announce grandly. 'I am Annabel. I've come from the future.'

Brenda's face pales, and she sways backwards.

My father steps in. 'She says she's a ghost, a ghost from the future. I know it sounds unlikely, but I'm relieved you can also see her.'

'But... but...' Brenda stammers.

My father puts a hand up, as if asking permission to speak again!

'I'm relieved you can see her too, because I was beginning to think I was going crazy. Either that or that my pills were giving me hallucinations.' An uncertain laugh!

'Aunt Rosie saw me too,' I cannot help boasting, but that only confuses her more. She doesn't know my Aunt Rosie. 'I am that baby in there,' I try to explain. 'As you can see, I've grown up and I'm visiting from Texas. I'm actually visiting from 1984. And I'm so happy to be here, seeing you all. I was at Victoria Station when my mother, Vivien, handed me over.' That seems to be the wrong thing to say because now she looks even more distressed.

Brenda stuffs her knuckles into her mouth. 'Oh my God, oh my God, what's going to happen to us?'

'You need some brandy?' my father speaks very softly.

'Don't panic.' Useless advice when both her hands are gripping the door handle. She wants to escape.

'But you're old, I mean how can you be so old?' Brenda asks.

'That's why you can't recognise me.'

She doesn't know how what to say, and I understand from her frightened eyes that it is too much for her to comprehend.

'This is my daughter.' My father is giving Brenda her some brandy from a flask that I've noticed he keeps hidden in his pocket. She takes the flask and drinks with her eyes tightly closed.

'Please believe me,' I say in an attempt to excuse my appearance.' I'm not here to hurt anyone. I'd just like you to know the war's almost over.'

Brenda rushes out, and I hear the dining room door swing shut. I know that sound. She returns in a minute with the salt cellar. This she shakes all over me. It is her defence against bad omens. She is not without courage, but I can't bear to see her babbling. 'Is someone going to die? Is that why you've come? And you, are you dead?'

'I hope not, and no one's going to die. You all survive the war.'

Brenda looks to my father for confirmation. He nods encouragingly.

I want to continue. 'Because I'm visiting from 1984 and because I've lived the years in between, you can ask me anything you like about what's going to happen. Well, I can tell you that your step-daughter Pat will marry an Australian, and then Paul goes out there to get a job and then you and Sidney sell up and move to Melbourne. That's some of the things that will happen when the war's over.'

Brenda takes a few minutes to work out what I've said. Yes, she has understood. 'Oh, that can't be right,' she says. 'We're not going to Australia. There's no way you're going to get me on a boat to Australia.'

'You fly.'

'It's good news,' my father insists. 'The trouble is, it's hard for people to believe in the future. We're used to accepting the past, but... let's leave, we're upsetting her.'

'So what exactly are you?' Brenda is now clawing at her chin. A familiar gesture.

'Can you accept it's me?' I hear anger in my voice.

'And you haven't come with bad news? What about Ray and Ev? They're fighting men, have you come to tell us Ray and Ev are not coming back?' She looks to my father for confirmation. He turns to me, expecting a reply.

'They will. They'll all survive the war. They come back alive. Your family is one of the lucky ones.'

She is giving me another chance. 'Tell me, if you've come on this... visit, you're a ghost then. You've died or something?'

'No, from my point of view, you are all ghosts.'

This uncertainty is too much for her. She turns her back on me and addresses my father. 'That's good news about Ray and Ev. Every time we hear that demon on his red motorbike, we hold our breath and, God forgive us, hope he goes past us on his way to someone else.'

At first, I think she's referring to the devil himself, but then I remember the 'Telegram Man', a red-helmeted rider on a red motorbike, bearing much dreaded news. 'I'm so happy you can see me,' I tell her.

And we win the war?'

'Yes!'

'Sidney's right, then. He does so like to be right. He never will come to the bunker.'

'Brighton's not bombed that much.' My father says.

'They dogfight over the Downs,' Brenda retorts. 'And last month they strafed the children on their way home from school. Why would they do a thing like that? But trust Sidney to be right.' She manages to laugh nervously about this, fidgeting with the brooch on her dress. She is wearing her Christmas best, a black crepe jacket over a chintz dress which was probably made on her sewing machine. I'm still not sure she really knows who I am, but I have discovered it's no use dwelling on the future. Brenda is now edging towards the dining room door and I'm disappointed that she wants this strange meeting to be over, to return to the ordinary and go back to her family. There's so much more I want to say. She puts a hand to her ample bosom, another gesture I remember clearly.

'And how long is the war going to last?'

'Only another few months.'

'Paul is so worried. He asks me every day whether he's going to have to fight. Now I can tell him he won't have to.' She gives my father a sweet smile. She almost wants to ignore me. 'This war's terrible, but let's hope good will come out of bad.'

I love it when she resorts to homilies.

'I'd like to thank you in advance for taking such good care of me,' I tell her.

She gives my father a furtive look and nods.

'Hope so,' my father sighs. 'Vivien is not very practical.'

'The baby will be better off with me.' Brenda takes us to the door and my father hands her several pound notes, which she immediately puts behind her back. 'I would look after her for nothing,' Brenda says.

'Of course!' My father bends in gratitude.

'We can adopt her if you want. Sidney has agreed that it may be the best thing. She will be well taken care of.'

My father does not immediately reply to this. He is struggling to find the right words. 'That won't be necessary,' he says.

Brenda tries to catch my eye as we go through the door, but I refuse to look at her. I'm afraid there will be a look of success on her face. She has saved my life, as she often told me. Her maternal instincts have been roused and she doesn't want to hand me, the baby, back, she intends to keep me.

Eliza Wyatt

****

'Release the past. It's gone, and the future is yours. Don't worry about the domino effect or the butterfly effect. Exaggerations. Your life is more important than your father's. It's up to you to take control!'

My father seems aware of my conflicting emotions and embarrassed to talk. He is limping badly. I walk a few steps behind him, noticing one of his shoulders is higher than the other. When we arrive at the station, we are informed the train to London will be delayed by four to six hours. I immediately want to know the reason: a bomb on the line, fire, or more likely staff shortages. No one else displays my curiosity and there's no one to ask. My father suggest we go to The Nightingale.

I wait while he relishes a pint of bitter, reading the newspaper on the counter. He looks up at last because he has a question.

'Did you ever learn to ride?'

'Yes, but I never liked it. There was a stable down the road and Sidney could not wait to get me on a horse. He came home one day with Maud, a thick-legged pony who was also a mean one. More than once, she threw me over her head and each time Sidney would make me get back up. Eventually Brenda was afraid I'd get concussion.'

I did not tell him about the expensive saddle my mother brought down from London, which sat unused for a couple of years before it was sold to put food on the table. I have become sensitive to shielding him from any facts that could shame him.

'Sad,' my father says.

'What's sad?'

'About Sidney and Brenda not being able to have any more children. Brenda told your mother that she always wanted another child, a daughter.'

This was news to me: the last piece of the jigsaw puzzle. I was the daughter she could never have.

He crumples up the newspaper, throws it aside, leans his head back and closes his eyes. I don't envy him reading about his country at war, and from the headlines there's a decisive battle about to be fought on the French and German lines. He looks tired. He may not be the young vibrant man I idealised when I saw him asking Gloria to marry him, but he's my father.

'Did you meet Sidney in the last war? Was he a soldier?'

No, no. He was a dairy farmer, they don't draft farmers.'

'How did you find them?'

'They advertised. The Longs have plenty of space in their house and were naturally in line to take in an evacuee. It was only a temporary arrangement.'

I remember Brenda's suggestion about adoption. They virtually adopted me, an open adoption. She wanted to keep me because she could not have any more children. Without criminal intent she effectively stole me from my own mother.

'As I told you, no one ever mentioned my father. Certainly not Brenda nor Sidney. They never once mentioned they'd met you, but of course it makes sense. I wonder why they never told me about you. Vivien once said you died in the war, but she was drunk and afterwards she told me she'd made that up and refused to say anymore. It makes me wonder if she murdered you.' I have to be amused by a look of horror on his face, but he does not take me seriously.

The more I see of my mother in this era, the more convinced I am that she could murder my father. I'm surprised that I am not shocked by this idea which would explain her secretive behaviour. Maybe I've come back to the past to prevent her. To prevent her would be a good reason for me being here but if I manage to prevent her, surely that will change my future completely. Is my voice right and is it possible for me to do that? When I go back to 1984, will that mean I won't be married to Ed, or have a son called David? Are these real people or abstract thoughts that a time traveller can disappear at will?

'You've convinced me you will be happy with the Longs but only if I'm not able to take you back.' At least I have made him realise that reality, which is comforting. A noise like a chainsaw fills the station, gradually becoming the noisy clatter and hiss of the steam train.

'Whatever happens to me, I can see you've had a good life and I'm glad you've grown up to be a…a…. thoughtful woman. Remember, you are my only child.'

'And what shall I call you? Dad, Pops, Papa?'

This makes him smile, but I cannot be glad about our increasing closeness because I'm worried about the effects our overnight absence is going to have on my mother.

'It's a pity we can't telephone; her to tell her how late we are going to be.' There is no sign of a pay phone, or the red telephone kiosk that is a London landmark.

'The restaurant downstairs at Adelphi Square was serving a free Christmas dinner. I hope she went without me and was the life of the party. Do you like cooking?'

'I'm not a good cook.' I confess.

'None of the women I have loved have been good cooks.'

'Must be in the genes.' I laugh, forgetting he will not understand the word. There's a lot of knowledge separating us, but I am glad he has used the words, 'women I love' to include me.

'You've never explained why you got divorced from Gloria.'

He squirms uncomfortably. 'Women always want explanations. She left me, not the other way around.'

I am silent, thinking that means he is what they used to call a 'leg over' man, an unfaithful husband. Like Ed! Or worse!

Adelphi Square is unusually quiet. Members of Parliament are probably visiting with their families. He goes straight to a wall of tin mailboxes and peers into a square of emptiness. He shakes his head. 'Nothing from Robert. What's this?'

Pinned casually on the wall is a telegram addressed to him. I can see my father is furious. He almost stamps his feet when he marches off.

'The telegraph boy is not supposed to leave a telegram like that! He should have left it with the receptionist. Christmas is no excuse!' His tone now rings with the brittleness of his mother's voice. 'No standards left.'

After opening it, he is silent for a good minute. Then he begins to tremble, and turns to tell me, 'Robert's dead.'

I look at the telegram. Printed on ticker tape in faint blue ink, the words ROBERT COOPER KILLED IN ACTION STOP GLORIA.

My father does not immediately cry. He stumbles down the corridor, his back to me. But then his shoulders shake, and I can hear his sobs. When he reaches 101, he gets out his handkerchief and blows his nose. He does not open the door immediately. He stands in front of the door, as if he does not have the energy to enter.

The dim lights shows the place to be clean and empty. Vivien must have done a huge cleaning job since we left. My mother loved her flats to look like furniture showrooms. Her white make-up case is the only item on the table. My father flips it open automatically.

'My present, she's opened it.' He points to a bottle of perfume half-hidden in the red silk lining.

He opens the bedroom door and sees that my mother has flung herself on the bed, still dressed.

'Drunk,' my father says knowingly.

'Sign of things to come.' I say accusingly.

'I need a drink myself. Wretchedly cold!'

He opens the bookcase and retrieves a hidden, half empty bottle of whisky. With slow movements he boils a kettle, pours a cup of hot water into a china cup and adds whisky as if his fussy mother is looking over his shoulder.

CHAPTER NINETEEN

1984

During one of his night vigils, Annabel came to Ed in a dream. She was surrounded by flowers, smiling a beatific smile that reminded him of Holy Cards given to him on his birthday. He was afraid to move because he felt her spirit getting nearer to him. He stayed with his hands clasped over her body. When the doctor arrived, he told Ed to go home and get some sleep. Ed stood in the doorway unable to make any decision about whether to leave the room or remain in case she stirred. A nurse came in and bustled about Annabel's bed, suggesting Ed go home. He said he wanted coffee, but he meant American coffee, not the coffee of the cafeteria. He decided to go for a walk.

Outside, the electric lights were so low they barely illuminated the city streets and made it difficult to walk over the bumpy sidewalks. In the distance he saw two men arguing and jabbing fingers at each other. He figured they were drunk and went out of his way to avoid them but for some reason they followed him. The three of them were spotted by a police car. The two drunks ran off, but Ed remained. One of the police officers, a woman, got out to question him. Was the country entirely run by women? Margaret Thatcher, the Queen of England? Ed's first instinct had been to run, but he was afraid of being shot down. Too late he remembered the police did not carry guns. He told them about his wife's critical condition, and they insisted on driving him back to the hospital. Ed suspected they wanted proof. The gates of the main hospital were padlocked so they had to enter via the Accident and Emergency Department where even the police had to wait in line. The three of them waited in a long line of injured and distressed people. The policeman and policewoman took advantage of the wait to hear more about Ed and his wife, and what they were doing in England. Being an American Ed was getting used to being under suspicion, but felt it was time to challenge the police. 'You people seem to have no idea why my wife was injured. Where I come from a bomb is a serious matter. My wife nearly died.'

They were intrigued by this complaint and when he told them the cause of Annabel's injuries, they listened carefully and displayed some sympathy for his story.

'Can you even tell me what sort of bomb it was, or who was the intended victim? Obviously not my wife.'

The policewoman blew her nose. 'More than likely it wasn't meant for her. It sounds like it was a letter bomb. That's what we call them; simple incendiary devices, which have become popular.'

'Popular?' Ed thought it an odd word to use.

'It's useless to speculate. For all we know, it could have been planted by anarchists.'

'Anarchists! Who are anarchists. '

'We have quite a few of them in this country. They want to blow everyone up, especially those in authority.'

'Is that the only explanation? Maybe it was a bomb meant for her mother, Vivien Langoni. She was a well-known figure and knew members of parliament and Lords and such.'

The policeman withdrew from them and got on his walkie-talkie. The policewoman picked up a magazine to read and Ed closed his eyes and was almost asleep when the policeman eventually reappeared.

'I've checked and as far we know your mother-in-law was no threat to the public unless she was drinking. We got her on a couple of DP's, Disturber of the Peace, but that's all. There was a court case against her, case of an injured eye, but the charge was dropped. The bomb could have been planted by one of her less than desirable friends to shake her up a bit.'

'You mean before they realised she was dead?'

The police decided they were no longer interested in Ed's case and it was time for them to leave. Ed was glad he had stood up for his rights, although that did not stop him feeling ashamed of his mother-in-law who had injured someone in a bar.

****

Back in Adelphi Square, the rain falls steadily through the night, gushing over inadequate water pipes. I don't want to be here. I want to go back to my foster family and enjoy Boxing Day. Now that I've visited Brenda and Sidney in my childhood home, I am a little embarrassed at playing the daughter with my own father. I am almost as old as he is, even if he's thirty years older than my mother. I wonder if my parents plan a future together as a family, maybe having another child. My father acts more like a father to Vivien and if he expects to start a family with her, he has chosen someone who does not know what family means. It is a long night, but I don't want the day to begin. My hungover mother will surely start a quarrel, and my poor father's already in pain from the death of his stepson. I'm imbibing his misery and that makes me fearful of never being able to escape, afraid I'll always be locked into this painful past, and seduced into accepting the reality of this distressed era. It is three o'clock before my father stumbles into the living room. He goes into the kitchen to boil water and turns down his mouth when he sees me.

'I've never liked Boxing Day.' He says.
'Boxing Day is not a holiday in the US,' I tell him.
'No parties for the children then?'
'I tried to make a party one year. David was about seven. I made jellies and blancmanges, and when the kids came, they began throwing the food at each other. Last time I did that!'

He goes into the bedroom to get his electric razor, which I'm surprised to see in this era, especially after hearing about the working women machine-cutting razor blades.

The noise wakes my mother. She stands framed in the kitchen doorway, beautiful and threatening, a Hollywood star in search of a role or maybe just a cigarette. She ignores my father. She is thinking about yesterday. I stand in front of her, but she blearily looks past me, still drunk from last night.

'I've got one of your headaches,' she accuses my father.

'I own headaches?' He protests. 'You should have had our journey back.'

'You and who?' She is alert to this slip.

'The train was packed. And there's nothing in this house to eat.'

'I suppose you stopped off to see one of your friends.' She is impatient for the story.

'The train was cancelled. I was stuck most of the night on Brighton station.'

'I don't know why you think trains run on Christmas Day.'

'Of course they do in wartime! For men on leave.'

'I thought you'd been bombed or something.'

'Just dying of hunger by the time I got back.'

'How am I supposed to guess that?' I hear in her voice the resentment of a woman who is supposed to provide nourishment when she doesn't feel nourished herself. 'Don't forget we're going to Fred and Michael's Christmas party this afternoon. There'll be food there.' My father groans expressively.

'I cleaned the place with a toothbrush, in case you haven't noticed. Had to do something with myself on Christmas Day. I never found that rabbit we bought for Annabel. You didn't risk sending it in the post?'

'No, I took it with me.'

'You took it to see your mother?'

'I went on to see Annabel.'

'You mean you went to see the Longs without me?

My father wilts under her angry glare. 'They don't live far from my mother.'

'You told me your mother lived in Surrey.'

'Sussex.'

'You said Surrey. You lied! And you saw Annabel without me?' How quietly she says this.

'I saw her briefly, yes, to check up on her since I was fairly close by. I thought it a good idea to visit the Longs without warning them. That's the best way to find out how they're treating her. And I'm glad to report she's put on weight and looks happy.'

Vivien is silent, standing dangerously near him with a kettle full of boiling water. She says very deliberately, 'You went to see her by yourself, without me.'

'I didn't plan to. It was a last-minute decision.'

I'm sure this is a lie, and she knows it too. She slowly puts the kettle down with such sinister control it makes me afraid of what she's going to do next.

'I didn't know the trains would stop running.' Guilt makes my father's voice low and weak.

'You deliberately told a lie about where your mother lives. I suppose the Longs are friends of your wretched mother's?'

'No! They're just a host family. I told you, my mother knows nothing about you or the baby.'

'You haven't told your mother about me, you haven't told her that your brother's dead. I can't trust you. One day I'll wake up and Annabel won't be at the Longs, and I won't know where she is because you're a liar.'

My father's mouth curls in a snarl, something I've not seen before. 'You're so very quick with these accusations maybe you were planning to steal her yourself.'

She is righteously outraged. 'You don't want this baby, you never have.'

With a thrill, I can see my mother is preparing to fight for me. Yes, this is the mother I want: one who will stand up for her child. My mother puts on her coat. 'I'm going down to Brighton to bring her back.'

'You know we can't have her at Adelphi Square. And even if they made an exception for us, you can't manage her.'

My mother is now searching in her purse. 'Give me some money!'

My father shakes his head. 'She's in the best place and that's where she'll stay.' My father's voice now has a military edge.

My mother reacts to that authoritarian tone. 'You've stolen her. Give me some money for the train fare.'

'There's nothing to do down there! You will upset them.'

'You don't understand. I'm through with you.'

'You've got to accept the baby's in the right place. Just for now!'

'You know what I'm going to do? I'm going to live down there in Brighton. I hear it's a party town and that's where I am going to live. Far away from you!'

Vivien beats him out the way with her fists. He backs off to a more logical argument. 'You neglected her! I could have brought in the police.'

'I'm going to call the police, you've stolen my child. All of you.'

My father moves angrily in front of her. I'm afraid he's going to hit her, but she is well within her rights and he does not have the strength of will to physically stop her. She pushes him away, but before she reaches the door there's a knock on it. I hate the sound of that knock. My mother flings open the door and a young man in navy uniform is standing there. His smile freezes on his handsome face.

'Ensign Brunelli, sir! Good afternoon, sir!' He puts out a hand, and my father's too confused to refuse it. He bravely addresses my mother. 'You told me to come round about this time, didn't you, ma'am? For the party?'

My mother recovers immediately. 'Come in, ensign.' She says this seductively, as if she has not been in the middle of a desperate quarrel. The young sailor removes his cap and looks unsure about accepting her invitation.

'Maybe I've come at the wrong time.'

'Your timing's perfect,' she tells him, flashing a smile. 'I'm dressed.'

My father interrupts. 'I don't know what impression you're under, er... ensign...?'

'Brunelli.' His Italian name fits his flashing brown eyes and good looks.

My father breathes heavily. 'There is no party here. Adelphi Square's party was yesterday.'

'He means Michael's party,' my mother calls out from the bedroom. 'Give me a few minutes, and please wait downstairs in the lobby.'

'Certainly, ma'am.' The ensign in happy to make a quick exit.

My father goes into the kitchen to make himself some toast. I'm glad to see him eating. He does not seem as confused as I am by the sudden end to the quarrel. Has she given up on going down to Brighton because she got distracted? Oh yes, I forgot; this is my mother, the woman who walks out the door with every handsome man who appears, the woman who cannot resist a party. We wait in ominous silence as we listen to my mother trying to flush the toilet. My father winces with every jerk of the chain. My mother eventually enters in a tight-fitting suit, carrying two coats.

My father gasps, 'Look at you!'

She ignores him and flips open her white make-up case with a bang, to aggressively anoint herself with the perfume he gave her.

'You're going to Fred and Michael's with this ensign?'

'Of course! They'll love him.'

My father is silenced by this inference that Ensign Brunelli is homosexual. He is not sure whether to believe her, but my mother always had a sure instinct for a man's preference; a woman ahead of her time.

'You've forgotten about going down to Brighton. True to form! You're going out now!'

'I told you about Fred and Michael's shindig. You're invited. But not by me! I'll stay over with them. I'm never coming back here. You and I are finished. Don't follow me. I can't trust you, and don't worry about Annabel. We'll be fine.'

It is a good exit line, and she makes the most of it. Except that she comes back to collect her make-up case. She is focusing on what will happen in the next few hours. She looks determined to enjoy her friends, almost as if she knows it is her fate to be known as a good time girl.

My father makes one last effort. 'I forbid you to go.' Not the right words!

'You never wanted that baby. You wanted a boy.'

My father backs away, and while I want him to deny this, he has forgotten I'm still there. While she checks herself in the mirror, he puts his hand in his pocket to bring out the telegram about Robert Cooper. There are tears in his eyes. He may be deciding whether to tell Vivien about the death of his stepson, but it is suddenly too late. She does not notice the telegram in his hand, and slams the door behind her. I follow my father into the bedroom. He goes to his bedside table and opens and closes a couple of cupboard doors.

'No pills left,' he murmurs.

He goes to the window to see Vivien and Ensign Brunelli, arms linked, walking down the street.

'A bit stupid, aren't I? Letting her go to a party after a quarrel? She wows them every time. I'm talking about the Yanks. She looks like one of their film stars or something. Now that they're in town, our Tommies don't have a chance with the girls.'

'I married an American.'

'Sorry, I forgot.'

My father passes a hand over his forehead and reaches out a hand to me; the first sign that he needs me. He is feeling upset over the quarrel. 'You're all I have left,' he says in a mocking tone. 'And you're a ghost!'

I do not appreciate that. I want to yell, I'm more than a ghost but then what am I? How do I describe myself, how important am I to him in this era? He sinks down on the lumpy sofa and picks up a cushion, which he hugs unselfconsciously.

'Do you know what I think?' He points a nicotine-stained finger at me. 'That you are only here to remind me not to drink too much, and not to take too many pills. That's why I've conjured you up. Now that I'm running out of them, you too may disappear on me.'

I do not reply. I'm not sure he knows whether he approves of my possible disappearance or not.

'I know a chemist,' he suddenly tells me. 'He lives above his shop and I can wake him up. I need my pills tonight.'

We head towards the river and turn off onto narrower, darker streets. Smoke billows in front of us and I hear the ominous crackling of a fire. Round the next corner is a barricade shielding us from a blaze of flames, steadily burning down a row of shops. 'That was the chemist's shop and the barber's,' my father says with a hint of hysteria in his voice.

He approaches the debris that has been flung across the pavement. His foot pokes at a drawer with brass handles that has miraculously escaped the fire. White packets of pills spill out and he peers down at them hopefully, but soon realises the uselessness of such a search. With an impatient curse he turns his back on the devastating scene and limps away, more bent than usual because he has forgotten his stick.

'We all want peace, yet we're always at war. How can we really change the future for the better?'

'Sorry?'

I didn't realise I was speaking out loud, but I want him to know my thoughts. 'If we can create our own destinies, who made this terrible time and place? I don't know why I've been forced to see so much destruction. It's true I have destructive thoughts, but doesn't everyone?'

My father does not understand what I'm trying to say. When he unlocks the door of 101, he ushers me into the flat with a strange admission. 'I may have cancer of the tongue from too much smoking.' His voice has never sounded so hollow.

'That's a very rare form of cancer.'

'I've got all the symptoms. Where are my glasses?'

He finds a hefty medicine book already open to an article underlined in red.

'My tongue hurts like hell. I hope this doesn't mean I'm going to die a painful death.'

This is a new twist to his despair, and I sympathise. He does not want my sympathy. 'We're all dying one way or another,' he says soberly. Except you, the ghost.'

'I'm not a ghost,' I protest. 'I'm a traveller through time.'

Now he's rifling through the medicine cabinet while I watch, fearful he's going to take some inappropriate cure for cancer and poison himself. He retrieves a bottle from the top of the medicine cabinet and shows it to me disappointedly. 'Aspirins,' he complains. 'Not going to numb me much; half a dozen miserable aspirin.'

He throws them down his throat and drains the bottle of whisky before slamming the bedroom door shut. I feel rejected but I can hardly complain about his behaviour because I know he's upset. I wait until I hear him snoring, then open the bedroom door. I want to see him in bed. There are sounds of dance music from the floor above. I'm glad people are playing music and not listening out, like I am, for more explosions. By his bedside is a book he has been reading. It is by Robert Graves, a paperback, with an eerie green cover of trenches in No Man's Land on the cover. My father's snoring suddenly stops. He is sleeping soundly in crumpled sheets and I give way to an urge to creep into bed beside him. I think back to my foster parents. I never dared enter their bed, but I have an urge to see my father's naked body. His skin is remarkably firm, and he looks younger than he does when awake. Not much sign of hair, faint tufts over his nipples. I cannot help joining him under the sheets in an attempt at a father-daughter snuggle. Even lacking tactile sensation, there's nowhere in the world I'd rather be.

I have no real sense of time passing, but when I hear people talking outside in the passageway, I jump out of the bed fearful of my mother finding me there and being able to see me. There's no one at the door. It is the noisy neighbours upstairs. When I return to the bedroom, I'm shocked to see my father's face is ashen. He looks ill. I lean closer to his unshaven face and cannot hear him breathing. My presence disturbs him, and his body shakes with a rattle and a spasm that lands him on the floor. What is happening? Is he having a heart attack? His lips gleam with saliva. Is this how my father dies? I turn this way and that looking for help from some object, a mirror to reflect his breathing, but even as I think of this, I know it is too late. How did this happen? It must be the pills, the pills and the whisky. Did he mean this to happen? I remember him drinking the whisky. Then I see the empty aspirin bottle on the bedside table. Looking closer I see my mother's spidery scrawl: 'Your Sleeping Pills.' He thought he was taking aspirins, and he'd taken barbiturates. My mother's writing is clear, but small. Was he wearing his glasses? He was reading the medical book and his glasses are resting delicately on the table. I look down at his body on the floor.

'Don't let him die!' I shout out.

'He wants to die.'

Ah, my voice. Hearing that voice gives me hope. 'No, no! Keep him alive!' I plead, straining to hear the voice again.

'Let him go.'

'He's got to live, bring him back to life, please.'

'You'll be better off without him.'

'I want him to live. I have the power, don't I?'

'Not over life and death'

The word death ends in a high pitched wail and a deadly cold from somewhere makes me shiver. It is too awful to think that demon voice could be my mother's. She never talked like that. The voice lied, and I never want to hear it again. I punch the wall without feeling it. I think of the real life Vivien. Is she ever coming back after the party? I hate to think of what she's going to find, and how it will change her forever. She did not murder my father, but if she sees that aspirin bottle, she will realise she was partly responsible. Always a neat freak, she transferred his pills to a neater bottle. 'It's not her fault,' I cry out, angry that she behaved for the rest of her life as if she was guilty of my father's death.

CHAPTER TWENTY

It is raining and I open my mouth to drink the rain. I'm on the verge of delirium with thirst, and this is the first time I notice a thirst. Does that mean I'm beginning to be a more real? The streets sign says Bayswater: good name for the place in this downpour. The streetlights in the dawn make the streets look like an Impressionist painting. Handwritten signs have directed the traffic around bombing debris so cars creep along as if exploring an unknown universe. In contrast the people are surprisingly perky. I suppose they are jubilant at having survived the night's bombing. I trail the embankment wishing I could relieve my pain by tearing the limbs off the bare trees I pass. Then I shock myself by discovering I can almost do that. I am becoming more alive, more solid. Possibly my father's death has done that, anchored me here forever. I am in grief and maybe grief will imprison me here in the past forever. I don't want that, so I must not give way to personal grief. I must keep my mind occupied, find a far-reaching perspective. Looking across the river I'm perversely glad to see houses and warehouses on fire, being destroyed. I mistake the sound of beating drums for a funeral march, until I see it is the sound of soldiers marching in regimental formation. The troop heads towards me, eyes front. I stand in front of them, glad they do not see me. Hypnotised by their mass, their syncopation, I want to join them. Together we march past Buckingham palace towards Victoria railway station which is crowded with soldiers and men in air force uniforms.

They look very young, boys with bare faces. They file into the waiting train throwing their rifles on the floor. I hope they're not loaded. Do soldiers travel with their own guns because they're afraid they won't be equipped with them? Green duffel bags and assorted gear threaten to topple down on them from the overhead rack.

There is one lone woman in a turquoise coat. She is offered a cigarette, even though she's delicately coughing in the smoke.

'On your way to a holiday?'

'Going to have some fun?'

A fresh-faced young man, with a generous smile, answers for her. 'You betcha!'

'Us an' all! Before we're shipped off to you know where.'

They bestow big smiles on the woman. She buries her head in her fur collar. I try not to think of my mother. Perhaps she is buying some cigarettes before going back to Adelphi Square, innocently letting herself in. I must focus on what's in front of me.

The train stops at what must be a military base. The size of the base astonishes me, fields upon fields of small aircraft. I am seeing England's only and final defence, it is the equivalent of a nuclear deterrent. Uniformed personnel are weaving in and out of long sheds and again I'm reminded of a film set. This impression is enhanced when an attractive woman strides by, wearing a smart jacket belted at the waist. Made in Harrods, I say to myself. The airmen come to a shouted 'Halt!' at a group of huts. These are clustered, ridiculously close to the runway. Inside one of the huts men of all ages are talking and relaxing, their flying jackets slung on the backs of their chairs. A few of the men smoke pipes, reminding me that pipes have completely gone out of fashion. The walls are covered with sheets of thin paper and closer inspection reveals them to be smudged carbon copies of names under different categories, pilots, navigators, rear gunners. Equally impressive are detailed weather maps with finely inked-in diagrams. This kind of meteorology must be a lost art since the advent of television. Snatches of small talk are coming my way in a mix of accents.

'Why do we call them 'sorties' like we're French? What's wrong with 'mission?''

'Too religious sounding?'

'The Huns have put up two feet high concrete blocks to stop our tanks.' No one comments on this. 'So how we ever gonna get over the Marginot Line?'

'They don't call it that. Used to be called the Siegfried Line.

'That reminds me...hey, isn't that like the Chorus Line?'

'The NAAFI's run out of tea, for heaven's sake.'

I move away to explore. The door at the end leads into an enormous hangar filled with aircraft. The one and two engine planes look like toys to me and remind me of Paul's Meccano set. They are painted with lurid cartoons but there's a reality about them that cannot be denied. A wall suddenly moves and huge doors are drawn aside to reveal the night sky glittering with stars. It is ominously quiet. Some night bird angrily squawks at us. I quickly draw back. Birds became my friends when I was with the Longs, but I don't want to remember that now. Young women in blue overalls jog by. I follow them fascinated by the beat of their feet. The column snakes its way across the concrete of the aircraft hangars. Near the planes the line breaks up into individual women who jump into low carts loaded with bombs the size of concrete mixers, These they drive merrily, if not crazily, round the hanger to line their carts up under the bombers. As I watch them taking such delight in their jobs, I think of the war in Vietnam and our protests against it. But Vietnam never attacked America. I remember marching arm in arm down Main Street defying the people who were unthinking patriots, but now I want to join the war effort and be one of the boys. These soldiers are preparing to sacrifice themselves to defend their country, like my father did in World War One.

The sound of a bugle draws me back to the classroom hut, which is now thick with cigarette smoke.

'Groupie coming!'

The warning silences casual chat and transforms the room into a classroom of airmen, leaning forward expectantly. Groupie is a weather-beaten man who has a permanent squint. His straight back and military bearing, the colourful medals he wears, all command attention and respect.

'Operation Chastise is well under way, and although this is a small unit, we're not going to be outdone by the Eighth...' He pauses as if he's made a joke, but no one laughs. 'Operation Transportation was a success and something to be proud of. I'm sure you've met Group Leader Colonel Jenkins?'

A balding but fresh-faced extremely young Colonel Jenkins glares at the men before he goes straight to the map of France and Germany.

'Still aiming to cross The North Sea here. Altitudes to aim for will be twelve thousand feet or below, dependent on cloud cover. There will not be much tonight.'

An audible groan sounds, which he ignores.

'Never go below eight thousand feet. Don't kiss any chimneystacks. That's an order! Is that understood, you cowboys? Enemy flak and interference expected. There will be no, I repeat no alternative targets. Observers will be present.'

A series of sharp shots ring out and shake the flimsy hut. The Colonel hesitates but is not going to be stopped. He bangs his stick even harder on the map. The men exchange frowns and quizzical looks. A scuffle outside the door stops the briefing. he has lost his men's attention.

'What the hell's going on out there?'

A voice rings out behind the door, 'It's Lever... Lever something, Sir.'

The Colonel covers his maps with a blank sheet and waves for the door to be opened.

'What has happened?'

A young man, his face pale and twisted with anxiety, hovers at the door. 'Lavigne's been on a shooting spree in the toilet, sir. Smashed the lights.'

The Colonel is momentarily at a loss for words. 'Is there any damage? Did he hurt himself?'

'Just lost his mind, I think, sir!'

Colonel Jenkins tries to think of something that will cover the situation. 'I want a full investigation. Good thing it happened on the base.'

Another air force officer arrives. Underneath his jerkin, his jacket is covered with ribbons. He salutes the group who lean in closer as if trying to compensate for the interruption. 'Okay, men let's stay together, keep tight and obey orders! As in all our missions, we are aiming for military installations; we are not aiming to bomb civilians.'

I'm glad to hear him say that. The pilots look indifferent. He dismisses them with a nod, and before he whips open the door, they are lighting up cigarettes. Once outside they crowd together like people who have a difficult job to do. Operation Chastise!

'I like the name. Appropriate for once.'

'I could think of a better one.'

'When are they going to give us Berlin?'

'Saving that for the Eighth!'

Having had their say, the men clank out the briefing room towards their aircraft, casually chatting with ground crew. The carts driven by the women are now used by men who stand on them which I cannot hear in order to secure the bombs on the undercarriages. An unexpected cheer gives the eerie scene a kind of warmth. Everyone on the tarmac looks up at the night sky. A pinpoint of light becomes a small plane that makes a velvet landing. A pilot climbs out as someone runs up with a ladder. He clambers down, but as he reaches the ground and takes off his helmet, we see the long hair of a beautiful woman. The airman standing closest to me murmurs, 'I'm in love.'

'Forget it,' an older pilot scoffs. 'While we're in the skies she'll be partying in the night away.'

The young woman, who is walking close by, looks as if she hears this and almost sneers at him. She nods vigorously to the airman who steps up to greet her.

'One A,' she says. 'But watch out for tightness on the left.'

'What a neat plane!'

'She's called Lenora, and she was a birthday present.'

The pilot grins, which I presume is a thank you, and leaps up the ladder. As the young woman walks away she turns back for a last look at her machine.

I make a quick decision and squeeze myself into a one-man aircraft, but then I change my mind. I need company to inform me. I choose a heavier model which is obviously a bomber. The pilot and co-pilot are squeezed into the nose cone. Behind them sits the navigator with barely enough space for his equipment. There is another man on board, suited up like the others but crouching where he pleases. I wonder if he is the observer. He takes the maps from the navigator and waves them about short-sightedly. The others call him Dick when they ask him questions I cannot hear over the noise of the engine on the tarmac. At the rear is a Perspex turret and I'm surprised to see a man hoist himself up there. There is nothing between him and the night sky, or enemy aircraft! A man on the ground clutches the tip of one of our wings to turn the plane. These hunks of metal are not as heavy as they look.

'One, Two, Three, Four!'

The noise of so many engines starting up is now deafening. I'm surprised they cannot hear the noise twenty miles across the Channel. At last we are being flagged for take-off, and rattle over the airstrip until we gain height with a tilt to the right and the left. There are no clouds, but also no moonlight. This must be why the night was chosen. Flying alongside us are a dozen other bombers, and below us I can spot a number of one manned fighters. These must be our escort.

Despite the savagery of the engine, which shakes the thin metal cabin, the pilot and co-pilot start to chat. I creep nearer to hear words exchanged about Rolls Royce engines, Flying Fortresses and Liberators. Strapped into this metal craft high above the ocean, I admire these men who are risking their lives for their country. I can only see their mouths under their goggles, mouths set in a firm grimace. They are suppressing the danger of such an expedition, and yet they are convinced of its importance. I sense the tension, but there's nowhere I'd rather be. I have forgotten my father, my bewilderment at being here. I'm in the grip of some tribal loyalty.

As we gain altitude, talk stops. The cold sets their teeth chattering, an awful reminder of the skeleton within, but they still manage to chat to each other, naming the reputation and 'downs' of other pilots and not only the names of the pilots, but their wives and girlfriends as if they were all going to an elite social gathering. As we approach our target, the mood changes. The pilot kisses the back of his gloved fingers; perhaps there is a special ring hidden there. This must be the time for rituals, fetishes. The navigator crosses himself and is murmuring something under his breath.

The cabin lightens.

'Thank you, Lord!' the co-pilot yells out.

The pilot turns and smiles. 'Beautiful clouds, beautiful!' We are now dropping fast. Commercial air passengers would have their oxygen masks out. The cabin is suddenly infused with an incongruous pink, and I hear the navigator report the release of the flares, which are now colouring the clouds a Disney pink. From the sound of winching and clicking, the bombing is under way. The business is being done smoothly, efficiently. I look out as we discharge our deadly cargo, but can see only little puffs of smoke, no sound of the explosions below.

'Success, I think!'

But not without retaliation as I hear syncopated puncturing of something, wing, body, I do not know. The plane veers off, leaving the smoking target below.

'Anti-aircraft guns on the ground! Didn't expect them.'

'How many bombs have we got left?'

'We can't risk going in again. We'll ditch them in The North Sea.'

While they're talking, small puffs of black smoke float by.

'Let's get out of that flak! We're being followed.'

We soar upwards and below us I see two fighters below chasing each other round and round like crazed dragonflies.

'We've lost our firepower! What's happened?'

The navigator is looking towards the rear of the plane. The man called Dick crawls there. The young airman is hunched over his gun, blood oozing out of his coat. His tipped-back face is angelic. He is about my son's age and weight. Why can't I remember the name of my son? Dick pulls the body out of the seat and yells out to his companions that the gunner is dead. The plane's listing dangerously to one side and then it does a complete roll, which silences everyone. When the plane levels out there are whoops and cheers. I don't know why we flipped.

Our plane soars upwards. The enemy plane disappears.

'We lost him. We're going to make it!'

'Saved for another round of hell!' The grating sound of false laughter. There is smoke in the cabin. Something's on fire and the navigator crawls into the rear with a fire blanket to smother the flames. He is cheered on by the crew.

'Let's go home!'

I see ahead of us the white cliffs of Dover and that comforting patchwork of fields and hedgerows that is the England I know.

'Fuckin' Hell!' Dick suddenly yells. 'We haven't finished. Go back. One of our spitfires got him. Way is clear now'

Both pilots shake their heads.

'You haven't finished the job!'

'There'll be others on our tail, we can't risk it.'

'Back! Go back!'

I don't like Dick's shrill tone and I wonder whether he outranks the pilots, but there is no way he is going to change their minds. Dick senses this as well because he throws himself at the wheel and wrenches it to one side, yelling 'Turn back!'

'You idiot!' The pilot is punching Dick in the head. 'We can't take that kind of turn!'

The plane swerves like a car on ice and a sickening noise surrounds us. With a shock I see the cabin buckle under the strain and blue sky shows through.

'You've ripped us clean apart, you idiot!'

'We're going down.'

'We're going down!' The way Dick repeats this makes me realise he's proud of what he's done, proud we are all going to die. I look at his face and it has closed up, like the face of a Buddha, serene and stern. Yes, he is prepared to die, even looking forward to it. I remember my father telling me it was a suicidal impulse that dared him to risk his life. I am sorry for the rest of us but there is nothing I can do, we are going down and I am no longer a ghost or a time traveller, I am one of them, a disembodied spirit hanging in the sky before becoming an infinitesimal part of the cosmos.

Part IV

CHAPTER TWENTY-ONE

1985

****

I'm speeding through the night of the world, a microscopic particle, many particles, blown apart by an explosion, I feel guilty about attracting so many explosions, but my mind is reaching the furthest ends of the universe. I'm not frightened of this expanding mind but when I look down at my body, I'm in a hospital room. I'm not sure I want to enter a body that looks like it's in pain. How am I going to adjust to the shock of being confined?

Eliza Wyatt

****

I can hear nurses talk about my injuries and from their accents know I am in England. They are talking to a man I gradually realise is Ed. What is he doing here? Because of my injuries, Ed has come to England for me. I love him for it.

****

I did not want to open my eyes but was reassured by the sound of Ed's voice. He was calling for a doctor to view the monitor. I wanted to talk to him before the doctors arrived but did not know what to say. Ed smiled at me and we locked eyes. Then, without consciously willing it, I began a long ramble which included my bombing mission, war, suicide, Gloria, Vivien at the orphanage. I'm sure Ed thought I had lost my mind because he told the doctor as much when the doctor finally arrived. The doctor ignored what I was saying and told Ed no doctor knew how much my mind was going to be affected by the coma. He also said the shock of waking up would confuse me at first, but hopefully it would only be temporary. Ed held my hands.

****

The next few days, or weeks, pass in an effort to get me out of bed and walking. I am upset that while the nurses anticipate my every want, they are barely polite to Ed as if he overstayed his welcome. Ed repeats everything he says to me as loudly as possible. I am not deaf, but I do have trouble focusing on what people say. Sometimes there's a mist surrounding the bed and I have to wait until it clears before I can put my feet on the floor.

I gave up trying to tell Ed something about my time travel but insisted he go to Adelphi Square where my parents lived. I told him the number of the flat. He promised to do that and said he hoped that would stop me murmuring to myself about my experiences in the past. I will do that if he takes me more seriously and gives me proof that my father lived in Adelphi Square. I heard him ask an overly cheerful doctor whether they should test my mental state. The doctor replied, 'let's wait and see. We are going to need that bed for another patient, and she'll soon be sent to rehab.'

The hospital arranged for me to be sent to a Rehabilitation Centre in the nearby countryside. Ed marvelled at the extent of social services and how much they were taking care of me. I was surprised to hear he had been living in Vivien's basement and understood he was not sorry to leave. The police have been making enquiries about the tripwire that had led to the explosion, asking why anyone would want to kill my mother. I thought up hundreds of reasons, but Ed told me none of them sounded likely. At least he was enjoying his new surroundings. In the evenings I rested after physiotherapy, and he joined the locals in the pub where they keep buying him beers.

Eliza Wyatt

****

I have the impression I'm flying through space, unconnected to life on earth. When I'm in this mind, I don't remember who I am. Someone in the past told me to practise dying. Is that what I'm doing? But I have another mind, one that's anchored in my body, trying to believe in what Ed calls reality.

****

The mist over my bed has disappeared but I'm still intensely distracted by the sensations given off by ordinary things. There had been no smells in the past. The smell of disinfectant jolted an unpleasant memory of toilets. When Ed brought me flowers their pink colour went right through me. If someone entered my room, I sniffed impolitely. When I reached out for a glass of water, I knew drinking it was going to be an overwhelming experience. Rain on the window made me long for a thunderstorm.

****

News from David. The family clubbed together to buy him a ticket to London. When I heard that, my stomach clenched and I broke out in a sweat. There was something frighteningly normal about David's visit. 'What about Trudy?' I asked. Ed said he was pleased I'd remembered her name. We exchanged a familiar look, confirming that we were still parents. We also decided it was time to tell David about Vivien's profession.

Juggling two minds does not make me feel smarter or sharper. My second mind is no longer speeding through outer space but speeding through my body, maybe it is healing me. It. My other mind, the one enjoying every sensation, loves the feel of my hands on my body.

I asked Ed to lie down on the bed next to me, happy that he smelled of himself, although he looked embarrassed when I told him so. We needed time to get to know each other again. Ed was nervous about my facial surgery. I told him it did not matter. He suggested that if I wasn't happy with the result, they could do another operation. I told him I had more important things to think about. I wanted news of Houston and Mara. I thought fondly about her and her belief in the transformational weekend. I had undergone a series of transformations. Now I needed the sensation of touch, my husband's touch. This was not easy in the Rehab Centre, but in the middle of the night we managed it. A hurried love making, as if we were aware of David's imminent arrival. It was like a first date, but there would be more to come.

****

I confess to Ed about my two minds, and my theory that the unreal one could be helping me heal. He says he is pleased to hear this. I then confess to Ed that my travels to the past have shown me that the present and the future are not as real as they seem. I can hear him thinking 'poco loco,'' and he immediately buys a calendar and talks about his business plans for the new year. This makes me nervous.

****

Seeing David was wonderfully intense. For me he could have come from outer space to visit me. His presence magnified the present, and invoked many other dimensions. He told me about Trudy, and showed me photographs of the garden to assure me the flowers had been watered. His concern for me was real. When he walked beside me, he grabbed my arm a little too tightly. Worry about me has changed him, but he does not see that I, too, have changed.

I was glad that he learned about Vivien's profession. Ed told me David had good memories of his grandmother hugging him, even though he knew she drank too much. When I tried to talk to him about her, I could see he was embarrassed because he abruptly changed the subject. 'I can't believe both your parents committed suicide,' he complained.

'It was the war,' I replied. 'I'm sure if there hadn't been a war both of them would be alive today. War and suicide are somehow connected. I took up the fighting myself only to discover I was as suicidal as my parents.' I could see Ed and David found this difficult to believe. 'I saw war up close,' I insisted, 'and I wanted to be part of the action. Me, a wife and mother, who was driven by despair at finding and losing my father. I leapt into a plane to defend my country, but it was an excuse. I wanted to pound someone into a pulp because I was in grief. Grief about death, don't you see? That's what makes us fight, fear of death, fear of grief.'

Ed said, 'You've always been anti-war.'

'War has a lot to answer for,' I continued. 'It's generally called sacrificing your life, but it is exploiting our suicidal instincts. If people believed that, maybe diplomacy would be taken more seriously. I remember the Japanese Kamikaze pilots attacking Pearl Harbour. We used to laugh at them, but why? Hitler committed suicide, after pushing his country into a suicidal war. And World War One! We put our soldiers in front of cannons, and the amazing thing is that they stood in front of cannons!'

My impassioned outburst makes them look at me as if I am a madwoman. I cannot impose my ideas on Ed and David. They have to take their own journeys and make their own discoveries.

****

Ed insisted on showing David the London that impressed him as a student, St. Paul's cathedral, the Houses of Parliament. I was glad not to be included in this, because it meant I could be alone with my thoughts.

It takes peace and quiet to get in touch with my other, my unreal mind. When I do it resonates through every cell in my body and energises me. I'm sure it's healing me.

I had a sudden desire to write about my time travel, but I had not got very far when a deliveryman came to the door. He left a small brown parcel from Wood Vale Cemetery: my mother's ashes. I felt like a child who had been given an unwelcome present. How do these ashes relate to my mother's complicated life? The box sat heavily on my lap for the rest of the evening.

When Ed and David returned from sight-seeing they were in a jubilant tourist mood, but soon sobered up by the sight of the box.

'Are we going to keep them?' Ed wanted to know. 'We could take them back to Texas.'

'Maybe I should scatter them in the wind,' I suggested. 'Unless the wind blows them back in my face.'

'I'm sorry you weren't close to your mother.' David said.

That remark brought tears to my eyes.

David had another idea. 'They must be buried in sacred church ground.'

Ed agreed 'Your father and mother should be together.'

I began to think about my father's funeral. Was he cremated? Who came to his funeral? Where was he buried?

****

We contacted Adelphi Square and the office told us that a Hugh Cuthbert died on the date we gave them, and that it was officially recorded as a suicide. They advised us to hire a private investigator if we wanted more information, someone to trace the funeral and the cemetery. We interviewed a man in a pin-striped suit who assured us he had enough facts to do the job.

A few days later the investigator came up with the location of Hubert Cuthbert's grave, the aisle and the number. I was pleased to hear it was located in a Brighton cemetery. 'That would be right,' I told him. 'My father's mother would have taken charge and held the funeral in Brighton, far from his Civil Service colleagues. If his death was recorded as a suicide, she would have wanted privacy because I'm sure she never believed it was suicide.'

'You mean it was murder?' David wanted to know.

'No!' I was firm about that.

****

Brighton and Hove Cemetery North covered a wide expanse of graves under thunderous looking clouds. We passed stone angels in attitudes of supplication and prayer. I found myself looking at the headstones of soldiers who had died in both wars. Ragged wreathes of poppies still adorned some graves. If only I could express to the two men in my life what it means to be living in a country at peace. How every sound is supported by that underlying fact; the planes overhead, cars swishing by, the rustle of leaves, all reasons to be joyful.

Ed and David tramped on ahead, chatting.

'Any turkeys this year?'

'Pedro got a four-pointer. Didn't mean to, of course. or maybe he did.'

'Leave the antlers behind?'

'No, he's found a place that buys them.'

Their conversation made me realise they were only visiting England. I was alone in my grief, regretting I had not been able to love my mother before she died.

'Here it is!' Rushing ahead, David was the one to find his grandfather's grave.

The headstone was in granite, my father's name etched in gold lettering. No dedication, just his name and above his name, also in gold lettering, the name of my grandfather, John Edgar Cuthbert. My grandmother's name was absent.

'Well, this isn't going to be any good.' Ed had brought a swiss army knife to bury the ashes. The grave was not covered in grass, but contained green glass pebbles sloping towards the middle where the concrete had collapsed.

'Look at the state it's in!' David protested. 'We should do something about that.'

I was taking a picture of the engraved headstone. 'No mention of my grandmother.' I complained. 'Nor of my uncle Charles! He died in the war. Sort of!'

'Was he my uncle?' David wanted to know.

'Your great uncle.' I replied.

I opened the box of ashes. 'If I hadn't gone back to the past, I would never have found my father's grave.'

'You paid the price.' Ed remarked.

David began to recite a prayer.

I scattered my mother's ashes on top of my father's grave and reached out my arms, like I'd seen that old man doing in front of the burning building in bombed out London. 'I'm sorry,' I cried out loud as the wind took my mother's ashes. 'You gave me the chance, but…' Tears ran down my cheeks, and appropriately it began to rain.

Ed and David retreated into their hoods and sheltered under a yew tree. I sat on the grave until rain soaked through my jeans and quilt jacket. Cold and wet, I yelled over to the two men in my life, 'And I'm not going back to Sunny Hills Country Club!'

That made us laugh.

Before going to sleep I'm afraid I'll go back to the past and on waking I have the fear that there is no such thing as the future. But I haven't seen any more ghosts, and I'm aware of my unreal mind healing me.

****

ABOUT THE AUTHOR

Eliza Wyatt was born in Brighton, Hove actually. She returned to her hometown after twenty-five years in her other home-town, Boston, Mass. where she was active in the theatre community as a writer, director and producer, enjoying more than twenty productions of her award-winning plays across the United States, Scotland and England. She also produced a prize-winning short, an environmental film, directed by Michele D'Acosta. Two of her plays have been adapted for the screen.

Eliza is a member of the Dramatist Guild as well as The Society of Authors, and she is a long-time member and director of the International Center for Women Playwrights.

Interview

Eliza answers questions she's often asked.

Is the novel autobiographical?

Eliza:
I'd say semi-autobiographical.

I drew on my childhood experience of being fostered for the character of Annabel in my novel. The main difference between us was that I was not encouraged to recognize my mother. She was presented to me in the guise of an aunt who lived in London. Annabel has the advantage of already knowing her mother from an early age.

Annabel's story is not my story even if we share a transatlantic experience. I lived in Boston for more than thirty years where I was active in the theatre.

Most of my play productions took place in the United States, Boston, New York city and L.A. and I've also had productions in London, and Edinburgh Theatre Festival, and the Brighton Festival.

The common thread between Annabel's life and mine is London. London is a forceful character in the book, and a town with a colourful past, and sorrowful history. To those who love the town, and want to visit it, I have mentioned some well-known places and landmarks. Adelphi Square is a fictional name of a real place which is still standing.

What made you choose a novel and not a play?

Eliza:
In my mind it was always a novel because of the detail I wanted to include. I wrote plays, screenplays, essays and poetry but Annabel Langoni is my first novel. I was shocked to find novel writing such a challenge. I learned the hard way, by constant re-writing and studying novel-writing. I learned that a novel gives the writer time to explore in depth the struggles of a character, a family, or even an entire community. The reader is invited to imagine many other lives within the structure of the plot, but hopefully by the end of the novel will be able to imagine the main characters living on beyond the end of the book with some idea of how their lives will be changed.

Creating an original character in a semi-autobiographical setting was a new writing experience for me. The difficulty with a main character is to ensure she is an active force throughout. Annabel in Texas is certainly that, and later in London, even after her injuries, she hires a private investigator to find her father's grave. In her time travels she's less of a participant than an observer but because time travel answers so many of her questions, we can see her character change as this happens; she is shaping a new reality for herself when she finally returns from the past.

When did you first have the idea?

Eliza:
I think it is hard to say when a book is first generated in the mind of an author. I was not interested in writing my personal biography, but when my son became a father, I decided he and my grandsons were missing out on important family history. I began by writing a fictional letter from my father to my son. It is fictional because I never knew my father. Then I wrote a memoir of my childhood called Beautiful Strangers, and I was encouraged to turn that material into a novel. I accepted the challenge not realising how long it would take me, and how many versions I would eventually write. A list of the titles I considered and rejected makes me smile, Mystery Solved, A Ghost's Story, War Hero's Daughter, Haunting My Parents, The Murder Mystery Fan.

It took me a number of novel writing years to have the confidence to call the book by the name of the narrator, Annabel Langoni. The name comes from my childhood because my mother called me Annabel and would sing the Nat King Cole song, Annabel, to me. Like Annabel's mother in the book, my mother did not raise me and satisfied her maternal instincts with songs of unrequited love.

It's taken you a long while to be published, hasn't it?

Eliza
I'd say it took me about ten years to write the novel and get it published. As I have said, I knew nothing about novel writing and less about publishing.

My first publisher, Stirling Ltd. in Edinburgh, listed my book to be published in October 2020. Unfortunately that publishing business did not survive the Pandemic, but I will always be grateful to them for offering my first publishing contract, and to the Editor-in-Chief, herself a talented writer, who praised my book. Soon after that I was diagnosed with cancer, so began the fight for my life, rather than for the book.

What have you learned from writing the book?

A sombre knowledge was gained by my research into what happened in London during the forties. The country had barely recovered from World War I before London was hit by Nazi bombing raids. Between 1940 and 1941, forty thousand people died and many more were injured. World War II impacted many people and many, if not all nations.

I discovered about 56 million people died, globally, in the Second World War if you include the Asian Pacific War, and why wouldn't you?

That figure shocked me because I was not aware until recently of the magnitude of human lives lost, not to mention destruction of the environment. The twentieth century can be accused of being the most diabolical in western history. Has this figure been purposely hidden from us? I understand the need to forgive and forget, but being informed we may be able understand more about our war-torn cities and the culture we have inherited.

You also found out about your family?

Eliza:
I did research on ancestry.com, as well as consulting voter registration and parish records to find out how long family members were in each residence. I went with my camera to houses where they had lived.

One of the unexpected delights I discovered while writing the book was bringing my parents to life. Talking about them with my friends made my father seem like a real person. I'm grateful to the writing process for that and because it also allowed me to reflect on my mother's life. I was forced to consider her objectively, which enabled me to put their love affair into perspective. I think that made me more secure in some important ways.

When I first began the book and wrote the dedication, I dedicated my book to my antecedents, or ancestors (a rewrite), but then, after I'd finished the book, I knew I had to dedicate the book to parents. That is because I now felt I knew them.

You learned about your extended family from your research.

Eliza
Yes, I was able to trace my mother's family and I met my four first cousins when I was thirty-six. Our mutual Italian grandfather we were not able to trace. An immigrant to England in the 1920's, no one knows where he came from or even his real name. There's reason to believe he gave a false name to the immigration authorities. Presumably he was illiterate, since the paper trail stops with his X on his marriage certificate to my grandmother.

In contrast, my English father's story is well documented. His medals are on record with the Imperial War Museum, and I was delighted to find English birth and death records as well as census information, which gives the occupation of each adult. I hired a private investigator to find my father's grave. My only visit there was five years before I started writing the book, but the book could have been motivated by reading his name on the gravestone. Curiously enough, that plot of English earth is my sole inheritance, since my name claims it.

Did this have a good effect on you, finding out this information?

Eliza
It certainly confirmed my believe in genetic inheritance. For instance, I was far from being a brilliant student, but yearned to go to college because I had an intellectual curiosity, probably from my father's side. I took my undergraduate degree in philosophy and loved the work of female philosophers. I also loved visual art.

When I took up sculpture as a hobby, I discovered a hidden talent, which I'm sure came from my mother's side, her Jewish and Italian roots.

How much of yourself is in the character of Annabel?

Eliza
At one point in my writing a helpful friend put Annabel under analysis, treating her like a patient in therapy. We discovered Annabel had never suffered from low self-esteem, which was due in part to having two mothers, but she is programmed by her upbringing to want conventional things. Ed's unfaithfulness shatters the ideas she has about love and marriage.

When we first meet Annabel, she is an ordinary wife and mother who is satisfied with the American dream of a nuclear family in a comfortable suburb, that is until her biological mother's suicide. In London, as a teenager, she went to classes in communism because they were free and she felt deprived of an education, but she is not politically active and shows no interest in Thatcher's England. The therapist and I concluded this is because she has unconsciously been trying to be the daughter Brenda and Sydney wanted her to be, deliberately turning her back on her mother's wayward life.

Like Annabel I presented a corporate persona and I thought I passed, except when I had to accompany my husband on corporate away days. Then I was questioned about my theatrical career, and soon learned I was considered eccentric.

Meeting her father, a war-hero, gives Annabel another point of view, and a unique opportunity to witness the country at war, and see history as a living force that shapes the life of every citizen.

Unlike Annabel I was more aware of governmental policies and the economic depression of the Prime Minister Heath era. I felt connected by media or design to the cultural life of London where I began my theatrical career. Growing up, I always knew that my mother gave birth to me sharing a room with Vera Lynn, who was the voice most heard on the Armed Forces radio, her most famous song being We'll Meet Again, which must have been the catchphrase of the war.

The book brings the past alive, and gives us a personal view of history by means of Annabel's time travel, do you believe time travel will ever be possible?

Eliza
We have not achieved this yet but I think when we do, it will not be with a time machine. We now know that our cells have memory, water has memory, and our DNA is affected by our experiences. I have Annabel attempt to explain something like this when she says she accessed the past through the mind of her mother. It is quite possible that in the future we will be able to project visually the past lives of our biological cells and our inherited DNA. If that is the case, we will be able to enter the minds of our ancestors. Then the whole of human history could be accessed, with no degrees of separation.